TERROR IN THE NIGHT

BEA CARLTON

ACCENT BOOKS
Denver, Colorado

Originally printed without a title, this book was named through a national *Name the Mystery Book* Contest. From the thousands of entries, the panel of judges selected TERROR IN THE NIGHT submitted by Geneva Stone of northwestern Idaho.

ACCENT BOOKS

A division of Accent Publications, Inc.
12100 West Sixth Avenue
P.O. Box 15337
Denver, Colorado 80215

Library of Congress Catalog Card Number 84-072788

ISBN 0-89636-153-5

Second Printing 1986

Lovingly dedicated to my husband, Mark, whose love, encouragement, and prayers have meant so much to me through the years.

1

Carole Loring stood with her hands on her slim hips looking every bit as angry as she was. Bitterly she surveyed the canvas tents, the open fire and the huge pines around her. How could Gran have done this to her!

Longingly she recalled her beautiful home, the well-paid gourmet cook she employed and her own personal maid. But now—now. . . .Her sputtering thoughts were interrupted by Gran's cheerful voice.

"Oh, there you are, Carole. I've been looking for you."

Carefully masking her anger, Carole turned to face her spritely grandmother. With only the slightest discernible trace of bitterness in her voice, Carole replied, "Just looking over the accommodations, Gran. It was very thoughtful of you to plan this vacation for David and me." Carole stopped, clenched her fists and continued, "I'm almost speechless over your thoroughness in getting us out here in the crisp mountain air to fish for two weeks." Carole's beautifully manicured nails bit into her soft white palms.

"It will do you and David both a world of good," Gran replied vigorously, not in the least intimidated by the frigid, lady-of-the-manor, social tone that her granddaughter had used. "And speaking of that husband of yours, where is David?"

Carole's aristocratic nose twitched and a sneer marred the perfect curve of her red lips.

"If I know my beloved husband, he's probably already out behind some pine tree with a bottle."

A look of pain crossed Gran's face at the harsh and haunted tone to Carole's voice, but she indignantly replied, "Drinking! I specifically told him that there was absolutely no alcohol allowed on this trip."

"Well, Gran, you may have told him, but the fact remains that David hasn't been away from a stiff drink for more than a day in the last four years of our marriage—let alone the two weeks of this little jaunt you planned."

"Carole. . ." Gran's voice changed to an unspoken appeal as she looked at her spoiled, willful granddaughter. Even in the designer jeans and silk shirt, she knew her granddaughter was one of the prettiest women she'd ever seen. Petite, finely boned, her dark silky hair was swept back into a tumble of shimmering curls. She stared into the stormy blue-black eyes. Surprisingly, she thought she saw tears there. But if so, they were gone in a quick blink of thick eyelashes.

"Gran, sometimes I wonder how David could have made such a mess of things."

"David?" her grandmother interrupted.

"Yes, David! We had a perfect marriage, the fairy-tale romance. Now what do I have? A drunken lush for a husband!

"When we first met in college, David was so—so perfect! So sweet, so thoughtful, so gentle. He was shy and handsome in that rugged sort of way." Carole's voice trailed wistfully away.

"And whose fault is it that your handsome, intelligent husband is what he is now?" The accusation in Gran's voice brought Carole's eyes back to her grandmother. "Who talked him out of his teaching career?"

"Gran! What do you mean?"

"You know what I mean, young lady."

"But, Gran," whispered Carole, aghast, "You surely can't blame me for David's condition. All I tried to do. . . ."

"All you tried to do was to possess his every waking moment, to greedily eliminate any outside interests and activities he had that didn't meet up to your specifications."

"Gran! I didn't!" Carole's voice registered her shock.

Softening at the look in her granddaughter's face, Mrs. Drake said, "I love you, Carole. I raised you from a little girl, and I love you. But I also know you. I'm not blind to your faults and if you want to save your marriage, you'll do some deep soul searching in the next two weeks. This is a very special wilderness camping outfit. I made some mistakes while you were growing up. There were some essential things I left out of your expensive education. Maybe— somehow—I can make up for that now.

"But, I better go find David. Supper will be ready in a little bit, and I need to unpack, too."

With that, Mrs. Drake left her granddaughter.

Carole drifted out of the circle of activity and the other arrivals. Finding a spot just beyond the campsite, she sank down on a log and let her mind wander back to her junior year in college. A smile tugged at the corners of her mouth as she lost herself in recollections of the strong, tall David Loring she'd met in her biology class. His unruly, red-gold hair and keen blue eyes had attracted her from the first day of the semester. For her the class had been a lark, but she'd known within minutes of talking to David that it was a passion to him. From the accidental pairing as lab partners, they had gradually progressed to coffee in the student lounge and then a concert or two. At first David could talk only of biology, botany and his lifelong desire to teach. But she had changed all that. In fact, something had changed a lot of things—she winced as she remembered. It had taken a bit of womanly charm, after they were married the summer following graduation, to persuade him to abandon his teaching aspirations. But like everything she had ever set her mind to get, she had succeeded.

Even without Gran's probing, Carole knew she had loved David so deeply that she was jealous of anything else that demanded his time. After all, she'd reasoned, with her wealth there was no need for him to work for a living. And at first David had seemed content to simply be her attractive, attentive escort at the many parties she gave and attended. Their marriage had been one long extended honeymoon.

When David had begun to change, she didn't quite know. But gradually she'd become aware of it. At first it was only an occasional drink, but then David had begun drinking

7

more and more at their parties where the alcohol flowed freely. And, it was as though the liquor had given birth to a new personality. Still the outwardly attentive escort, he'd also become the uninhibited host who captivated their guests with his scintillating—sometimes biting—wit and charm. The shyness and quiet reserve that had drawn her to him were gone. Carole knew she wanted the "old" David—sometimes moody and withdrawn, sometimes boyishly unsure of himself, but always slavishly devoted to her.

Carole lifted her eyes in mute appeal to the majestic, towering mountains around her. The smell of the pines, the deep whisper of the river not far away, and the soft chatter of the birds lulled her. Maybe two weeks away from their normal routine would help. She knew David cared for her somewhat crusty, world-traveled grandmother and had honored her request not to bring any alcohol with him. She'd just been angry and had struck back without thinking. But fishing! Carole shivered at the thought of touching the cold, slimy, dead fish. "No way!" She said aloud to herself. "I'll find something else to do." And with that resolved in her mind, she turned back to the central activity of the camp.

2

After an evening meal that even Carole grudgingly admitted had been cooked to perfection, she lay back in her camp chair. In the darkening sky, a myriad of stars blinked silently, and a huge yellow moon moved serenely overhead like a lonely sentinel. The cool, tangy air was laden with the heady scent of spruce and fir from the thick forest around them. The evening was pure joy. The magic of the high-mountain night seemed to cast a spell over everything and everybody. Even David sat back in the chair beside her—relaxed and sober.

Silently Carole let her eyes inspect the other campers in

their group as the dusk gathered slowly around them. Besides herself, David and Gran, there were two middle-aged school teachers who called each other Miss Nell and Miss Katherine and who had talked non-stop since they arrived. In addition, a family of three had arrived just as supper started, a Mr. and Mrs. Judson Adams with their thirteen-year-old son who had already pulled three practical jokes and had been insolent to everyone. Carole could recognize a spoiled brat when she saw one. Judson Adams II qualified. Completing the party were two businessmen who had arrived together and talked avidly of trout, lures, bait and fishing equipment—none of which had interested Carole in the least, although she had smiled politely at them throughout dinner. There was also Slim, the pack wrangler; Manuel, the small, lithe, Mexican cook; and Steve Morgan, the dark-bearded, green-eyed camp boss.

"Now he looks like a man who can take care of himself. That quiet air of assurance is inbred," Carole thought to herself as everyone gathered around the campfire.

Suddenly the soft strumming of a guitar lent its own magic to the night and Manuel began to sing in his own language. What the song was, Carole didn't know, but it seemed to fill her heart with a strange longing. When the song ended, Steve rose in his slow, deliberate way and began to speak. His first words were shocking to Carole.

"I know you're all familiar with the routine of this camp since it was discussed when you signed on."

Carole sat up and listened. This was all new to her since Gran had done the registration for them.

"We always have a brief time of Scripture reading and worship each evening after supper," Steve continued. "It seems the Lord is especially real out here in the wilderness like this, away from the rush and noise of the city. Let's begin tonight with an old song I'm sure you all know."

Scripture reading! Worship! Carole turned her startled gaze first to David who seemed mesmerized by the fire, and then to Gran, who also stared straight ahead, seemingly unaware of her granddaughter's scrutiny.

What had Gran done! All the years she had lived with Gran they had never gone to church except on Christmas and Easter. In fact, Gran had never seemed interested in religion before.

Manuel began strumming and singing a second song and the words were familiar to her this time. Carole had sung "Amazing Grace" a few times in the fashionable church she infrequently attended. Steve joined Manuel, their voices harmonizing and filling the night. Others, hesitant at first, joined in until most of the group was singing. Carole was strangely stirred—first to an unexpected, inexplicable longing, then to anger. She turned to Gran.

"Did you know they were going to have church up here?"

Gran looked slightly annoyed at being disturbed and a little guilty. "Certainly, I did. Sit still. A little preaching might do us all some good. It certainly won't hurt us."

So! Gran had deliberately tricked her into coming up here to listen to preaching! Well, she didn't have to stay for the worship service.

Turning to David on the other side of her, she spoke sharply, "David, let's go for a walk. I don't like this, and I like being deceived even less." Her voice shook with anger and a strange unrest had permeated her being.

To Carole's utter amazement and consternation, David covered her clutching hand gently with his own and said, "Let's give the thing a chance. We might like it."

Carole felt totally deserted. Indignation and frustration boiled up in her throat, almost choking her. Snatching her hand away, she rose quickly and stalked away. The others seemed too absorbed to give her stiff departing back more than a passing glance. Marching to her tent, she missed the look of agony that crossed David's face and the pain that blurred the longing in his deep blue eyes.

Pausing only long enough to get a flashlight from her tent, Carole turned down a well-beaten path toward the noise of the river. At first the moon was so bright the flashlight was unnecessary. She walked swiftly but the music and singing seemed to follow her, increasing her agitation. Her pride still smarted from the scant attention David and her grandmother had paid to her wishes.

As the hum of tumbling water grew more pronounced, the sound of music and singing grew dimmer. Carole slowed her steps and began to notice her surroundings. The wide path led through brush and scattered trees, but just a few yards from the path was a heavy forest. She looked toward the river, then caught her breath in amazement! Directly ahead of her, where the trail forked, stood a little girl, like a diminutive angel dropped from heaven! She was tiny with blond hair that fell like shimmering gold in the moonlight about a pointed, pixie face. Bare feet peeked from beneath a white nightie. She was standing very still, staring at Carole.

Carole stopped instantly, petrified with shock, her heart beating wildly. Could this really be a child out here in the wilderness? She passed a hand over her eyes in bewilderment. When she looked again, the tiny figure was gone.

Carole stared at the spot where the figure had been. Had she seen an apparition? Her knees felt trembly and she was a little faint. "Get a hold of yourself," she said aloud, surprised at how her voice shook. "Stop acting like an idiot," she told herself sternly. "There *was* a child. Perhaps there are other campers nearby. Of course! That must be it."

The thought spurred her to action. She walked swiftly to the fork in the trail and looked down each end of the path. There was no sign of a child. She charged down the right-hand path and in just a few minutes came out in a clearing— a campsite but no campers. It was also the end of the trail.

Hardly stopping to catch her breath, she walked swiftly back to the fork and took the other path, following the river. Excitement beating in her throat, the worship service at camp forgotten for the present, she plunged down the trail at

11

a reckless pace.

Shortly she noticed a dim path on her left that headed straight toward the river. The trees pressed more closely there so she switched on her light. Proceeding more slowly and cautiously down this new path she soon saw a small swinging footbridge. A few quick steps and she was standing on the bridge.

She stopped in fascinated amazement. Across the footbridge and beyond a wall stood a castle! Built of gray-white natural stone and covered here and there with dark vines, it loomed mysterious and lonely in the moonlight. There were no lights in the castle windows and no sign of a child.

Swaying with the bridge, Carole stood for long moments, gazing at the huge castle-like mansion. She felt her spine tingle with excitement. Entranced, she felt transported into a far dim yesterday of princes, princesses, and knights with shining armor astride powerful, black horses.

The faint sound of music and singing wafted by a gentle breeze broke her reverie. She turned and began to make her way back to camp. Her anger was gone. Quickening her step, she was soon at the edge of camp. The worship was over.

Steve Morgan was strolling toward his tent. Carole called to him and he turned and came to meet her. "Yes, Mrs. Loring?"

"I went for a walk just now down near the river. Does someone live in that beautiful old castle-like mansion across the river?"

"Yes," Steve said. "Charles Prentice, a rather eccentric old artist, lives there. He built Thunder Mountain Manor many years ago for his bride. They lived a life of seclusion until their only daughter moved to the city. I understand that the old lady didn't live long afterward. She died four or five years ago. Old man Prentice lives there alone now with only a middle-aged couple to keep house for him. Even they are a little strange. Isolated from people too long, I guess."

"Who does the child belong to that I saw near there tonight?"

Steve's head jerked up shortly. "Child? Where did you see a child?"

"She just suddenly appeared where the path forks a few minutes after you started the singing," Carole explained. "She seemed to be about four or five years old and had long blond hair."

Steve looked at her closely. "Are you sure you saw a child. Shadows and moonlight can be deceiving."

"Of course I'm sure," replied Carole indignantly.

"Where did she go?"

"She just—sort of—vanished." Carole felt a little foolish.

"Mr. Prentice's housekeepers are childless, and with his dislike for people, he has no friends that I know about. His daughter is in her twenties and hasn't been seen in these parts since she left for the city several years ago. No, there are no children in these parts," Steve declared emphatically.

"Maybe there are other campers in this area?"

"No, there is no one here except our camp. I keep close tabs on things like that. Are you sure you didn't just imagine you saw a little girl?" Steve asked again.

Carole's temper flared, "I know what I saw! I did not imagine it! I saw a child!" She turned on her heel and stalked away without even a goodnight.

3

The delectable smells of smoke, coffee and frying ham awakened Carole. It was still very early but the camp was astir. Manuel's voice rose softly on the crisp morning breeze in a haunting Spanish melody. David's cot was empty.

Carole stretched lazily and shivered in the brisk

13

mountain air. Her thoughts drifted to the events of the evening before and she was wide awake. What of the child? Could she have imagined it? Impossible! She had seen her and that was that!

She had tried to talk to David last night but he had been in one of his withdrawn moods. When she had told him briefly about seeing the tiny figure in the pathway, he had told her it was probably her imagination. And when she had flatly declared she knew what she had seen, he had merely shrugged, then promptly turned over and went to sleep.

"I'm not going fishing today," she stated aloud. "I'm going calling at a certain castle." Having decided on her plans for the day, Carole dressed quickly and was soon seated in the dining tent, eating a delicious breakfast with enormous appetite.

Conversation drifted about her. Everyone was excited about trout it seemed. Plans had been made to walk to Silver Lake, a small lake nearby, where the fishing was reported to be extra good. Even Gran was jubilant over the prospect of catching the sought-after creatures. David was unusually quiet and looked grumpy. Carole wondered if he hadn't rested well. He looked tired but at least he was sober and that was a pleasing thought.

As the campers scattered to collect fishing gear, Carole spoke apologetically to her grandmother. "I think I'll stay close to camp today."

Tying on an enormous floppy hat, Gran nodded absently, "Suit yourself," she said, and went on selecting fishing materials from those supplied by the camp.

David raised an eyebrow quizzically, "Want me to stay with you?"

"No—no." Carole spoke hastily. She didn't want any help in her snooping. "I'll make out fine. If I want to fish, I can fish in the river nearby."

When the fishing party was gathered and ready to depart, Steve strolled over to Carole in his deliberate manner. "Mrs. Loring, Manuel will see that you and Mrs. Judson have some lunch. She also has decided to stay in camp. We should be back before dark. Please don't stray too far from camp. If you fish, just stick to this part of the river. We want to take back the same number of guests that we brought." His weathered face crinkled into a smile.

Carole thanked him but he continued to stand there for a moment, stroking his short, neat beard, apparently turning something over in his mind. "By the way—" His demeanor was serious again. "The land across the river is privately owned and posted against trespassers. Also, the old fellow who owns Thunder Mountain Manor doesn't take kindly to visitors. He is reputed to have run off his last visitors with a shotgun." Steve Morgan's green eyes twinkled. "We aren't equipped to handle casualties."

Carole was annoyed, but she spoke patiently, "Thank you for your concern, Mr. Morgan."

Steve gave her another long searching look, seemed about to say something else, then decided against it, and with a friendly wave of his hand went to join the departing fishermen.

Carole leaned back in her chair and closed her eyes. The voices of the fishermen drifting back into camp gradually grew dimmer and dimmer. The only sounds that could be heard then were the gurgle of the river, the feathered camp-robbers scolding in the nearby trees, Manuel's soft humming, and the clink and jingle as he put his camp kitchen into order.

Carole dozed—but not for long. Mrs. Judson emerged from her tent and discovered Carole. She plunked herself down in a chair nearby and began a wearying tirade of all the clubs she belonged to and how she never had enough time to attend all the meetings and functions connected with them.

It must be tiresome to feel a need to impress people as the Judsons seemed to, Carole thought. Smothering a yawn, she interrupted, "I believe I'll go to my tent for awhile, Mrs. Judson. Please excuse me."

A short while later, Carole was hurrying down the trail toward the river. As she left camp, she saw that Mrs. Judson had cornered Manuel and his expression was so woebegone that Carole could not suppress a soft giggle. Poor Manuel, she thought.

About twenty minutes later Carole stood at the edge of the swinging footbridge, surveying the old gray stone mansion with searching eyes. She felt a tingle of excitement. An emerald-green expanse of lawn sloped toward the steep river bank; a four foot stone wall stopped its descent. Several huge old trees and flower beds lent grace and beauty to the landscape. In front of the great house, on Carole's left, a gray-haired man was busily working in a spacious flower bed beyond a natural stone sidewalk.

Crossing the swaying bridge and approaching the wall, Carole observed several "NO TRESPASSING" signs. There was a wide, arched gate. She found it locked. Ignoring the signs, she climbed over the stone fence and walked swiftly toward the old man.

Although she approached almost noiselessly, he seemed to sense her presence, raising his shaggy head and looking about warily. His face had no doubt once been handsome but now it was lined, and the dark eyes looked fierce and belligerent under heavy, shaggy gray brows. As soon as he saw her, he came hobbling toward her, shaking a three-pronged cultivating fork.

"Young woman," he shouted, "can't you read?"

Carole stopped and smiled appealingly. Speaking in her most beguiling voice, she ignored his questions and said, "You have a beautiful castle, sir. I am fascinated by it. But that isn't the reason I am trespassing on your property." Even her sweetest smile, with a dimple thrown in for good measure, didn't seem to melt him. The old man stood his ground fiercely, like an angry bulldog.

"What do you want, then?" he growled.

Carole scanned the windows of the old castle before she turned her lovely blue-black eyes to his face. "I took a walk the other night, from our camp on the other side of the river, and I saw a little girl. She disappeared in this vicinity. Is she your grandchild?"

For just a fleeting second, fear was mirrored in the old man's fierce eyes. She was sure of it! Then he thundered, "I don't have a granddaughter! Get off my property with your idiotic prattle!" He shook his fork menacingly.

Carole, unused to such abuse, took a step or two back, but curiosity and determination made her try again.

"But, Mr. Prentice, who could she be, then?"

The veins stood out in the old gentleman's neck, and his face became livid. "I'm wise to you scheming, conniving females! You never saw a child, or anything for that matter! That's just tomfoolery you concocted to get past my 'no trespass' signs to gawk. 'Tain't the first time it's happened. Lazy, good-for-nothing silly women! All they've got to do nowadays is gadabout the country, gawking and taking pictures. Now, get out of here before I go get my gun!" He began to hobble toward her again, his dark eyes smoldering angrily.

Carole turned quickly to flee, but in turning she lifted her eyes to the ivy-covered walls of the old mansion—and gasped. There in a second story window was a child's face— a little white pixie face, surrounded by long, shimmering flaxen hair. For a few seconds it was there and then it vanished as though snatched from its perch.

The old man had stopped when Carole did. He bellowed, "What you gawking at now?" Carole saw stark fear in his eyes. Then, sputtering threats, he charged toward her. Carole ran.

Safely back across the wall and the swinging footbridge, she looked back. The old tyrant was standing at the stone wall, still waving his wicked cultivating fork, shouting vindictively.

4

As Carole was going back to camp, she saw Manuel busily scouring a large iron skillet in the sand at the riverside. When he saw Carole descending the steep path to the river, he smiled a welcome.

"Manuel, can you tell me anything about the old man who lives in the huge mansion across the river?"

"Only that he is mucho mean man!" Manuel spoke expressively, "I go over one time, when we have camp here, to have neighbor-talk. He run in house and get big gun before I get across river good. I no stay to talk!" Manuel laughed at his own joke.

"Slim say he hear in town that old man get mad at his girl 'cause she want to live in city, and he tell her to go and never come back. She never come back either!" Manuel spread his hand over his chest, "That man must be much miserable inside to act so bad. He sure need Jesus in here, " he said, patting his chest.

Feeling rather uncomfortable at the mention of Jesus, Carole thanked Manuel and strolled on down the river bank. The river flowed deeply and smoothly here, rippling softly around rocks and boulders, clear as crystal, yet where it neared the mansion the riverbed was narrow and the water tumbled and foamed over and around huge boulders, spilling over rocky shelves into little waterfalls and narrow rapids.

The murmur of the river, the warm sun spilling through leafy branches, the whirring of insects, and the chirping of birds were soothing and restful to Carole's spirit. She sank down in the warm sand between large white rocks, resting her back against a smooth boulder, and tossed small stones into the water not far from her feet. Small minnows darted about in the shallow edge of the water.

Gradually her mind drifted from the peaceful scene about her to the rather frightening encounter with Mr.

Prentice awhile before. Why did he deny so vehemently that there was a child in his huge castle-like home? Who was the little girl and what was she to the old man? He was afraid of something or someone, and it seemed to be somehow connected with the child. In her mind, Carole could still see the tiny white-clad figure, her long hair shimmering like silver in the moonlight. Although Carole had never especially liked children, she was fascinated with this one and the mystery surrounding her. Who was she and where had she come from?

Carole had had very few dealings with children, but it seemed to her they were forever crying or demanding attention in some manner. Perhaps she was even a little frightened of them. David wanted children, but she had managed so far to change the subject adroitly or forestall discussion. She couldn't bear the thought of sticky fingers clutching at her, drooling baby lips and smelly diapers. Was something the matter with her? Perhaps some women were just not made for motherhood. Sometimes she wished she could present David with a baby but she just couldn't face the idea.

Carole's thoughts swung to David. She really loved him, but could she stand to be married to a sickening alcoholic? He was headed down that road unless he changed. Was their marriage doomed, headed for divorce? She shuddered at the thought. She had always been highly contemptuous of those who shed mates and donned new ones as nonchalantly as changing clothing.

Where had her marriage gone wrong? Gran seemed to think she was to blame! Perhaps Gran was right. If so, was it too late to rectify the matter? David had wanted so badly to teach. Should she encourage him to go back to school and get his teaching certificate, if that's what he desired? She detested the idea of his teaching school but if that would cure their marriage, maybe it would be worth the sacrifice.

Maybe she *should* give him a child. The thought was revolting! Surely she wouldn't have to go that far. After all, why should she do all the giving? She wasn't even sure any of this would straighten out their marriage anyway.

Carole jumped up. She'd had enough of her musings. They were unprofitable anyway. She'd go back and see if Manuel had lunch ready.

After eating, she rested in her tent for awhile, then decided on a walk. A few minutes of brisk walking and Carole was standing once more at the end of the footbridge, surveying the huge old stone house. There was no movement anywhere. She backed into the shadows of a tree and sat down on a log. She was determined to find out more about that child and what was going on in that mysterious place! But after half an hour of intermittently pacing about and sitting on the rough bark of the log, she decided to walk on down the river. Sleuthing was very boring this afternoon.

At first Carole enjoyed the brisk pace she set for herself. It set her blood to pumping and made her feel alive and healthy. The solitude, the rustling forest sounds, the splash and ripple of the river, and the colorful busy birds and darting chipmunks were refreshing to her spirit. But soon she grew tired and began to feel lonely and desirous of human companionship.

She turned around and soon was back at the footbridge. She glanced at the mansion but there was still no stirring on the grounds or at the house so she set out for the camp, feeling somewhat depressed. She was actually looking forward to seeing David. She missed him! A frightening thought surfaced in her mind. What if she and David parted? Could she bear to come home to an empty house? She recoiled at the thought. Maybe a drunken David was better than no David at all!

Evening came at last and with the long shadows came the weary but exultant party of fishermen. Gran complained of tiredness but Carole could tell she was pleased, even elated, with the day's adventures. David sought out Carole immediately and told her jublilantly of the day's happenings. He was the old David she had married—bubbling over with life and laughter, not giddy but fun to be with, gentle and thoughtful.

Carole felt lighthearted as they sat down for supper, but a little barb kept pricking her conscience. Had she caused the changes in the old David that she loved so well by trying to force him into a mold that was foreign to his nature? One he could never adjust to? She knew he didn't really like her way of life. The thoughts marred the merry meal for her.

Supper over, Carole saw Manuel reach for his guitar, and she felt that uneasy feeling slip over her. She rose to go to her tent but David laid a detaining hand on her arm. His voice was almost pleading, "Please stay, honey. I—I—" He hesitated, seeming to search for words, "Maybe we can find some answers here to our. . . ." He broke off abruptly, but there was a mingled wistfulness and imploring in his eyes. Touched, she decided to stay.

Manuel was singing now. The words she didn't understand but the music stirred a yearning, a longing for something—something vague and intangible but, nevertheless, very real.

As if in answer to what the something was, Manuel laid aside his guitar and began to speak, not loudly but with much simplicity and earnestness, about something called salvation that he seemed certain he possessed. He told briefly about an unhappy selfish life of drinking, fighting and carousing.

"But one day," he said, in his Spanish accent, "I invited Jesus into my heart and Jesus make me into a new man! I never quit thanking Him for the joy and peace I have down here." He patted his chest. "My kids run to meet me now with no fear because Jesus, instead of devil, is master of Manuel."

Manuel picked up his guitar again and began to sing softly in his pleasing voice, "Amazing grace, how sweet the sound, that saved a wretch like me." Others joined in and Carole found herself singing and thinking as she did: Does he really have something that I do not have? Is this experience Manuel calls salvation something real?

Steve was speaking now. He had just finished reading from the Bible. Carole caught only the last few words, "Take my yoke upon you, and learn of me; for I am meek and lowly in heart: and ye shall find rest unto your souls."

Steve's earnestness matched Manuel's as he closed the Bible and looked out over the campers, his green eyes intense with feeling. "I, like Manuel, had filled my life with many things which should have brought happiness but, in reality, seemed to make my life more meaningless. But several years ago Manuel came to work for me and through him I met Jesus Christ. Then I, too, found that peace Jesus promised."

Carole had never felt so perturbed in her life. Why, she did not know. She turned to David and saw that he was soaking up every word, and Gran sat with rapt attention, also. Carole's unease and agitation grew through the last song— an unfamiliar one which spoke of joy and peace. Angrily she thought, this worship doesn't bring *me* peace and joy! She was glad when it ended.

But it wasn't over. She didn't rest well and all through the next day of fishing, resting and excellent meals that Manuel prepared on a huge wood stove and large barbeque grill, the words of the little service kept popping into her troubled mind. Words of Manuel or Steve; a line or so of a song; and the words from the Bible, "Ye shall find rest unto your souls," traced their way across her memory time and time again.

But David did not seem troubled and Gran appeared to enjoy every activity of the day. David fished with enthusiasm, and he tried to draw Carole into the thrill of trout fishing, whooping with delight when she landed her first cutthroat. She could have lost herself in the sport, also, if those haunting words had let her alone. But they continued to pour through her consciousness like liquid fire.

5

Eagerness and desire were etched in David's face when the devotional service began that evening. Carole felt almost frightened and very alone. Had she lost David to this thing called salvation? She pled a headache and escaped to her tent. But there was no escaping the words and music of the singing which carried clearly until she covered her head with a pillow.

When that didn't work either, she groped in the semi-darkness of her tent for her radio and turned it on. Thankfully the batteries were strong. A news program was on the first station so she turned the needle back and forth, trying to find some music that would come in strong enough to cover the annoying worship service. But there wasn't anything, so she went back to the news station. At least it was a strong, loud noise.

"There has been no new development in the million dollar jewel heist," a newsman was reporting. "A week ago in Spokane, Washington, two armed gunmen were surprised by the owner of Johnson Jewelry in the early hours of the morning as they were about to make off with an estimated million dollars worth of jewels. It is still unknown how the burglars opened the vault where the jewels were stored. The store owner, Raymond Johnson, was shot in the chest. He is reported to be in serious but stable condition at a local hospital."

The newsman went on to describe the two robbers as Caucasian in their late twenties. "One man has a trim mustache, dark curly longish black hair, and is about six-foot, with a medium build. The other burglar is a little shorter, heavily built—like a prize fighter—with reddish hair and a ruddy complexion. He is clean shaven and has a scar running from the corner of his right eyebrow up into the hairline. Police Chief Ronson says the description fits recently released convicts Ferron Kyle and Max Parrish, well-known jewel thieves.

"The men escaped in a stolen car which was later found abandoned. Anyone seeing persons fitting this description should contact his local police station. The men are considered armed and dangerous.

"A fire in Southside Spokane which destroyed a warehouse, has been brought under control before it could spread to other businesses in the area. Faulty wiring in the older building, and not arson as was first suspected, is believed to be the cause of the fire. Mayor Farrell praised Spokane firemen for bringing the fire under control so quickly. At first, it appeared the whole block was in peril.

"The governor has called an emergency meeting. . ."

But Carole heard no more. The droning voice of the newscaster had drowned out the music and singing of the offending worship and calmed her down. She hadn't rested well the night before and the strenuous day in the high, clean mountain air took their toll. She fell sound asleep before the news broadcast was over.

A short while later, when David came in search of her, the radio was blasting out rock and roll music and Carole was sound asleep. He turned down the volume, gently eased Carole's boots off and covered her with a soft, warm plaid blanket before returning to the campfire. He wanted to ask Steve Morgan some questions he had been wrestling with since the first camp devotional service.

6

When she awoke the next morning, Carole felt refreshed from her long sleep and ravenously hungry. Delectable odors were coming from the large, open cook tent. As she made herself presentable, she mulled over the happenings since they had arrived at camp and made some resolutions:

24

Number one: She would forget about the child. It was possibly her imagination, but if not, it was of no concern to her.

Number two: She would throw herself into fishing, camping, eating and enjoying this beautiful Idaho wilderness.

Number three: She would not attend another church service while here. It made her miserable and destroyed her peace of mind, so why should she subject herself to it?

With these decisions firmly established in her mind, Carole went to the dining tent with a light heart.

This morning Manuel had prepared fluffy baking powder biscuits, fried salt pork, which Carole had never tasted but found delicious, creamy gravy, scrambled eggs, and hot, stewed dried apricots. She had never tried these before, either, but with a dab of butter and buttered biscuits they were delectable. And there was plenty of good, hot coffee. Even the odors of food seemed stronger and more pleasing to the senses in the heady, clean mountain air. It whetted her appetite to the point where it seemed she couldn't get enough.

Steve Morgan had recommended a hike to Cougar Lake where the fishing was unusually good and the scenery spectacular. All the campers decided to go and by seven were dressed and on the trail. The trail was wide, and though there was climbing, it wasn't extremely steep except for a place or two. David and Carole were both in excellent physical condition so the hike was just comfortably invigorating for them while some of the others protested and panted, resting often.

The trail was well marked and Steve assured them they couldn't get lost as it led straight to the lake, so David and Carole hiked on ahead of the others. Gran decided to come with the rest at a slower pace. The morning was cool and crisp as Carole and David set off. David was obviously delighted that she had come with him and was his old cheerful, thoughtful self today.

She stayed true to her resolutions. When any words of the annoying devotional service tried to creep into her mind she decisively turned her thoughts to other things. Carole determined to enjoy the day and she did.

After the others were left behind, there remained only the sighing of the breeze through the trees, the drone of insects, and the chatter of birds and squirrels. It was peaceful and soul-resting. When the path wasn't too steep, and where there was room, David would take her hand and they would stroll together, not talking much, just relaxed and contented.

Once they stopped dead in their tracks, hardly daring to breathe, as a cow elk crossed the path ahead with her awkward youngster pressing close behind her. Cute little chipmunks darted here and there, stopping long enough now and then to nibble at seeds held in tiny paws as they turned inquisitive little heads to follow the movements of the intruders into their domain.

At last they reached the shore of a small lake lying like a blue-green jewel set in a ring of reddish-gold rock. It was so beautiful they were content to sit on the rocks and soak in the tranquility of the scene spread out before them. After awhile they heard the others trudging up the trail and they reluctantly arose to fish.

The morning was an enormous success fishwise. The fish seemed hungry and grabbed the bait almost as soon as it hit the water. Shouts of glee reverberated around Cougar Lake as elated fishermen pulled out one shiny, flipping fish after another. Slim, the camp wrangler, and all-around handyman, filleted the fish—mostly pan size, pink-meated silver salmon—and packed them in the ice chests brought up by two surly, long-eared mules. Tonight Manuel had promised them a mammoth fish fry. Having a part in bringing in the meat satisfies a certain primeval hunter instinct inherent in mankind, whether ultra-civilized business-man or back-country aborigine, and these campers were no exception.

However, by midmorning most of the exuberant

26

fishermen and fisherwomen had taken their lawful limit and had to find other diversions. Steve told them about a picturesque canyon that contained a waterfall and a colony of nesting swallows high in the cliffs that was within easy walking distance. Some, including Gran who was an enthusiastic bird-watcher, had brought binoculars, so it was decided unanimously to go. Taking the sack lunches Manuel had sent along, the party set out, leaving Slim to return to camp with the balky mules and fish.

David and Carole shared Gran's binoculars and were amazed and entranced with the variety of birds the area sheltered. When they arrived at the waterfall, everyone shared the four pairs of binoculars, watching the swallows. The cliffs were thickly populated with mud nests from which the nesting parents flew endlessly, in search of food for their voracious offspring. Steve explained that mountain sheep frequently were sighted on the rocky mountain top near the waterfall, but though everyone kept a vigilant watch, the elusive creatures didn't put in an appearance all day. No one seemed to mind, though, as they investigated the canyon, which wasn't over a quarter of a mile long. It contained, besides the spectacular waterfall, a gorgeous array of wild flowers, lofty trees and multicolored boulders and the crystal clear, ice-cold stream, rippling and gurgling over a rocky, pebbly bed.

Late in the afternoon Carole climbed a grassy knoll to observe more closely a patch of wild flowers. Sitting down to rest before returning, she saw Steve Morgan glance that way and then leave the others to join her. She stiffened when she saw him coming. She avoided Steve because she had known two other Christian fanatics who couldn't talk to anyone very long without trying to push their religion on them. She had long ago decided when, and if, she wanted religion she would seek it out herself; she didn't want someone pushing it down her throat. As bold as Steve was in his camp devotionals, she was sure he was one of those fanatics. Not wanting to be rude, she remained where she was but resolved to listen to no preaching.

Sitting down near her, Steve inquired if she was enjoying the camping trip. She answered in the affirmative, but remained on her guard while they exchanged some other small talk. She had the decided feeling that Steve had more on his mind than birds, flowers and fish. It probably had to do with religion and she planned to have no part of that.

Steve told her a couple of comical incidents that had taken place on other camping trips. In spite of herself, Carole found herself warming to this man. His humor and obvious enjoyment of life were contagious. His broad shoulders and easy, confident, controlled manner spoke of strength and dependability without arrogance or conceit.

Steve rose to go, walked a few steps away, then turned and walked back to stand before her. "Mrs. Loring," he said, "I have hesitated about asking you this lest you think I'm pushy. I don't mean to be, but I noticed that you have not been staying for most of our devotional times. Is there something in them that is offensive to you?"

When he began to speak, Carole's instant reaction had been: Here comes the sermon! Standing up, ready to do battle, she answered his question coldly, "I just don't like 'church' with my fishing!"

"Then your grandmother didn't tell you there was to be a devotional time each evening in camp?"

"If she had, I wouldn't have come!"

Steve studied her face gravely for a moment before he said slowly, "Is the fact that you feel you were deceived disturbing you or is it the actual service that you find objectionable?"

Carole hesitated, considering, before she answered candidly, "I'm not sure. I was angry about Gran's deception, but I don't like your worship service, either!"

Steve spoke softly, "Why don't you like it?"

"Because it makes me uncomfortable and—and—" Carole's dark eyes flashed fire, "you and Manuel talk so smugly about the peace and happiness you have! Your worship service doesn't bring me peace and joy—it makes me miserable! I don't know why it does but it just does!"

"Mrs. Loring," Steve said gently, "the only time God's Word makes us feel miserable is when we are fighting against it. I was the most miserable man alive before I asked God to come into my life. I had all the comforts of life, was a success in my occupation, had the love of a great gal, two good-looking, intelligent kids, but life seemed empty and devoid of meaning. Then I met Jesus, and now every day is full and satisfying. If you want this, it's yours for the asking. Just believe that Jesus, the Son of God, died to pay for your sins and invite Him into your life. It's that simple."

Carole had been expecting a "sermon" from the camp leader but when it came, Steve spoke with such earnest sincerity that she was completely disarmed. Now, suddenly, with vivid clarity, she realized—he was preaching to her! Fury exploded in her.

Lifting her chin haughtily, every word she spoke was a brittle icicle, "Mr. Morgan, I'm not a heathen! I was baptized when I was a baby. I'm a member of a church. I give to charities and to the church generously!"

"Those are good and commendable things," Steve reasoned, "but they do not bring peace into a person's heart, only Christ living and ruling in our lives can do that."

"When I want a sermon, I'll attend your nightly service!" Carole said venomously. Stepping around Steve, she stalked away. She felt a twinge of guilt at her rudeness—but she had no intention of apologizing.

She hadn't taken a dozen steps before Steve fell into step beside her. "Mrs. Loring, I'm sorry if I have offended you. Will you accept my apology?"

Carole tried to be gracious, but it was difficult because she was so angry. Through stiff lips she mumbled, "It's okay, forget it." But as she walked toward the group David was with, strange questions began to surface. Why was she so angry with Steve Morgan? Why did the devotional time so distress her? Why did a couple of Christian songs, a

Scripture verse or two, and a few words about serving God upset her so much? Was Steve right? Did she need something she did not have? She thrust the thought forcefully away. She was a Christian just as much as he was! But the uneasy feelings refused to leave her mind. Angrily she thought, "I wish I had never heard of this camp, Steve Morgan, Manuel and especially their worship service!"

But a few minutes later, as she stood leaning against a tree, watching David laughing and talking with the group, clear-headed and obviously enjoying himself, she had second thoughts. She had not seen David like this for many, many months. Here in the mountains David was relaxed, cheerful, and—sober. In fact, he was the David she had married and loved with all her heart. The David he became after drinking too much was the life-of-the-party with scathing wit. Her guests loved that David and often told her how fortunate she was to be married to such a fascinating man. She always agreed, with an artificial smile, and then secretly longed to have her old David back. He was the one she loved, and wanted to be cherished by.

After one of their lengthy parties where alcohol flowed freely, Carole frequently had the strange feeling that an alien had invaded her lovely home, a person that she wasn't even sure she liked, much less loved. This foreign person was polite but in a supercilious way, arrogant, mocking, sarcastic and crass—all the things she disliked in a man. When the alcohol wore off, he was contrite, humble, and apologetic. Filled with self-reproach, he tried to make up for his misbehavior by being overly attentive and especially thoughtful. This demeaning conduct repulsed her almost as much as the one for which he was apologizing. Apparently David could not stomach it either, and usually he was hitting the bottle before the day was over and the vicious cycle would start all over again.

As she stood watching David, her heart swelled with love and wifely pride. He made a striking picture. His lean, muscular frame was enhanced by the blue denim jeans and blue and yellow cotton flannel shirt, open at the throat. The long shirt sleeves were rolled back and revealed strong, tanned wrists. There were comfortable, well-cut walking boots on his feet.

Gathered about David, giving rapt attention to what he was saying, were the two women teachers, Mr. and Mrs. Adams and their son, Gran, and even one of the almost inseparable businessmen. Curious as to what subject David was captivating his audience with, Carole shoved herself away from the tree and started toward the group gathered at the edge of the wide stream.

The movement caught her grandmother's eye and Gran slipped away from the group to join Carole before she came close enough to really hear what David was saying. Stopping Carole with a slender, jeweled hand on her arm, she spoke softly in her abrupt way, "I like your young man!"

Gran had never said much about David since their marriage and his heavy drinking had begun, so this remark came as a surprise. Now Gran was observing David with a speculative gleam in her eyes. "That boy has a good head on his shoulders! And when he talks about those water plants, they're no longer a handful of weeds—they are fascinating creations! Look, Carole, even that smart-aleck Adams boy is listening! Can you beat that!" And Carole saw that it was true—the boy was leaning forward, completely absorbed in the plants David was holding in his hand and what he was saying.

"David should have been a teacher," Gran continued. She turned her head slowly to look at Carole. "He was studying to be a teacher wasn't he? Before he married you?" It sounded like an accusation, and Carole was immediately on the defensive.

"Why should a fine young man throw his life away in a stuffy old classroom, teaching a bunch of empty-headed, stupid kids that don't even want to be there? I could see him teaching in college classrooms, but no! David wants to teach in high school or even in junior high!"

"You mean a college professor sounds much more dignified and sophisticated than a junior high school teacher?"

Carole's face flamed and her anger flared, "Yes, it does! If he insisted on teaching when he doesn't have to, at least he could do it in a distinguished college somewhere!"

"So, it's just as I feared. You have used your charm to turn a highly gifted teacher into a worthless but sophisticated drunk!"

The words fell like searing coals of fire upon Carole's heart, and she did something she had never done before in her life. Her brusque little grandmother had been both mother and father to her and Carole had always treated her with utmost respect, but now—cut to the quick—she lashed out with words that were meant to wound and hurt.

"What have you done that has ever been a worthy contribution to society? Given a few paltry dollars to charity out of your abundance! You speak so condescendingly of your granddaughter for wanting a sophisticated, dignified husband! That's the example you set for me! You were ever the sophisticated socialite, flitting here and there about the world, entertaining and being entertained!"

Carole was crying now. Her voice had risen and she realized with horror that David and the others had heard her last words as they turned startled eyes in her direction. David rose quickly and started toward her. Mortified because she always prided herself on self-control, she turned away. But Gran laid her small, strong hands on her forearms and forced her to look at her. Her voice showed no anger or censure.

"You are right, Carole. I loved you dearly but I was far from the best example for you. I never realized it, though, until I saw myself mirrored in you and your ideals. I have been trying to find a way to rectify the lack in our lives. I thought perhaps God could help. I found Him last year and that is why I came and brought you two with me to this kind of camp."

Carole reeled under the impact of Gran's disclosure. Humility and this manner of confession were foreign to the grandmother Carole thought she knew so well. Then she felt David's comforting arm around her, leading her away. When a screen of trees and brush hid them from curious eyes, he kissed her tenderly before seating her on a fragrant carpet of pine needles. With his arm still protectively about her, love and concern glowing in his blue eyes, he asked, "What was that all about?"

Carole tried to laugh lightly but it came off poorly and sounded more like a sob than a laugh. "It really wasn't much of anything. We just had a little disagreement."

David didn't look convinced. "And it had you shouting and crying?"

"I didn't shout. I just raised my voice a bit."

"But you were crying."

"Okay! I was angry and I was crying. Grandmother accused me of not letting you teach and making an alcoholic out of you!"

David went very still and dropped his eyes. When he didn't speak and the silence lengthened between them, she blurted out, "You think that, too!"

David still didn't speak for a long weighted moment, then he moved around until he was facing her. "No, Carole, you did not make me an alcoholic. In fact, I don't believe I am an alcoholic—yet. I drank because it made me forget—temporarily—what a coward I am." She noticed he used the past tense and her heart leaped. "And—no, you didn't make me give up teaching. I laid it aside because I loved you so much I hadn't the courage to risk losing you over it. But for a long time I have known that loving and being loved is not enough. A person must have a purpose or goal in life."

He paused, but Carole just waited silently for him to continue. "Up here, away from the parties—and alcohol—my mind has cleared and I have come to some decisions. I had planned to discuss them with you later but perhaps now is as good a time as any."

David took her hand in his strong brown one. Lifting it to his lips, he kissed it before proceeding. "I have made three definite decisions and commitments.

"Number one, I have given my life to God.

"Number two, I plan to resume my studies and become a teacher.

"Number three, I will never drink again."

When David enumerated his first decision, her heart gave a wild lurch. Now, as he finished, she burst out, "You mean you're going to be a priest?"

David laughed, "No, honey! I just mean that I'm planning to serve God. I've invited Christ into my life and I've asked God to direct and guide me."

Suddenly Carole felt fury building in her again and she spoke accusingly, "Steve Morgan has been talking to you and convinced you that you have to be a religious fanatic like he and that Manuel are! Didn't he? And he's the one who convinced you that you need to go back to school. You've been discussing our business with him instead of with your wife! And I guess he told you that if you take one more drink it would send you straight to hell when anyone, except those goody-goodies, knows that a drink now and then doesn't hurt you. It's just when a person doesn't have the sense to know when to quit that alcohol does any harm!"

Stricken, David's face went ashen. Slowly he got to his feet. She could see anguished hurt play over his sensitive face. When she stopped spewing, he spoke very quietly. "You have everything wrong, Carole. After the first evening worship service I knew that I needed God in my life. I went to Steve last night. He prayed with me, and I committed my life to Christ. I did discuss my returning to school with Steve, but he just listened and advised me to ask God for direction, which I did. However, I have known all along that I should be a teacher, and to teach I must finish my schooling, and I plan to," he said decisively. "As for the drinking, it has to be all the way or not at all."

Carole sprang to her feet. "And what am I to do while

you go to school all day and study all night?"

Troubled, David studied her lovely, indignant face, her dark velvety eyes practically shooting sparks. "I'm sure it won't be as bad as you think. I will always make room for you in my life."

"How charitable of you!" she said scathingly. "Well, let me tell you something! I'll never play second fiddle to your old school! Never!" She turned and marched stiffly away. She fully expected David to come after her and coax and caress her back into a good mood—he always had. But this time he didn't!

7

On the hike back to camp, Carole was frigidly silent, and after a couple of futile attempts at conversation, David left her and made himself useful to the older ladies when the trail was steep or talked to the other campers. Gran's efforts at communication Carole also rebuffed.

Back in camp she went immediately to her tent to lie down while final dinner preparations were underway. But the longer she lay there the more her rage grew. She finally could lie there no longer. Grabbing her flashlight since it was nearly dark, she went for a walk.

As she was starting down the trail toward the river, Steve called to her. "Mrs. Loring, it isn't real safe for you to be wandering about by yourself after dark. There are wild animals in the woods. And it is almost suppertime, so please don't be gone long."

Carole didn't turn around or answer, and acted as if she hadn't heard him. This childish rudeness gave her a sense of defiant satisfaction. She knew her actions were immature and churlish but at the moment she didn't care.

Carole took the trail that led to the artist's castle. She walked swiftly and as she walked her anger began to cool and remorse set in. She wished she had not cut her little grandmother down. Shame flooded her innermost being as she recalled her denunciation of the grandmother who had willingly made a home for her when her own mother and father would, no doubt, have shuttled her into a boarding school.

Nearly all her life, Gran had been the only one home to hear Carole's "little girl" talk and her dreams, and to kiss away the loneliness, or the hurt of a bumped knee. Gran was always busy with her own social life, charities, and business matters, true, but never had she been too busy for Carole. When she was older, Carole shared her aspirations, discussed her boyfriends, and ran to Gran with all her problems. And Gran was always ready to listen, to give a little sage advice or to help her solve a problem. She, and not Carole's mother, had taught her manners, etiquette, how to dress, and all the little things a mother normally teaches a daughter. There was nothing she could not discuss with Gran, to the envy of some of her friends who weren't as fortunate.

Gran and David were the two loves of her life and she reproached herself as she realized she had treated them both abominably. "I must go back and apologize to them. But not yet," she said aloud to the forest. "First I have to sort some things out in my own mind. Why am I acting this way?" Carol exclaimed in despair. She knew she must examine her feelings and emotions and answer that question. The explosiveness of her feelings about David's new resolves and her verbal attack on her grandmother frightened her. And why did she so resent and even abhor the brief, simple camp devotional? She had never minded attending a long church service before. A tiny, annoying suspicion kept buzzing in her brain that her repulsion went deeper than just being angry with her grandmother for not telling her about the nightly camp devotional before she came.

Carole had walked rapidly and now was standing at the swinging footbridge. There still remained a dusky light and the old castle-like mansion seemed gloomy and mysterious in the eerie half-light. A faint light glowed in two downstairs and three upstairs windows. As she stood watching, an outside light on the left side of the building went on, illuminating a long shed-like building not far from the house. "It's most likely a woodshed," Carole thought and wondered idly if they had electric service or a strong power generator. Electric service probably. It could be extended into the remotest areas, she was sure, if money was no object. And to build and maintain a mansion of this size the artist must have a sizable fortune.

There was no movement on the grounds of the old castle to hold her attention so Carole's mind reverted to her former troublesome thoughts. Why did she object so strenuously to David going to work? She had told Gran that she wouldn't mind as much if David would teach in a college, but truthfully, she didn't want him to work at all. When they were first married, Gran had suggested that David begin to learn all about the family's businesses and gradually take over a leadership position. Now Carole remembered that she had promptly vetoed the suggestion. David also had expressed a desire to work into one of the companies or go to work elsewhere. He told her he enjoyed work and felt like a "kept man" when he contributed nothing to their upkeep. But she parried or put off every proposal.

What was the *real* reason she panicked—and panic she did—when she thought David might leave her side for a job? She recalled the reason she gave Gran. "I don't ever want David to become so engrossed in business that nothing else matters, like my father and mother did."

She had dim, almost forgotten memories of when she was very small. Her mother had been home to read to her and play with her during the day and to tuck her into bed with a warm hug and kiss at night.

But her father, Thomas Drake—whom Carole had idolized—had been home very seldom. And when he was, he'd had little time for Carole. She recalled inventing excuses to go to his study on his infrequent visits home. He never came to her, so this was the only way she got to see him. But most of the time when she sought him out he was impatient with the intrusion and sometimes even angry with her. Once she overheard him telling her mother, "Can't you keep that kid out of my study? I'm a busy man!" She wondered why Daddy didn't like her, and tried all the harder to please him but was usually rebuffed or scolded for her trouble.

Then her mother began to travel with her husband. Perhaps she also longed to be with Carole's father, Carole reasoned now. She became more and more his "right hand man" and home less and less. Soon she was as engrossed in the family businesses as her husband—an astute business-lady, everyone said admiringly.

Carole saw very little of her parents after she was four years old but received many lavish, expensive gifts from different parts of the world where they traveled. At first she had lived in ecstacy for days after an exotic gift arrived from her parents—it was like a longed-for caress from the missing parents. She slept with the object and would hardly lay it down even to eat. Then one day she accidentally discovered that the gifts were all selected, wrapped and sent by her mother's secretary. Grief-stricken, she had realized that usually neither parent saw or even knew what had been sent to their daughter. After that, the gifts were only objects to be shown to her friends for their envious admiration, and then they were usually cast aside and never looked at again.

Carole leaned on the corner post of the swinging bridge, gazing at the old castle with unseeing eyes. Absorbed in her meditations, she was unaware that night had settled upon the river and stars were beginning to blink silently overhead.

It seems logical, she reasoned, that the fear and panic I feel when David speaks of becoming involved in a job of any kind is brought on by the remembrance of first my adored father and then my warm, loving mother becoming so involved with business that they deserted their daughter completely. I'm afraid of being forsaken again!

But surely, David would never leave her out of his life. Her heart quaked at the very thought. It had been unthinkable that her mother would abandon her only child, but she had! Would David do the same? I'm a coward, she thought. I'm afraid to take the chance of losing David to the world of business. Too many make a profession lover, God and master. I'm terrified of being deserted again. Thank heaven Gran has always been there! But though Gran has done her best to be father and mother to me, my husband's place she could never fill.

This was the first time Carole had ever fully analyzed her feelings. For one thing, she had tried never to think about her parents—it was a painful subject. They had been killed in a plane crash when she was twelve, but she had tried to blot them from her life and memory long before that. Their memory spelled rejection with a capital "R." They hadn't been home in over a year when they were killed, and in that year she had received only one short note from her mother, dictated to the secretary. There had been no personal note, no expressions of love.

Carole recalled now that she had considered her parents' deaths a final and complete desertion and had been angry, rather than grieved. They had spent their lives rejecting her, and now they had abandoned her for good. It was typical of her parents, she had illogically reasoned. Well, she didn't care, she had raged in her young heart. But she had cared—terribly. She had covered her grief with a nonchalant smile and even her grandmother had never known the depth of her pain.

Now David had determined to go back to school and become a teacher! Carole felt cold, though she wore a warm sweater. Panic traced icicles through her inner being. He was leaving her, too! And if the school and teaching didn't take him from her, his new religion would. Helpless tears rolled down her cheeks.

The salvation that Manuel and Steve spoke of so

glowingly would take away her thoughtful, handsome husband as surely as the earth was round! Like those two religious persons in college, that's all he would talk about or care for—religion. It sickened her to think of David becoming a pious, obnoxious creature that everyone avoided! Feeling absolutely bereft and desolate, she put her head down on the bridge post and sobbed.

8

So absorbed was she with her own grief she only dimly heard the first shout. At the second shout, she jerked her head up and, dashing the tears from her eyes with a quick swish of her hand, she stared at a strange panorama spread out before her startled eyes. Through the dim, starlit night, a small white figure was racing across the lawn straight for the swinging footbridge. Sprinting behind her in hot pursuit were two large figures, obviously men, their light-colored shirts showing plainly in the dim light. Carole ducked down and backed into some prickly, concealing brush that lined the path, being careful she wasn't seen but in a position so she could still observe the running trio.

The tiny, white-clad figure was at the edge of the bridge when the first large figure caught her. Across the narrow expanse of the river, Carole saw the child struggling in the arms of the tall figure. She heard a breathless, angry, male voice cursing violently. "Be still, you troublesome little vixen."

The tiny figure continued to struggle and Carole heard a resounding smack. With shocked horror she knew that he had struck the child. Carole felt a fierce urge to spring to her defense, but caution laid a restraining hand upon her.

The child cried out once and then began to sob, "I want my mommy. I want my mommy."

The other heavier, shorter figure had now reached the pair. "Hand that brat over to me and I'll make her afraid to run off again," said the newcomer in a coarse, nasal voice.

"She's my kid, and I'll handle her in my own way," replied the hard, decisive voice of the first man. "You better remember that this kid is the only hold we got on the old man. If anyone puts a bruise on her, he might not be so easy to handle."

"Yeah, I guess you're right," grumbled the nasal voice, "but my hand sure itches to put a bunch of bruises on her. Come on, we better get back to the house before some nosey fisherman from the camp over there gets a yen to fish at night and sees us."

The taller man grunted something Carole couldn't hear, tucked the sobbing little girl under his arm, and both men moved swiftly back toward the house.

Carole's heart was pounding with suppressed excitement. There was a child at the castle—and others as well! The old artist had lied. Why? She must find a way to get closer to the house and find out what was going on over there. The old man had disclaimed any knowledge of a little girl at the castle. But there was a little girl! And also at least two other men. The tall man had said the little girl was his own child but spoke of her more as a useful and necessary object than his own flesh and blood. The little girl certainly didn't act like he was her father. Where was the mother that the child was crying for—back at the house? If so, why would the child run away? Something very strange was going on in that old castle. She must, someway, get closer and learn why these men did not wish to be seen and what connection they had with the belligerent old castle owner.

Surveying the area with swift, calculating eyes, Carole made a quick decision. Her jeans and shirt were inconspicuously dark and the quickly retreating men had their backs to her. If she dashed silently across the bridge, crouched low and ran along the wall to the woods which pressed in not far from the old mansion, perhaps she could stay inside the edge of the tree line and come close to the house without being seen. A prickle of fear ran down her back but she refused to let it deter her. She was too close to uncovering the mystery she was sure the castle concealed to give up now.

Carole swiftly unlaced and removed her boots. Holding them in one hand, she crept to the edge of the bridge and took a step out on it. Thankfully, no squeak or sound betrayed her presence. The men were still moving rapidly toward the house and were not looking back. She glided lightly to the other side of the bridge, paused briefly to ascertain if she was observed, saw she wasn't, and— crouching to make herself as small as possible—she sprinted to the wall, and hidden, glided to the line of trees.

Standing in the sheltering shadows, she stood still for a moment to catch her breath. Her heart was pounding heavily from the exertion of her wild dash, plus excitement and fear. Leaning against a tree, Carole breathed slowly and deeply for a couple of moments before seating herself on the prickly pine needles to pull on her boots. Then she began to creep stealthily among the trees until she reached a position near the dark shadow of the long woodhouse.

It took only a minute to dash across a small clearing to the end of the woodshed. Moving cautiously along the wall, she quickly discovered that the building was really just a frame and roof. Racks of neatly stacked, sawed and split logs made up what had appeared as walls from a distance. At intervals, aisles were left open to make the wood easily accessible.

Entering one long, dark aisle, Carole moved slowly in the almost total darkness. Dim light shone at the other end. As she crept along, every six feet or so she passed other, shorter passageways crisscrossing the longer aisle she was following. Nearing the end she could hear a low murmur of voices but couldn't see anyone. Surmising that the voices were coming from the left of her aisle, she turned into one of the shorter paths. Feeling her way along until she came to the next long aisle, she turned back to the right again, toward the faint light. Now she could see figures.

Stealing to within five feet of the end of the passageway, she saw old Mr. Prentice and two younger men standing on a small side porch. Clinging to the old man's hand and leaning against his leg was the tiny, blond-haired sprite. The child was dressed in a white nightie that reached almost to her feet. Peeking out from under the nightie were furry, pink house slippers.

Although Carole couldn't hear every word, the three men were obviously engaged in an argument that was growing hotter by the moment. Suddenly Mr. Prentice silenced the other two with an angry shout, "Listen, you two!"

Perhaps the shout shocked the other two into silence. At any rate, they clamped their jaws shut and listened as the old artist continued in a loud voice, "You've been here a week now! You said when you came that you didn't plan to stay long. You made me send away my hired help! The house is getting filthy! I'm sick of eating out of cans! And if I don't send for them soon, they'll begin to suspect that something strange is going on here. I followed your orders and told them I was giving them an extra vacation this year. I've never done that before and they know I don't enjoy taking care of myself. They could come back to see if I've had an accident or fallen ill!"

The shorter, nasal-voiced man roared, "If they come back you'd better have a good story ready to send them away again unless you want something to happen to that brat!"

"Pipe down, both of you," the third man said roughly. "You'll have the people over in that camp across the river coming to see what's going on!"

Carole couldn't hear the next words so she inched her way closer. The older man had lowered his voice but he was still angry. She caught only the last of his next words. ". . . you harm my granddaughter and you'll see how much help you get out of me!"

The tall man spoke soothingly, "Calm down, old man, before you have a heart attack. We aren't about to harm that kid as long as you—"

Carole couldn't hear his last words so she took another step forward—and fell sprawling! Her foot had tripped over a piece of wood lying in the passageway. Carole sprang to her feet and ran, but she had fled only a few steps when powerful hands closed on her arms and dragged her struggling figure into the light. She had never been so frightened in her life! For one awful moment after she was hauled from her place of concealment she was too petrified with fear to open her mouth. The stocky, short man had captured her. His steely fingers bit into her arms as he propelled her across the narrow space into the brighter light of the small porch where the other two men stood.

Finally Carole found her voice. "Let me go! Take your hands off me! How dare you treat me like this!" She protested angrily, struggling fiercely against the powerful hands which pinioned her arms behind her back.

Pitting all her strength against her captor in the struggle to free herself, Carole realized how utterly helpless she was and how futile her struggles were. She felt like a tiny kitten in the clutches of a large, overpowering bulldog. Hearing a harsh, grating sound, she suddenly realized that he was laughing at her efforts. Furious, she struggled even harder, but he still held her effortlessly. Roughly he shoved her onto the small porch, facing the other men.

"What are you doing snooping around here?" the tall man demanded in a chilling, authoritative voice.

"I just went for a walk down by the river, heard voices and came over to see what was going on." She tried to keep the quiver that was threatening to take possession of her muscles out of her voice as she told part truth and part fabrication.

"And what did you see?" The black eyes which stared

into hers reminded her of a snake's eyes—glittering, expressionless and cold. Her legs felt like jelly and she longed for a place to sit down. Before she could attempt a rational answer she felt with relief the pressure released from her arms. The stocky man moved around her left side and stood with muscular arms folded, glaring at her.

"Lady, who are you trying to kid?" her captor's nasal voice was laced with sarcasm. "Taking a walk by yourself here in the woods at night?"

Now the light shone fully on the man's face and Carole gasped. Her eyes fastened in horror upon a wide scar which started at the corner of his right eye and extended up into the hairline! Her mind tried to remember where she had heard about such a scar. Then she remembered! The radio broadcast the night before when she had turned on the radio to drown out the devotional service! The newsman had reported a million dollar jewel robbery where the store owner had been shot and wounded. The robbers had escaped. One of them was heavily-built—like a prize fighter—and had this distinctive scar! This man was the jewel thief!

Carole was so caught up in her own reflections that she didn't realize she was staring fixedly at the brawny man or that shock was registered clearly on her face until he reached out a thick, hairy hand and gripped her arm.

Startled, she tried to break away but he jerked her back and snarled, "You know who I am, don't cha?" When she tried to stutter a denial, his eyes narrowed to diabolical slits as he continued, "How do you know who I am?"

Carole lowered her eyes. Terror lanced through her body. She was in grave danger, and she knew it. A clear, calm mind was needed, but the fear pulsing through her body and pounding heart had almost paralyzed her reasoning capabilities. She fought to control the quivering in her body and to calm the stupefying panic in her brain. Then sudden pain cleared the cobwebs from her mind. The powerful, beefy hand that clutched her arm had tightened into a cruel, hurtful vise.

Carole gasped, "D-Don't—you're hurting me."

The steely grip slacked off slightly, but the evil eyes bored into her dark, frightened ones. "You haven't answered my question. You know who I am! How come?" When she hesitated, the vise began to tighten again.

"Okay—okay!" she cried out. "I'll tell you. But you don't have to break my arm!"

The man took his hand from her arm but continued to stare at her balefully. "Out with it, then. I ain't got a lot of patience!"

"I heard on the radio a day or so ago that a man with a scar had robbed a jewelry store."

The tall man spoke up, "Are you from that camp across the river?"

"Yes, I am, and my husband and grandmother will be looking for me anytime now. So you had better let me go!"

The old artist, Mr. Prentice, spoke for the first time. "The lady's right. Someone will be looking for her soon and then you'll be in a lot of trouble. Holding this lady against her will is kidnapping. Let her go, Ferron."

Ferron? Ferron? Where had Carole heard that name? Her mind groped in the recesses of her memory to recall. She had it! The news commentator had said the description of one of the robbers fit a Ferron—Ferron—she couldn't recall the last name.

The man standing before her was tall, in his middle twenties she would guess, with dark curly hair and a small neat mustache. Except for the thin cruel mouth and the glacial, obsidian eyes, he could be considered good-looking. With a sinking feeling in the pit of her stomach, she knew this man fit the description of the other jewel thief. She had foolishly blundered into the hiding place of the two men who just a few days before had robbed a jewelry store and left a man badly wounded!

Ferron's glittering eyes upon her filled her with dread. These men would not release her. She knew who they were and where they were hiding. These thoughts raced through her mind. She must escape before they dragged her into the castle!

Taking them all by surprise, she leaped away from the men—avoiding the hands clutching at her—and fled down the slight slope of the hill toward the swinging bridge. Putting all her strength into each racing step, she ran as she had never run in her life.

She might have made it if a lace on her boot had not come untied. Tripping on the long cord, she almost fell, and before she could recover, the tall man was upon her. She had not screamed before as she had needed all her strength to run, but now she screamed with all her might. Almost instantly a hand was clamped over her mouth. She tried to bite the hand but it was clamped too tightly about her mouth and jaw. She struggled fiercely, kicking, twisting, and flailing with her arms. The other robber arrived, and between the two they half-carried and half-dragged Carole into the side door of the huge old house, through a wide, pleasant screened-in porch and into a very large kitchen.

The old man, with the wide-eyed child clinging to his hand, followed the two men and Carole into the house. The men dumped Carole into a leather arm chair and the snake-eyed one threatened to "knock her head off" if she screamed again. Turning to the artist, he ordered, "Get me some rope!"

Mr. Prentice began to sputter angrily, "See here, you two-bit punks, turn that girl loose! I refuse to allow you to keep her here against her will. This is my house and I say what goes. You'll have the whole sheriff's department down on us. Don't you have a lick of sense?"

The brawny robber pounced on him like a hulking bear. Grabbing him by the shoulder with one large, hairy hand he growled menacingly, "You ain't got nothing to say about what we do! Got that? Remember that you doin' what we say is the only thing keepin' that little brat healthy. Look," he continued gleefully, "the poor little thing is shakin' in her boots!"

And indeed, she was. Her face was pale and a couple of tears slid down her cheeks before she pressed her trembling, white-clad shoulders and tiny head against her grandfather's trouser leg. The old man's face blanched. Bending stiffly to a squatting position, he wrapped his arms protectively about the small quaking figure.

"You lay a hand on my granddaughter and I'll—I'll—" His blustering was squelched by the mirthless, mocking laughter of the younger man.

Without bothering to answer the artist, he turned back to Ferron. "I'll get some rope. I saw some in the basement."

The thought of being tied was overwhelming to Carole, and she burst out passionately, "Please don't tie me up! Please—" Near tears and with anguish etched into every line of her lovely face, she turned beseeching eyes to first one and then the other of the two thieves. The thick-set man turned back from where he was about to go out the door and looked questioningly at Ferron. Seeing that it was Ferron who made the decisions for the pair, Carole raised her hand in a gesture of appeal and began to implore the hard, cold eyes before her, "Please, please don't tie me up. I—I—"

Ferron shifted his black eyes to the face of his accomplice. Grudgingly, he said slowly, "It really would be wasted time and energy. We have to lock her up somewhere anyway until we leave." He turned back to Carole, "If you can behave yourself, we'll not tie you up."

Not waiting for a promise from Carole, he turned to the old man who had moved to another large leather chair and had lifted his small granddaughter onto his lap. "Where can we put the girl so she'll be out of the way if someone comes looking for her?"

The artist seemed to ponder a moment then said slowly, "You could put the woman in the tower. There's a bed up there and a small bathroom so she'd be okay."

"Good—the perfect place," said Ferron. "Let's get her up there now before we have visitors."

"And what will we say when her family comes searching for her?" the older man asked sarcastically.

"We won't say anything, old man. Remember there isn't supposed to be anyone here but you! You will say you haven't seen the missing lady and make them believe it! We'll be out of sight—with your granddaughter. So you had better make it good!"

The old recluse seemed to wilt before their eyes. Gently, he put the child off his lap and rose stiffly. He spoke in a weary, resigned voice. "Someone could be here at any minute. Go on up. Mitzi and I will be up as soon as I get some bed linens." Taking the child's hand he turned to leave the room.

"Mitzi goes with us!" Ferron commanded. "I don't trust you, you old geezer." The child let out a cry of dismay but subsided meekly when Ferron strode over and grabbed her arm.

Her grandfather patted her shoulder comfortingly. "I'll be up right away, kitten." She nodded solemnly and allowed her father to lead her toward the door without further protest.

"Bring the girl, Max," called Ferron over his shoulder.

Max grasped Carole's arm with a curt, "Let's go."

9

As they were leaving the room, Carole swept her eyes over the well-lighted kitchen for the first time. Even the frightening, grim circumstances did not obliterate the warm pleasure the beauty, harmony and homeyness of the room kindled in her.

The spacious room was painted a sun yellow, the many cabinets and closets were a warm walnut. A massive fireplace of native stone filled most of one wall, with comfortable-looking leather and cushioned chairs drawn up nearby.

A gigantic black cat reposed at the end of the wide hearth. With his paws curled-in he looked like a statue except for the glowing green eyes which followed every move that anyone made. Gleaming, glossy black, copper-bottomed pots hung on the wall near the copper-brown stove. The huge refrigerator was also copper-brown. A round walnut table, with yellow placemats, was surrounded by matching armchairs with colorful yellow cushions. A squatty vase of fresh flowers was on the walnut table. Walnut buffet and china cabinets glowed invitingly. Obviously much time must be spent in this inviting room, thought Carole as she was ushered out.

As the four moved quickly down a wide hall toward a curving stairway, Carole glimpsed a large, formal dining room furnished with gleaming oak furniture and sparkling chandeliers. Farther on, through double doors, was a spacious, elegantly appointed drawingroom. At the end of the hall, through an open doorway, she observed walls lined with books, obviously the library. Each room was dimly lighted but there was no mistaking the wealth and luxury of this fine old mansion. Everywhere she looked was polished wood, rich draperies and fine paintings; the carpet beneath their feet was plush and resilient. Under different circumstances, Carole's aesthetic soul would have reveled in the beauty.

They climbed the wide, gracefully curving stairway and came into what must be the artist's studio. Hanging on the walls of a long wide gallery were pictures of all sizes, and of many and varied scenes. To her left, at the end of the gallery, was the artist's cluttered working place with easels, paints and brushes lying about on the tables, cabinet top, and even on the floor. Near the enormous windows a canvas stood on an easel. To the right she saw several doors, all closed.

None too gently, the burly robber urged her on up the stairs with a steely grip on her arm. These stairs ran up the side of a wall and were wide and easy to climb. The third floor contained a long hall with several doors on each side, all closed. Other lesser halls branched off to what Carole assumed were still other rooms.

As they walked down the hall, Carole felt a surge of pity and then anger. Ferron walked with long strides, tugging Mitzi along. The little girl had to practically run to keep from being dragged. Her little face was pale and the fair hair about it was damp with perspiration. She was panting from the exertion. An angry denunciation almost burst from Carole's mouth but she quickly checked it. She could make things worse for the poor little tyke. Anger, she was finding, did not have a good effect on these men. She must have a cool head and speak with calmness.

Ferron opened a door about halfway down the hall, and they entered a room which contained narrow stairs that spiraled upward, around and around a pillar about five foot thick.

Before Ferron could take a step up the stairs, Carole spoke breathlessly, "Couldn't Mitzi and I go up together? You men have longer legs than we do and we have trouble keeping up with you!" Truthfully, she was having a little difficulty herself, but her main concern was for the small child.

Ferron hesitated and Max ejaculated, "Oh, let them go together! I'm tired of dragging this dame along!"

Carole held out her hand, and Ferron released Mitzi's hand. Solemnly, the little girl moved to Carole's side and, looking up at her with large, trusting blue eyes, she placed her tiny, soft hand in Carole's. A strong emotion surged through Carole, unlike any she had ever experienced—protectiveness? Joy? Love? She wasn't certain she could have labeled it, perhaps it was a dash of all three. It was gone almost as quickly as it had come, but it left a lump in her throat and a quiver in her heart.

The men went up ahead of Carole and Mitzi, keeping a watchful eye upon them. It was a very strenuous, steep climb, but shortly they stepped out into a room which would have been the dream of any storybook princess. The tower room was octagonal shaped and was almost solid windows. While the men were searching for a light switch or a lamp, Carole moved to the window. The large yellow moon rode the ridge of a mountain, and the stars glistened like jewels in the dark velvet blue of the night. Mitzi was still clinging to her hand and now she said in a voice filled with wonder, "It's just like the picture in my storybook when God made the world!"

Ferron found the light switch and flooded the room with light, only to turn it off almost instantly. "The drapes!" he exclaimed. "Help me pull the drapes, Max. The old man said this glass is the kind that we can see out and no one can see in, but someone could sure see that the tower is lit up." The drapes were drawn, shutting out the lighted heavens and shutting them in with the surly captors.

Carole felt fear building up in her again—nauseating, stupefying fear! What did these men plan to do to her, to this pitiful child and to her irascible old grandfather? Would they really set them free when they felt their danger of discovery was past? It was unlikely, she thought, and shuddered. She pushed back the fearsome thoughts. She must have a clear mind. She must not let fear paralyze her. She must escape!

By this time David, her grandmother and Steve Morgan would be worried about her and would be looking for her, she reasoned. Would they remember her interest in the old castle and come here? At least they knew what direction she had gone. If only she had had the forethought to drop something to let them know where she was.

It was cool in the tower room. As she pushed her free hand into a jacket pocket, a sudden realization hit her! Her flashlight had been in the large left patch pocket of her suede jacket. It was no longer there! Where had she dropped it? Slowly she thought back. She had had it when she got to the swinging bridge and even after her wild dash into the trees. It was unlikely she had dropped it in the woodshed or she would have heard it—or would she? The ground had been covered with bits of wood and bark, she recalled.

"Dear God," she prayed silently, "please let someone find my flashlight and know I am here." A thought rose in her mind to mock her: what makes you think God would answer your prayer, when you wouldn't even stay for a simple service honoring Him? She suddenly felt desperately lonely and desolate. Quickly she shrugged away the feeling and turned her attention back to what was going on about her.

Mitzi still had a firm grip on her hand as Carole's eyes explored the room. The stairs came up in the middle of the room, off which was a tiny bathroom—containing only a toilet, wash basin, mirror—and a small closet. The few furnishings in the room were a little four-shelf bookcase, complete with books, a small desk and chair, a floor lamp, a couch and a small rocker.

Ferron and Max were standing close together, speaking in low tones but keeping a close watch over their prisoners. Suddenly Max raised his voice and said in an exasperated voice, "What's keeping the old man?"

"Stay here and I'll go see," commanded the other robber. He strode swiftly to the door and down the stairs. Max closed and locked the door, then stretched himself upon the couch with a grunt of pleasure.

"Let's go over and see what books are in the bookcase," Carole said to the still-clinging little girl. Suppressing a yawn, Mitzi acquiesced.

As she browsed through the four shelves of books, Carole suddenly realized that this tower room must have been a favorite haunt of Mitzi's mother when she was growing up. All were children and youth books. Many of them were worn copies of familiar children's classics.

Mitzi had finally released Carole's hand and was fingering the books with the gentle touch of one who loves and respects books. Suddenly she drew out a volume with an excited, "This is like *my* Bible storybook!" Her blue eyes were wide with pleasure and anticipation. "Can I look at it?" she asked.

"Certainly," said Carole with relief.

A wide, comfortably cushioned, continuous window seat about two feet high was built into the wall under the windows. It extended completely around the room. Mitzi carried the large, illustrated book to it and climbed up. Curling up with her head and shoulders supported by cushions, she was soon absorbed in the brightly colored pictures.

Carole sat down on the floor and began to idly look over titles of books on the first shelf. She reached out and removed one of the books. It was the old classic *Little Women*. The title page had the name Joy Prentice written at the top. She noticed a couple of lines at the bottom.

"I wish I had some brothers and sisters," she had written. "I am so lonely."

Carole felt her heart reach out to the girl who had written them. She put the book back in the shelf and took out another—*Tom Sawyer*. Opening it to the front page she found Joy Prentice inscribed at the top and at the bottom a hand-written sentence, "I wish I had a friend like Huck." That was all.

"How strange!" she thought. She put the book back in the case and selected another. The title was unfamiliar but it also bore the name Joy Prentice and a single line, "Please, Jesus, will you be my friend?"

How odd, she thought, as she replaced the book and removed one from the second shelf. The name Joy Prentice was on the front page in the book, but that was all. She removed several others on the bottom three shelves but there was no writing except Joy's name.

She returned to the top shelf and began to take books out, one by one. There were about two dozen books on the top shelf. Each contained a handwritten line. Each line had to do with being lonely, or wishing she had a friend like someone in the book, or "I wish I had a sister," or "I wish I had a brother."

"This is almost like a diary," Carole thought. When she

came to the very end of the books she noticed that the books had progressed from children, to teen and then adult level. She took out a book of poetry, the last book on the shelf. It said, "Today I found Mother's secret. It was hidden behind the peacock. It has given me courage to go against Daddy's wishes. I'll be sorry to leave my dear castle home but I must. Please forgive me, Daddy, and try to understand. Dear Jesus, make me strong."

Carole continued to hold the book in her hand and reread the little message, a longer one than any of the others. I wonder what she meant by "Today I found Mother's secret. It was hidden behind the peacock"? How very odd she mused. This must've been written just before she went away.

Carole looked about the room half expecting to see a peacock somewhere, but there wasn't one. There were several pictures, but none with a peacock, no peacock ceramic pieces or statues.

The strange little diary written line by line in each book had given Carole quite a bit of insight into Joy's life. Apparently Mitzi's mother had been a very lonely little girl and teenager. Then apparently she had discovered a strange secret which had given her the courage to leave her home and go to the city to find some friends. Carole was caught up by this strange drama. She wondered, what was the secret? What had Joy's mother been hiding?

Thoughtfully, she slipped the last volume back into place just as she heard a knock at the door.

Max heaved himself up and lumbered across the room to unlock the door. Ferron came into the room followed by the old artist. Mr. Prentice deposited sheets, pillowcases and two small pillows on the couch and then sank down, breathing hard and raggedly.

Mitzi's eyes lit up when her grandfather came in. But glancing covertly at the man who called himself her father, she seemed to try to make herself very small and stayed very still. She obviously was terrified of him.

55

"What was keeping him?" asked Max, nodding toward Mr. Prentice.

"We've had visitors," announced Ferron. Carole, standing by the bookcase, felt his cold eyes upon her. Her pulse quickened and her heart began to thump.

"The girl's husband and the camp boss from across the river came to the door and asked if we had seen a missing lady—a Mrs. Loring." Ferron chuckled wickedly. "You should have seen the performance the old man put on! If I hadn't known they were here, I would have believed him myself. He acted mad at being disturbed, hadn't seen no woman and didn't expect to. How come they thought he might a seen her! He was gettin' ready for bed!" Turning toward Mr. Prentice he spoke admiringly, "You did great, Gramps! You shoulda been an actor instead of dabbing paint on canvas."

The old artist said nothing, and Ferron turned back to his fellow conspirator. "The camp boss said they were going to get the other fishermen back in camp to help search but if they didn't find her pretty quick they wanted to come back and call the sheriff. But it'll be morning before they can get the sheriff out here, so let's leave the kid and the woman up here for the night. Tomorrow we'll probably have to move them to a better place if the sheriff starts snoopin' around. For now, let's go raid the old man's wine cellar again and play some cards."

Max smacked his thick lips in anticipation and agreed. Ferron turned back to his father-in-law, "Come along, Gramps."

The old man rose stiffly. "I have to make up this hide-a-bed first," he said, indicating the couch, "and tuck Mitzi in for the night. Go on down and I'll be down directly."

Ferron looked annoyed. "I don't trust you, you old coot. We'll wait right here. Make it snappy!"

Snapping the hide-a-bed out was simple, but the old man's movements were tortoise-slow as he began to slip a fitted sheet on the mattress. Carole wondered if he was ill or perhaps had a bad heart. Not knowing the first thing about making a bed—a maid had always done that sort of thing in Carole's home—but wishing to help the old man, Carole stepped to the other side of the bed. Awkwardly emulating him, she managed to get her two corners tucked around the mattress. Mr. Prentice brought two colorful blankets from a shelf in the tiny closet and between the two, the bed was quickly made up. At his call Mitzi came running and climbed into bed.

"Will you read me a story, Grandpa?"

Glancing at the two men impatiently waiting, Grandfather demurred, "Your father is waiting for me now, kitten. Maybe tomorrow. But I'll hear your prayers before I go."

Mitzi seemed to be considering. Casting a furtive glance at her father, she said "Thank you, Grandpa, but I'll say them for the nice lady this time."

Mr. Prentice kissed his granddaughter and tucked the blanket about her. Bidding her and Carole goodnight, he left the room.

Before he followed, Ferron searched the room with his eyes. Switching on a powerful flashlight which he handed to Max, he went to the lamp. Using his handkerchief he removed the hot bulb and also the one in the bathroom—the only two lights in the tower room—and carried them away with him, Max lighting the way. His mocking "Sweet dreams" floated back to Carole and Mitzi in the pitch black room.

10

As soon as she was sure the men had gone, Carole felt her way to the windows and pulled back all the drapes. The welcome moonlight spilled into the dark room. Mitzi's small quavering voice said, "Ohhhh—that's better. I don't like the dark."

Hearing the fear in Mitzi's voice, Carole called softly, "Do you want to come see the stars and moon again before you go to sleep? They are really lovely."

There was a soft rustle and Mitzi was at her side, tucking her small hand trustingly in Carole's and snuggling her white-clad form against Carole's side. Carole knew that earlier, delicious rush of warmth and felt again the catch in her throat and flutter in her heart. Was this what one felt for one's own child? She had never thought about this aspect before, only what a bother children would be. The ones she had known were so demanding, always crying or whining, and sticky or drooling. But this little thing clinging to her hand was like a tiny angel and drew from Carole a protectiveness and warm response that surprised her. Maybe it was because they were in this terrible dilemma together.

They slowly circled the room and viewed the panorama of the velvet blue, star-studded sky and sharply outlined skyline. Everything appeared mysterious and beautiful under the light of the huge white moon and blinking stars. Their distressing plight seemed unreal under the spell of beauty and the stillness of the night.

Suddenly Carole felt a nip of the chill that was beginning to invade the room and hustled Mitzi back into bed. Snug under the blankets the child's wide blue eyes studied Carole's face in the dim moonlight. "You're the lady on the trail," she stated.

"Yes, I'm the 'lady on the trail,' I had gone for a walk down by the river. When I saw you, I thought maybe a little angel had fallen out of heaven."

Mitzi giggled delightedly.

"What were you doing out on the path by yourself at night?" Carole asked. "And where did you vanish to when I went to find you?"

"I hid in the bushes when you came after me." Mitzi sobered, "I had run away to look for my mommy. Do you know where my mommy is?"

Her voice trembled and Carole realized she was near tears. She would have liked to change the subject as the thought of a crying child almost sent Carole into a panic, but she needed to find out what was going on here. So she prodded gently, forming her words carefully.

"How did your father get you?"

"Mommy went to the hospital for her eye. I stayed with Mrs. Carroll. He got me from Mrs. Carroll."

"Who is Mrs. Carroll?"

"She owns the big house where we live. Her girl is all growed up so she likes me to keep her company. Mommy pays her though."

"Why did Mrs. Carroll let your father have you?"

"My father told her that he was staying close to the hospital and visiting my mommy. He was supposed to take me to the hospital to see her—but he didn't. Instead, he and that other mean man brought me here. He told me I was his 'kid,' too, and he wanted to keep me for awhile." Her little face screwed up in a perplexed frown. "I don't know why he wanted me 'cause he doesn't like me! I—I'm afraid of him."

"So you ran away to try to find your mother?"

"My mommy will c-cry when she finds out I'm gone. I'm all she's g-got." A fat tear ran down her cheek.

"But you have your grandfather," soothed Carole quickly.

Mitzi dabbed at her wet eyes with the sleeve of her nightgown. "Mommy said Grandpa doesn't like us—but he does! And I like him—a lot!"

"I'm sure your grandfather likes you," murmured Carole.

"Mommy's name is Joy. She said Grandpa used to tell her she was the joy of his life. But now she isn't," Mitzi said sadly.

"What happened, Mitzi?"

"When she got growed up, she wanted to go away from this big house so she could meet other people. Grandpa said if Mommy went away she could never come back. Mommy cries sometimes when she looks at Grandpa's picture. She doesn't know I see her," she confided, her expressive eyes wide with concern. "She cries when she thinks I'm asleep. But Mommy says that God will change Grandpa's mind and he will love Mommy again because we are praying." Carole steered the conversation away from the uncomfortable subject of praying.

"Did your father ever live with you?"

"Mommy never talks about my father. She just said he went away before I was born."

"I imagine your grandfather was happy to see you, wasn't he?" Carole felt guilty to be prying but felt it necessary to learn as much about the circumstances in this house as possible.

"At first he just yelled at my father that he didn't have a granddaughter. I was scared of him! But my father showed him some pictures and then he got real quiet and looked at them a long time—then he let us in."

"Your grandfather seems to love you very much."

"He holds me and calls me 'kitten.' I don't look like a kitten!" Mitzi giggled, "But I like the way he says it."

Carole had been sitting on the side of the bed. Now she stood up. "I think it's time you got to sleep."

"Will you listen to my prayers?"

"If you want me to," said Carole uneasily. She had no idea what was expected of her.

Mitzi hopped out of bed and knelt beside the bed. When Carole continued to stand uncertainly, the child asked quizzically, "Aren't you going to kneel? Mommy and Grandpa always do."

Carole knelt obediently. She had never said bedtime prayers or ever seen it done.

Mitzi promptly bowed her head over clasped hands and recited,

> *"Now I lay me down to sleep,*
> *I pray Thee, Lord, my soul to keep.*
> *If I should die before I wake,*
> *I pray Thee, Lord, my soul to take.*

Dear Lord, bless Mommy and Grandpa
and this nice, pretty lady."

Carole felt a prickle of tears under her closed eyelids at this.

"And, please don't let Daddy and that other mean
man hurt any of us."

The child knew the danger!

"In Jesus' name. Amen."

Mitzi hopped up, clasped her tiny arms about Carole's neck, and planted a kiss as soft as thistledown on her surprised cheek. Jumping back into bed, she snuggled down under the warm blankets. Carole tucked the blankets about the small shoulders and touched the white forehead with her lips.

"Mmmm, you smell good," murmured the little girl sleepily. "Goodnight, nice lady." She closed her eyes and was asleep almost at once.

11

Carole stood looking down at the little girl. The moonlight streaming into the room made her long blond hair look like shimmering silver, and the softly molded lips, the long lashes resting on soft cherubic cheeks, the little pointed chin with a slight cleft, turned her face into the face of an earthly angel. Small, perfectly shaped hands lay curled near her face. She seemed so relaxed in the face of the danger that crouched just beyond the door. Could her little prayer and faith in the One she prayed to so trustingly and sincerely have anything to do with the peace the child apparently possessed? Carole thought of Manuel and Steve Morgan. Their words rang with the same trust that Mitzi displayed. Did God really care—in a personal way—like these people seemed to feel He did? A great longing welled up in her being. Almost—she would like to find out more about this.

Abruptly, she shoved the thought from her mind. She would never desire to be like the sanctimonious goody-goodies she had known in college—the only two she knew who professed to be more than mere indifferent church members.

She continued to gaze at the peacefully sleeping child. If I could have a child that looked and acted like this, she thought, perhaps it wouldn't be so bad to have a baby. But what do I know about raising children? Mine would probably be like the brats I have seen.

Truthfully, she had never been around children at close quarters. She had no close relatives and no brothers or sisters. Moving in the circles of the very rich, and visiting in the palatial homes where she was a guest, servants had, for the most part, kept the children out of sight. This was the first time she had ever seen a child asleep. She's like a beautifully sculptured piece of art, she thought, but living and breathing.

Her mind reverted back to the thought of having a child. David wanted children so badly. He would probably be a wonderful parent, she mused—gentle, kind, patient. At the thought of David, loneliness enveloped her and she moved restlessly to the window to look out into the star-strewn heavens. She ached to feel David's strong, comforting arms about her. A lump formed in her throat and tears stung her eyelids.

It seemed like an eternity since she had left the camp in a huff that evening and gone for a walk. If only she had listened to Steve's warning! He had warned her of wild animals, but the animals who held her captive were more to be feared than wild animals, she thought. She sensed a barely restrained savagery about the two jewel thieves that was terrifying.

She had been pacing restlessly around the glass walls of the tower when suddenly she saw several pinpoints of light weaving in and out, and farther over she saw a circle of light.

That must be their camp! The tiny lights must be David and Steve and others from the camp searching for her! Her heart began to beat wildly as she pressed her face against the glass trying to see better.

"If only I had a light to signal with," she whispered. Leaving the window, she raced to the small closet in the center of the room and threw open its small door to the searching moonlight rays. Carefully she felt along the only shelf. It contained nothing. She searched every inch of the floor—nothing. A careful search of the closet revealed only an old bathrobe draped on a hanger.

Carole next examined the tiny bathroom, feverishly exploring every inch. If she could even find a mirror, she reasoned, she might be able to flash a signal—the moon was very bright. There was a large metal framed mirror but it was securely attached to the wall. She prowled about the room, searching, but there was only a roll of bathroom tissue in a recessed holder. The room contained no small objects of any kind, only the sparse furnishings. Ferron and Max had probably seen to that, she thought bitterly.

Totally disheartened, she went back to the window. The tiny pinpoints of light were still flitting here and there. She counted them. It was hard to get a perfect count as the tiny lights were weaving back and forth and sometimes couldn't be seen, but there seemed to be at least ten which meant that all the men and even some of the women were searching.

It was agonizing—realizing that David and the others were so close—probably within shouting range—and she could not contact them in any way! She leaned her arms against the glass wall of her prison, buried her face in them and cried.

She raged at herself. It's your own stubbornness that got you into this mess! Think of the trouble you have caused everyone and the unnecessary pain you are putting Gran and David through! It isn't enough that you callously castigated them both this morning and then rebuffed their overtures.

You should have been the one to ask forgiveness for the way you treated them. But no. Instead of that, what did you do? What you always do! You pouted and acted like a spoiled brat. And look what it has gotten you into this time!

Finally, exhausted from weeping and the mental flogging she had administered to herself, she crept to the little rocker near the stairwell. She could no longer bear to watch the weaving lights below and know there was no way to reach them. Rocking slowly back and forth seemed to somewhat alleviate the tension in her body.

Suddenly she realized she was hungry, ravenously so. It was hours past dinner time. She recalled they were to have had an enormous fish fry of freshly caught salmon tonight. Her mouth watered as she thought of Manuel's simple but sumptuous culinary delights. Never in her life had she ever suffered hunger pangs. But suddenly she was so hungry that she felt she could eat anything! Perhaps the trauma of the past hours had taken its toll, at any rate she was voraciously hungry.

She considered hammering on the door to ask for food, but the thought of Ferron's cold, snake-eyes and Max's powerful, cruel strength drove the notion from her mind. They probably couldn't hear her anyway and would be unlikely to honor her request. Indeed, they likely would take pleasure in her discomfort. She tried to take her mind from food but her taste buds could almost savor the delicious flavor of crisp, fried salmon fillets.

Unable to get food off of her mind, she was about to drag her tired body out of the chair, when she felt a strange sensation. The large throw-rug under the chair seemed to move slightly! Her body went numb with fright. There it was again! She was sure the rug under her feet moved ever so slightly. Regaining her ability to move, she sprang from the chair and backed away, her dark eyes wide with terror. Her heart was hammering and her throat was so constricted she couldn't have made a sound if she had tried.

There! The small rocking chair moved. She backed

further away. Then she heard a faint tap. Then another. It sounded like someone was rapping with his knuckles on the floor directly under the chair. As the faint tapping continued, Carole began to lose some of her fright. Was someone trying to frighten her? That didn't sound likely. Was someone down there trying to contact her? If so, why didn't they call?

The fleeting thought came to her that the place was haunted and that a disembodied spirit was making its presence known, but she quickly forced that thought away from her. The real persons in the spooky old castle were terrifying enough to deal with. She certainly couldn't cope with the thought of ghosts. Nevertheless, she felt her scalp prickle.

The tapping stopped and the chair moved a little more this time. Then it moved again. Her hand flew to her mouth to suppress the scream that hovered there. Was someone— or something—trying to break into this room? She looked around wildly for something to use as a weapon, but even as she did so, she remembered there was nothing in the room except the few pieces of furniture.

The chair had stopped moving and the tapping was not resumed for a minute or so. Carole's violently beating heart began to slow. Then she heard a sound. Was it a voice? It came from beneath the floor. She heard it again, a little louder this time. It *was* a voice and it *was* coming from under the chair! She came nearer and the voice spoke softly again, urgently. "Move the chair and the rug so I can get in."

"Who are you?" Carole managed to quaver.

"Prentice—hurry, let me in."

Carole hastened to remove the chair and then the large, heavy rug. Almost instantly a small square of floor raised up and Mr. Prentice climbed stiffly into the room. He lowered the trapdoor before speaking in a loud whisper.

"Is Mitzi asleep?"

"Yes. How did—"

The old man interrupted, "I can explain later. We must

get out of here before Max discovers I'm not in my room. We'll have to go back down the way I came and it's very steep and narrow. We'll have to descend single file. Can you do it?"

"Yes—yes, I can do anything I need to do!"

"Good!" Mr. Prentice was moving toward the bed, "We'll waken Mitzi. She'll have to climb down herself as there isn't enough room to carry her. But she's a spunky little tyke, she can do it," he said with pride.

When they had little Mitzi up and standing in her furry shoes by the trapdoor, the old man urged them not to speak unless they absolutely had to and then in a whisper.

He arranged the chair as close as possible to where it had been before and the rug so it would fall back over the opening when the trapdoor was closed. Then he disappeared into the dark hole carrying a small flashlight. Carole helped Mitzi find the rungs of the ladder and slowly she descended into the narrow shaft until she was out of sight. Carole was almost petrified with fear of climbing down the steep ladder, but she would have tried anything to escape. So she followed Mitzi into the darkness and let the trapdoor down.

She thought she heard a sound above them just as she took her hand from the trapdoor, but she wasn't sure. She could see a faint glow below her as she moved slowly and cautiously downward. She was careful where she placed her feet, so she wouldn't tread on Mitzi's hands.

After what seemed an eternity, Carole felt a breath of fresh air and heard the faint swish of a door being opened. A few more steps and she was standing level with a small door, illuminated by Mr. Prentice's flashlight beam. He helped her step from the ladder to the floor where he and Mitzi already stood. They were in a large, unused walk-in closet.

After closing the door at the back of the closet, he whispered for them to wait while he checked to see if the robbers were about. He was back promptly. Urging them to walk quickly but without a sound, he led the way out of the dim room into the long hallway which Carole recognized as the third floor hall.

Taking Mitzi's hand, the old man moved away down the hall, with Carole right behind them. They passed the stairs and proceeded swiftly but silently toward the door at the end of the hall.

Just as Mr. Prentice raised his hand to open the door a figure moved swiftly from the last doorway along the hall, glided to within a few feet of the three and demanded in a loud voice, "Going somewhere?" It was Max, wearing an evil, sadistic grin on his beefy face.

Carole felt her heart lurch. Her knees went weak and she felt so faint that she put her hand to the wall to steady herself. She fought off the fear that washed over her. The nauseating gall of despair welled up in her throat, threatening to choke her.

After one little bleat of fear, Mitzi wrapped both arms around her grandfather's hand and stood mutely still.

The old man also seemed to have lost the power of speech. Even in the dimly lighted hall, Carole saw the sag of defeat in his shoulders and the fear in his eyes.

Max chortled as he stood facing them with his hands on his hips; then he broke out in guffaws of sardonic mirth. Mincing ridiculously about, he reviled them for their stupidity in thinking they could outsmart him. As the harangue continued, Carole decided that the robbers had raided the wine cellar and Max was well on his way to being intoxicated. A little bell of warning rang in her brain. The barely restrained savagery that she had sensed earlier could erupt and this swaggering thief could become a shaggy, angry grizzly.

She hoped the irascible old artist realized the tenuous thread restraining Max's anger. Covertly she cast a quick glance at the old gentleman and saw him furtively looking at her. A look of understanding flashed between them. Emulating Prentice, Carole put on a facade of dejection and defeat—it wasn't hard under the circumstances—and waited humbly for Max to run down.

Suddenly they heard the clatter of footsteps on the stairs

and Ferron came striding down the hall toward them. He immediately took command of the situation. Ordering Max to take Carole back to the tower, he curtly informed Mr. Prentice that Mitzi would be sleeping in his room, saying, "If you pull any more shenanigans, the kid will pay the penalty."

Max marched Carole back up the winding stairs to the tower. As they climbed around and around the large pillar, Carole suddenly realized that the steep, ladder-like stairs she had descended a short while before must run down the center of that pillar. How ingenious, she thought.

Idly she wondered what other surprises this storybook castle held. Were there other hidden passages and escape avenues? If there were, she had to find one. She had already had enough of castles to last her a lifetime.

Max demanded to know where the hidden trapdoor was located. Carole showed him and he tried to open it from the tower. Satisfied that it could only be opened from the under side, Max locked the tower door and went hurrying away— probably back to his booze, surmised Carole.

Lack of food and the strenuous activities of the night, plus the strain and tension she had endured, had rendered Carole very weak and utterly exhausted. She took off her jacket, washed her face in the miniature washbasin, dried on bathroom tissue since the old fellow had forgotten to bring up a towel, and taking off only her boots, she fell into bed. Then, remembering she hadn't checked to see if the search for her was still in progress, she forced herself out of the warm bed and dashed across the cold floor in stocking feet.

The camp was still lit up, but she saw no lights around the river. Had they given up so soon? Or were they searching somewhere else? If only someone would find her flashlight on the castle lawn—at least that was where she supposed it had fallen from her pocket. Or could it have fallen out when she fell over the stick of firewood in the woodhouse? At any rate, she no longer had it and if it were found, David would know it was hers because he had bought it for her—a powerful, expensive one, and one just like it for himself—just before coming on the camping trip.

"Dear God," she prayed softly aloud, "please let them find my flashlight. I know I don't deserve to have you answer my prayer, but I still have to ask. I'm in deep trouble, and there's no one else to turn to!"

Feeling the chill, Carole padded back to bed, climbed in and pulled the warm blankets up closely around her neck. Moonlight spilled its soft rays through the glass walls into the room. A light breeze sighed and murmured about the tile rooftop. She thought she would never get to sleep, alone in this lonely belvedere, but lulled by the crooning of the gentle wind and totally exhausted in mind and body, she fell asleep almost immediately.

12

Hours later, Carole awoke with a start. What had wakened her? She didn't know, but something had because every sense was tinglingly alert. She heard and saw nothing, so she was about to conclude she had dreamed something frightening when suddenly the air was rent by a blood-curdling scream which rose and fell, sending shafts of terror through her. Just as suddenly it ebbed away, ending in a quavering sob.

The nerves in Carole's stomach were in knots, her heart was pounding and her body trembling. What was it? It didn't really sound human. Was it some kind of wild animal? A mountain lion, perhaps?

The scream came again, closer this time, like it was just outside the windows. Carole pulled the blankets up around her ears to shut out the chilling sound. Huddled in the bed, she wondered if a mountain lion—if it were that—could break through the glass into the room. Again, the sound ebbed away, finishing on a moaning sob.

Carole watched the glass windows fearfully. Abruptly, a large, dark shadow catapulted into view. Carole felt her heart lurch with fear and begin to pound almost out of her body. Was that animal about to get into this room? There was no doubt now that it was of the cat family. The dark shadow moved along the glass walls with lithe, supple grace. It turned its majestic head toward the window. Catching the moonlight, the eyes glowed with green fire. Carole was petrified with terror. Now it let loose with that bone-jarring scream again. Carole pulled the covers over her head just knowing something terrible was about to happen to her.

For long minutes after the quavering wail had faded away she waited with bated breath and trembling body. There was no sound of shattering glass and the scream did not come again, so at last Carole peeked from under the covers. The shadow was gone. Drawing a long sob of relief, Carole slipped out of bed and crept to the window.

There was no sign of the animal, though she walked the complete circle of her prison. There was a brilliant glow along the eastern skyline. The sun was coming up! It was almost morning and she was still alive! Being alive had never meant much to her before. But this morning, although she was still a prisoner, at least she still was among the living.

The floor and room were chilly so Carole went to pull on her boots and slip on her suede jacket and then went back to watch the sun rise. Most of her life she had been a very late riser and had never seen the sun rise. Now, as she watched the breathtaking natural exhibit, she wondered why she had never thought to watch the sunrise before. Because it was something I've always taken for granted, she decided, just as I've taken the breath of life itself.

The fiery red ball blazed over the forest. The view from the tower was spectacular. On the east, where the river and camp lay, there was timber as far as she could see, and also on each side of the castle, but on the west, the castle had been built right against the side of the mountain. Rugged, moss-covered rocks and cliffs poked gray, white and rust heads through the dense green brush and vegetation. Even a scattering of pine trees had managed to take hold in the rocky soil.

Walking slowly around the octagonal glass walls she saw that the castle room she was in was really at the top of at least a two-story tower, very high above the roof of the rest of the building. The room beneath her was about ten feet wider and formed a wide circular walkway outside her windows, surrounded by a parapet about three and a half feet high. On one side a stone stairway with an artistically crafted, black wrought-iron railing curved downward and disappeared from view.

Suddenly a large, sleek, black head appeared on the stairway, followed by a graceful, ebony black body. With one agile, effortless spring, he leaped to the parapet, stretched luxuriously, and then sat on his haunches to daintily wash his face. It was the artist's huge cat.

Watching him, Carole wondered if the mountain lion—or whatever kind of big cat it was that had frightened her so last night—had come up those stairs. He probably must have. Wasn't it strange, she mused, that a wild animal would come up on the top of a building? She knew nothing of wild animals, but that seemed odd behavior for a mountain lion when he had the mountain behind and the huge wilderness all about in which to roam.

Finished with his bath, the huge feline rose and began a slow promenade along the top of the parapet wall. His supple, flowing movements made her think of the huge cat that had terrorized her before daylight. If he were only much larger, he could be the same animal. A tiny suspicion was born. It couldn't have been this animal—could it? The size, the bone-chilling wild scream. Then she remembered the gardener who lived for a time in a small bungalow on her parents' estate when she was a child. He had owned a very large, blue-eyed Siamese cat. He was very friendly to people but if other male cats invaded the grounds, he screamed much like the animal had last night. She remembered the gardener had begun to shut him inside his little house at night because her grandmother complained that he kept her awake.

Curiously, Carole followed the black cat's slow march as he paced along the parapet, protected from his detection by the one-way glass. Even if this could account for the terrifying screams she had heard, she mused, this cat was not nearly the size of that cat last night. Suddenly she noticed the cat's shadow on the platform outside. It was much larger than the real animal. That was it! The moon had been very bright last night and she had seen only a shadow! The cat had been walking the wall as he was now, and the distance of about ten feet had made the huge shadow on her window. Her mountain lion had been only a very large house cat!

She suddenly felt very foolish but at the same time extremely relieved. If she had to spend another night here—perish the thought, but it was a definite possibility—at least she wouldn't have to fear that a mountain lion was about to break through and attack her!

Carole searched the area in the front of the castle but saw no one astir near the river or elsewhere. She could not see the camp itself as it was set up in a site with numerous huge spruce, pine and fir trees sheltering and shading the tents. She felt keenly disappointed. She had expected that everyone would have been searching feverishly as soon as it was light.

Depression settled on Carole like a heavy, smothering cloud. Did no one care for her enough to get up early when her life was in danger? Quick tears filled her eyes. She turned away from the window and wandered disconsolately about the room. Hunger pangs gnawing at her stomach made her feel lightheaded.

Perhaps some water would help. She went into the tiny bathroom. There was no glass so she cupped her hands under the water and drank several large handsful. The water didn't help much; she was still ravenously hungry. The thought floated through her mind that she could live a long time without food, but without water she would die quickly. A morbid thought!

Suddenly part of Mitzi's little prayer popped into her mind:

"If I should die before I wake, I pray thee, Lord, my soul to take."

Mitzi had prayed that little prayer so trustingly. But Carole knew she could not pray because she wasn't willing to go the way of God. She wanted to go Carole's way. She had always been headstrong and willful. If she couldn't get her way by smiles and dimples, she tried tears and pouts, and if that didn't work, a haughty, blistering tongue-lashing usually wilted all opposition.

She sensed that the predatory two who held her, tiny Mitzi and the old artist captive, did not hold life sacred and when their usefulness was past—she shuddered to think what might lie ahead for them if someone did not rescue them.

An alien thought surfaced in Carole's mind. If I am facing death, shouldn't I make peace with God? She tried to push the thought away, but this time it seemed to resist and bounced back with renewed vigor. She had informed Steve when he had talked to her about God—was it only yesterday?—that she was a church member and had been baptized as a baby, but in her heart she had always known that those things were not enough.

The thought of having peace was desirable, but what would God expect of her? Could she never have any fun again—if she escaped from this castle alive? Would He expect her to dress like that dreadful girl in college who seemed to feel that drab unattractiveness was godliness? And both she and the other fanatic—a male counterpart— spent most of their free time on campus lecturing the other youth on their sins and their frivolity.

She remembered that Steve and Manuel didn't seem to feel it was an unpleasant mode of living. They spoke glowingly about living for God. Could it be that she had based all her theories of Christian living on two poor examples?

She had always had a yearning for "something," an undefinable "something" that seemed to elude her. Could it be as she had heard one time, that man and woman were equipped with a space that would always feel empty unless it was filled with God? The thought was intriguing.

Manuel's singing had stirred her strangely. Had God been trying to get her attention while she'd been so busy trying to run away and trying to insulate herself from anything Christian that she couldn't hear? Could she be missing the boat altogether because of false, preconceived ideas? Excitement began to build in her.

Her musings were interrupted by the sound of the door being unlocked. The two robbers entered. Ferron brusquely ordered her to go below with Max. "I'll check the room, to see that she hasn't left anything in case they come up here," said Ferron.

Carole's heart missed a beat. The thieves must have reason to believe that the house was about to be searched. Had someone found her flashlight?

Carole braved a question. "Is the sheriff here to search the house?"

Max's nasal voice answered, "He wanted to search the house but he ain't got a search warrant yet so the old man didn't let 'em in. But the sheriff said he'd be back with one." He laughed, an ugly, unmirthful sound. "But *you* won't be nowhere to be found!"

Carole felt as if he had struck her in the stomach, knocking the breath from her body. "What are you going to do with me?" she asked fearfully.

Max laughed unpleasantly again. "I'll let it be yer surprise for the day!" He cackled again at his own private joke. "Now, get on down them stairs. I ain't had my breakfast, and you're holdin' it up."

Max began a swift descent and it was all Carole could do

to keep from being dragged along. Ferron came clattering after them.

A few minutes later the three joined Mr. Prentice and Mitzi who had apparently been waiting for them on the third floor. Without a word, the artist took Mitzi's hand and led them all down the main hall to a room at the end. It was an unused room. There were dust shrouds on the furniture. He moved stiffly across the room and pushed back the sliding door of a spacious, empty walk-in closet. He felt along the wall at the back of the closet and presently a section of the back wall rolled back silently to reveal a small platform and a flight of steps descending on the left. The old gentleman did not turn toward the stairs, however, he crossed the platform and fitted a key into the lock of a door that Carole had not noticed.

Swinging the door back, he pressed a light switch and several lights flashed on down the full length of a narrow tunnel. A stale, musty, dank odor assailed Carole's nostrils and she drew back, but Max pushed her forward into the corridor. The old artist moved on down the tunnel with Mitzi clinging to his hand. Ferron and Max pushed Carole ahead as they followed. Carole shuddered. The place was like a tomb!

13

When David had seen Carole go stalking off toward the river, obviously still very upset and still very angry, different emotions struggled together in him. He had seen how she ignored the warning that Steve had called to her, and how she had rudely walked away, her head held high and haughty, her back stiff and proud.

"Always the little princess," thought David bitterly as he watched her go, his hands thrust deeply into his pockets. When she was out of sight he turned and walked slowly away from the camp in the opposite direction. Entering a copse of aspen, fir, and spruce, he slowly began to climb the gentle slope.

Walking on a pine needle carpet, the fragrance of the evergreens filled his nostrils. In spite of the confusion and turmoil of his mind, his senses registered pleasure, and he stopped for a moment, threw back his head and breathed deeply of the crisp, heady, fresh mountain air. Then sighing deeply, he moved farther up the mountain. Soon he came to a fallen log with moss clinging to its sides and sat down.

A plumy-tailed gray squirrel ran partway down a nearby tree and scolded him for invading his privacy. When David tossed a piece of bark in his direction, the squirrel momentarily stood his ground, little ears erect, bright eyes inquisitively searching out what this strange interloper meant to do, then he flashed back up to the top of the tree and disappeared.

David rose to pace slowly back and forth. He just couldn't sit still. "What is to become of Carole and me and our marriage?" he murmured aloud.

Two days before he had unreservedly given his life to God. He had thought God would work out all his problems, and for that one day he and Carole had had such good fellowship—almost like the first days of their marriage—until he had told Carole about his decision. David wondered now, as he had so often the past few months, if their marriage was going to work.

He knew Carole loathed his drinking—not a few drinks, but when he drank too much. So he had been shocked, surprised and deeply disappointed when Carole had turned on him when he had told her his intentions to serve God and quit drinking. She had even defended drinking! Nearly everyone indulged, she'd said. Drinking was not undesirable in their elite social circle. It was just when someone consistently drank too much that anyone disapproved.

David sat down on the pine needles in the shade of the tree and sank his head into his arms. He had felt God was the answer to their marriage and now it seemed that this might not be the case. He might have to choose between God and his marriage! Was he strong enough? David loved Carole so deeply! Yet he couldn't give up God.

David thought back to the time when he had met Carole. He'd walked in a glorious daze of joy and wonder when Carole had begun to show that she wanted to be friends. Awestruck, it had been weeks before he could summon the courage to ask her for their first date. Things had moved quickly from there, and just after graduation, he and Carole were married.

In the back of his mind he knew, even then, that it would be difficult to merge their two ways of life, but with the youthful confidence of fresh, joyous love, he knew that a way could be found. To his chagrin and consternation, he soon discovered that the way involved giving up his teaching. At first David had protested vigorously, but over and over his remonstrations were abruptly parried by imploring, velvety, midnight-blue eyes and ultimately extinguished. David couldn't win.

Carole was an expert at getting her own way. Beautiful, popular, wealthy and sought after, she had skillfully manipulated the adoring David.

After repeated defeats at asserting his will, David began to retreat from the line of battle into a bottle of alcohol. It was only after indulging quite freely that he could again feel he was master of his own destiny.

As David paced back and forth, pondering the situation, he came to a realization. His attitude about Carole had defeated him. He considered Carole—in a true sense—a princess. He felt privileged to worship at the foot of her shrine. Even now, as he envisioned Carole—her quick, infectious laughter and sparkling wit, her shapely head and melting, long-lashed dark eyes—his heart quickened. In the early days of their courtship and marriage, he had felt himself unworthy to be the husband of such a beautiful, talented creature of wealth from the best circles.

77

His own family had been middle-class working people. His father was a truck driver who lived from payday to payday, living comfortably enough, but certainly never affluently. David had worked his way through college.

Now that he had accepted Christ, he suddenly saw that no human should receive the homage and adulation he had given Carole. He loved Carole deeply, but worship belonged only to God!

14

David was so deeply in thought that he was unaware of the muted footsteps approaching from the direction of the camp. Gran was just a few steps away when she spoke his name. He looked up, startled.

"May I join you?" she asked.

"Certainly," said David sensing the uneasy feeling creep over him that he always had when Carole's crusty little grandmother was around. Gran seated herself on the log and David sat near her. He wondered what was on Gran's mind.

"I saw you leave in this direction awhile ago," Gran said. "I hope you don't mind my intrusion, but I wanted to talk to you, away from Carole."

David assured her she wasn't intruding.

Gran cocked her gray head to one side and looked squarely into David's face. "I saw the way you captivated your audience today out there on the hike," she said. "You have a great ability to teach, but I suppose I don't need to tell you that. I understand that at one time you had aspirations to become a teacher."

David nodded, wondering what Gran was building up to.

"What did you plan to teach?" she inquired.

"Biology. However, I would probably be teaching other

subjects as well because my desire has been to teach the younger grades, fifth, sixth and junior high—certainly no higher than high school. I just have a feeling for young people of that age."

"And Carole objects to your teaching." Gran's words were a statement not a question.

"Yes," David said.

"And that's what the argument was about today, I presume," Gran said.

David hesitated. He didn't wish to discuss their private conversation with Gran. "Partly," he said cautiously

"And what do you plan to do?" Gran asked. "Have you decided to teach after all?"

David breathed deeply. "Yes," he said, "I have decided to teach. But of course I will have to finish my schooling first. I need another year to receive my certification in education."

"Good," said Gran. "I would like to finance that year's education, if I might."

Puzzled, David studied Gran's face before he said somewhat stiffly, "Thank you, Gran, but I worked my way through before, and I believe I can do so again."

Gran spoke impatiently, "You need your time for study. You shouldn't be working. I have plenty of money to do whatever I wish with and I would consider it an investment if you would allow me to put you through that year's schooling."

"Thank you," David said. "I appreciate that, but I really would prefer to swing it on my own."

"Because Carole disapproves?" Gran asked.

David wished this conversation had not begun. He didn't wish to discuss Carole and his problems.

"Perhaps I can talk to Carole," Gran said. "I know she is a very stubborn girl. But part of her reason for not wanting you to teach, I'm afraid, stems from the fact that her parents—my son and his wife—became so involved with their business that they had no time for her. As you probably know, I raised her. I believe Carole is afraid that if you become involved in a profession, you, too, will desert her."

"I never knew this," David said in astonishment. "Surely Carole wouldn't think my teaching would make any difference in our relationship."

"Bitter experience," Gran said, "tells her it would. Once, when she was small, she and her mother were very close. Then her mother began to help in her husband's business, becoming more and more a part of it, until Carole rarely saw her parents. I think they tried to make up for their abandonment by sending her many expensive gifts. But they traveled to many different parts of the world and were scarcely ever home. Then, as you know, when Carole was still quite young they were both killed in a plane crash."

"Thank you for telling me this." David suddenly realized his uneasiness regarding Gran had disappeared and a warm comfortable feeling had taken its place. He'd always admired Carole's feisty grandmother, however, he had known she didn't approve of him. But she had not known him before Carole and he were married, and what she had seen of him since would certainly not have inspired her confidence in him as a good husband.

"I still would like to finance that year's education," Gran said. When David started to protest, she raised her hand and stopped him. "Please don't give me an answer now. Think about it. You could consider it a loan, if you wish, and repay me at a later time. But I just feel you have a contribution to make to the youth that you will be teaching, and it would be a privilege to have a part in preparing you."

At that moment the dinner bell began to ring and Gran stood to her feet. "Looks like our dinner is ready and the way my stomach feels, it's ready for it. Shall we go?"

"Yes," said David. "I feel that I could use some food, too, and I will consider your offer, I appreciate it."

A few minutes later when they entered the camp David looked for Carole. Not seeing her anywhere, he excused himself to Gran and went to the tent to see if she had returned. Finding it empty, he looked up the trail and didn't see her. It was getting later than he liked her to be out, but it still wasn't completely dark and he knew she had taken her flashlight. So he sat down with the others and began to eat.

As the meal progressed he kept looking down the path but Carole did not appear. It was growing darker and darker. Finally he pushed aside his plate and spoke to Gran, "I think I had better go check on Carole. I don't like her being out in the dark by herself."

Steve Morgan was sitting across the table from him and he spoke up, "I have been rather anxious about your wife, too. I think I'll get my flashlight and go with you, if you don't mind."

In a few moments both men were swinging down the path that Carole had taken. They walked quickly because darkness was falling rapidly. When they came to the fork in the trail, Steve said, "Most likely she's on the trail to the Prentice mansion. That castle seems to fascinate her."

David agreed and it didn't take them long to reach the swinging footbridge. They looked up at the old castle. There were a couple of lights on in the first floor and one outside on the left side of the building. As they looked across the expanse of lawn in the rapidly approaching twilight, they saw no sign of Carole although they looked in every direction.

"Perhaps she went on down the pathway," David suggested.

Steve nodded and the two men followed the path for several moments. On the trail they startled a small yearling deer which went bounding away through the brush, and further on they saw a skunk marching down the path toward them. They moved quickly out of the way, but when the little animal saw them, he scampered into the underbrush and disappeared.

By this time it was quite dark and they switched on their flashlights. "I don't like this," David said, "I wish I had stopped

Carole."

"Don't worry," Steve said. "Surely she is just a little late getting back, and she did have a flashlight, if I remember correctly."

"Yes, she did," David said. "Perhaps she went the other way," he said after a minute. "We have gone quite far this direction."

Steve agreed that she probably wouldn't have gone any further down the river. "Let's go back to the fork and take the other trail."

It wasn't very long until they were back at the fork. They hiked up the path to the old deserted campsite, but found neither Carole nor any evidence she had been there, though they searched the area thoroughly and called repeatedly.

"I really am getting worried," David said.

"So am I," Steve declared. "Let's go back to camp and see if she has returned there. If not, I believe we should go over to the castle and see if she has gone there, become acquainted with Mr. Prentice or his hired help, and been invited in."

"That's a logical thought," David said, relief in his voice.

When they came into camp Gran hurried to meet them, anxiety etched into her face. "Carole hasn't come back. Do you suppose she's all right?" she said.

"Now don't you go worrying," Steve said. "We'll go back and look some more. She hasn't been gone too long. Remember, she went for a walk the other night and returned safely."

He and David retraced their steps to the swinging bridge. They paused, flashed their lights up and down the banks and under the bridge where the water rushed deep and turbulent. There was nothing. They crossed the swinging bridge, the lawn and mounted the flagstone steps to the front entrance. They knocked and waited. All was still inside the creepy old house. They knocked again but no one came to the door.

"There must be someone here," David said. "There are lights on."

"Let's go around to the side door," suggested Steve. "There's a light there."

They followed the flagstone sidewalk around the building to the lighted doorway. David knocked on the door. No answer. He hammered on the door and still no one appeared. They turned from the door and flashed their lights all around. Not far from the side entrance was an open-sided shed with firewood ricked clear to the ceiling.

Steve walked around it with David trailing him. There was no one anywhere about and still no sign of Carole. The men silently walked back to the side door and knocked again.

"The place appears deserted," David said. "But let's try again." He knocked again, very loudly. Suddenly the door swung open and there stood the old artist, a frown upon his face. "Why are you trying to knock my door down?" he demanded belligerently.

Steve stepped forward. "Mr. Prentice," he said, "I'm sorry for the intrusion but Mrs. Loring, one of our campers, disappeared late this afternoon and we're searching for her. Have you seen anything of a young woman?"

"What makes you think that I've seen her?"

"Mrs. Loring seemed fascinated with your castle-like mansion, so we thought perhaps she had come here and you had invited her in for a chat."

"Not me!" The artist glared at the two men. "I don't have time for gadabout females." He started to close the door.

"Please," Steve said, "could we speak to your handyman? Maybe he has seen her."

"Jasper's gone."

"His wife, then," Steve suggested hopefully.

"Stella and Jasper are both away," the old man declared. "Gone on a trip. Now if you'll excuse me." The door began to close again.

David spoke for the first time. "Please, Mr. Prentice, it's

83

my wife that's missing, and I'm very worried. Could you suggest any place she could have gone?"

The old artist stared at David for a moment. It seemed that his expression softened somewhat. "Sorry, young fellow," he said at last, "but I can't help you." Reluctantly Steve said to the closing door, "Thank you for your time, Mr. Prentice, but if she does show up here or you see anything of her, please let us know."

Silently the two men retraced their steps to the swinging bridge. Again they examined the tumbling black waters underneath with their flashlights.

"Do you think she could have slipped, fallen into the water and been swept away down the river?" David's face was tense and pale.

"I can hardly imagine that," Steve said slowly. "Mrs. Loring seems well coordinated and alert. Let's search the trails again. Maybe she went farther than we thought or got away from the path and is having trouble finding her way back. Or she could have sprained an ankle and is waiting for help to come."

They followed the path that led down the river for about twenty minutes, calling at frequent intervals and probing into the darkness with their strong flashlight beams. But only the rush and gurgle of the nearby river and the twittering of birds settling for night in the trees overhanging the path answered them.

Suddenly Steve stopped, "I think we had better get some help. There are only two of us and we're very limited. I'm sure the others in camp will want to help."

"Agreed," David said as they turned around and walked swiftly back to camp.

When Steve and David strode back into camp a short while later, the campers surged out to meet them, asking questions and offering assistance.

Steve then organized the searchers into three groups with himself, Manuel and Slim in charge of different sections to be covered. The three groups would break into pairs. He urged everyone to stay within calling range of each other so no one would become lost in the woods. Everyone was to report back within two hours. Every ten minutes a shot would be fired from camp in case someone lost his bearings.

Two hours later the weary searchers came straggling back into camp. No one had seen or heard a sound from the missing Carole. When all the campers were accounted for Steve spoke decisively, "We must call in the sheriff. He can organize a large search party and be out here by early morning, I'm sure." He left the campground to make the call to the sheriff from the Manor's phone.

He was back very quickly. "Sheriff Murphy will be here at daybreak. He's calling in the forest rangers as well as all the men he can enlist from the Granite area. Now, it is past midnight. I would advise you all to get to bed and get as much rest as possible in the next few hours. Tomorrow could be an extremely hard day. But before we scatter, let us pray together."

Faces were serious as Steve prayed—a simple petition for Carole's safety and for the guidance and safety of those who would be searching for her.

Gran, who had remained in camp at Steve's insistence, had been the one who fired the gun at ten-minute intervals. Now her face was gray with fatigue and anxiety. David urged her to lie down and rest till morning. "What about you?" she asked David. "Are you going to rest?"

"I couldn't sleep with Carole out there," he said.

Steve heard his words and tried to reason with him, backed up by Gran. "In the morning the search party will be here to help. You should at least try to rest whether you sleep or not."

But to Steve's urgings and Gran's pleas, he only shook his head stubbornly. Catching up his flashlight, his face showing grim and set in the dancing firelight, David strode off toward the river.

An hour later he found Carole's flashlight on the castle lawn.

15

Their feet echoed hollowly along the narrow concrete path. The tunnel was only about four feet wide and no more than six and a half feet high. Surprisingly, it was relatively free of cobwebs, so it must be cleaned on a regular basis, Carole noted, wondering where it led. This was another of the castle's secrets—and a very spooky one! Was there a dungeon in this strange castle-mansion?

After a walk of several minutes, the five came to another door which Mr. Prentice opened with the same key, a single large one on a chain. They passed through the massive door into a large room with irregular walls, obviously a cave. Rocks protruded here and there as no attempt had been made to smooth and shape the walls. The floor was paved with concrete but the walls and the ceiling had been left as they were—a natural cavern.

Carole recalled that the castle was flanked on the back side by a mountain so this must be a cave on the other side of the steep slope she had seen from the tower, connected to the castle by a tunnel. In spite of her foreboding and fear, the secret passageway and cavern hideaway intrigued her. What had been the original purpose of this place, she wondered.

The old artist was moving about, checking cupboards and closets. Carole approached him hesitantly. "Mr. Prentice, why did you connect this cave to the castle?"

An odd expression came on his face as he turned thoughtfully to face her, "In this isolated location, Esther, my wife, was always afraid robbers might break in and harm us so this was meant to be a secret place to escape to and even live in for awhile, if necessary," he explained. "We have always kept it stocked with staple foods and essentials and had it cleaned monthly."

Ferron had been listening and now he spoke mockingly, "Esther didn't know she was preparing a fine hideout for the robbers she was afraid of." His bold, obsidian eyes glittered with malicious glee.

Mr. Prentice turned away without a word. Pity for the old gentleman surged in Carole's heart. His usual fierceness was gone. Now he was a beaten old man.

The cave was divided into one large room and a small bedroom that Carole glimpsed through an open doorway with a tiny bathroom beyond. The area they were standing in was the living room, with the kitchenette at the other end. Nearly all the furniture was built-in: chests-of-drawers, two cushioned benches—which as Mr. Prentice demonstrated presently, let out into comfortable beds. There was an electric cookstove and a small refrigerator. A butane heater had a smooth top for cooking—in case of power outage, Carol surmised. A built-in closet, a drop-leaf table, four chairs and a small platform rocker completed the main room's furnishings.

"We'll put the girls in here," said the old man, nodding toward the bedroom. The two robbers, busy poking in cabinets and closet didn't object.

Carole stepped into the little bedroom. It contained a double bed, a tiny nightstand, a built-in closet and a small old-fashioned rocker with a colorful cushion, and a small desk and chair. The bathroom opened into it and also into the kitchenette. It boasted a small shower stall, wash basin and toilet.

"There are plenty of towels, wash cloths, soap, shampoo and even sealed toothbrushes in the bathroom cupboard. And there are plenty of clean sheets, pillowcases, blankets and pillows in the closets in each room. We tried to be prepared," Mr. Prentice said, a trifle bitterly.

Carole could hardly wait to shower and brush her teeth but decided to wait until after breakfast as she was feeling weak and quite faint. She wanted to be present when food was prepared and get her share, if possible.

Apparently Max was feeling hunger pangs, too. "What's for breakfast?" he asked the old artist.

"If you two will come upstairs, we'll collect some eggs,

bread, meat and other perishables," he told the burglars.

"I'll go with you and Max will stay here with the hostages," Ferron spoke emphatically. "We don't want anymore escapades like last night. From now on, one of us will be with the girls and one of us with you. I'll hide when you get visitors but I'll never be far away. Remember that! And if you give a hint to the sheriff or anyone else, you, the brat, and the pretty lady won't live to see another day!"

Carole turned away from Ferron's cold, granite face. That he was capable of carrying out his threat and never batting an eye, she had no doubts.

The men returned quickly with paper sacks filled with food. Carole had seen, as Mr. Prentice checked the storage cupboards in the kitchen, that a large amount of a varied assortment of foodstuff was already stocked on the shelves. Carole watched the old man put away eggs, milk, butter, cheese, meat and some fresh vegetables in the refrigerator. He laid frozen, homemade bread out on the table. "What's your name?" demanded Ferron of Carole. When she told him he ordered, "Carole, make yourself useful and fix us all breakfast."

Carole didn't know what to do. She hesitated to tell the thieves that she had never cooked a meal in her life. Dressed in jeans, her dark silky hair hanging in a braid down her back, she didn't look the part of an heiress. She decided to be as honest as she could and still not reveal her position in life.

"I don't know how to cook," she said candidly. "But if someone will show me how I'll be glad to try," she hastened to add.

Max was gawking at her in undisguised astonishment, "A dame that can't cook!" he jeered. "I'll be switched! I've seen it all."

Carole felt her face turning red under his scornful stare. She turned away only to meet Ferron's glacial eyes, now narrowed in thoughtful speculation. She had to get the attention off herself!

"All women don't like to cook," she said crossly. "In our house I did other things while others did the cooking." She hoped they didn't ask her what "things" because being a good hostess and playing the piano beautifully might not be considered very worthwhile things in some circles. "Now, come on, someone show me how to start and I'll get breakfast."

She was suddenly aware of the artist's keen dark eyes watching her intently and she perceived that he understood the situation perfectly.

He casually moved to her side and said nonchalantly, "The frying pan is in here." He removed a large skillet from a shelf and set it on the electric stove. "The toaster is there," he said pointing to another oilcloth covered shelf. Thankfully, she did know what a toaster looked like, and quickly picked it up and set it on the table. "If you'll slice the bread," he suggested as he extracted a large serrated-edged knife from a holder and handed it to her. "Cut it rather thin so it will fit in the toaster."

Remind me to hug you sometime, thought Carole gratefully. She carefully watched everything Mr. Prentice did as he broke eggs in a dish and stirred them, added a dash of cream, salt, pepper and bits of chopped ham he had asked her to prepare. He smoothly directed her to put water on to heat for instant coffee and cocoa and, with Mitzi's help, set the table. She kept a watchful eye on the cook as he melted butter in the skillet, poured in the raw egg mixture and presently dished out a perfect omelet. The robbers had taken charge of the two cushioned benches and were stretched out like kings waiting to be served.

The old saying "hunger makes a good sauce" is certainly true, thought Carole awhile later as they ate the delicious meal of home-cooked wheat bread—toasted and spread liberally with sweet fresh butter, the delectable omelet, and homemade strawberry preserves. She had never been hungry—*really* hungry—before and she had to restrain herself from gobbling her food ravenously. Nothing, not even

Manuel's savory cooking, had ever tasted so good. She also had a warm feeling of well-being and self-satisfaction at the part she had played in preparing the meal.

After the meal, Ferron and the old artist both went through the tunnel, presumably to await the sheriff's return with the search warrant. Carole wished she had had the presence of mind to drop something for the sheriff to find. But I suppose, she thought gloomily, that Ferron will remove all signs of anyone except the old man being there, so it would have been a waste of time anyway. She felt like sitting down and crying from frustration, anger and fear. But with Mitzi there to be frightened and Max there to gloat, she controlled herself.

Max went back to his couch and stretched out luxuriously. "You girls can clean things up," he said grandly, "I'm taking me a nap."

He closed his eyes but Carole noticed soon that he was feigning sleep, and in reality was watching them through narrowed slits. It made her nervous and she finished the dishes as quickly as possible.

Mitzi saved the day for her now, as her grandfather had earlier. The child begged to help. When Carole gratefully agreed, Mitzi ran warm water in one twin stainless steel sink, added liquid detergent, and ran some hot rinse water in the other sink into which she dropped each dish as she washed it. "You can dry," said Mitzi, very grown-up-like.

Carole found a brightly colored terry towel with toadstools on it in a drawer and presumed it was for drying dishes. She took the dishes from the hot water and laid them on the drainboard to drain before drying them and putting them away.

As soon as they had finished, she whispered to Mitzi, "Let's go into the little bedroom." Feeling Max's evil eyes upon their backs as they retreated, Carole led Mitzi into the smaller room and softly slid the bolt on the door. They had hardly gone inside before Max was trying the door and then hammering at it, ordering them to open up. Assuming her most haughty demeanor, Carole opened the door.

"What are you up to?" asked the thief suspiciously.

"Mitzi and I just want a little privacy, that's all," said Carole. "There's no way out of this room, as you can see! We will probably do a little reading," she nodded toward a well-filled bookcase in the room, "if we can find something interesting."

"Maybe I will, too," stated Max, as he pushed his way into the room and went to stand before the bookcase. Carole and Mitzi eased themselves back into the main room, not wishing to share such close quarters with the hairy, grizzly-like man. Thumbing through a few books, he finally selected a large illustrated travel book and went back to his cushioned couch.

Returning to the bedroom with Mitzi, Carole didn't attempt to lock the door again. When she heard his snores, she slipped to the door and peeked out. He was sprawled out, the book had dropped to the floor, and he was snoring loudly with his mouth hanging open. Carole closed the door surreptitiously and slid the bolt.

Leaving Mitzi occupied with a puzzle she had found, Carole took a quick shower, brushed her teeth—oh joy, to have a toothbrush again—brushed and re-braided her hair. Afterward, when Mitzi begged to have her hair done like Carole's—a request which caused a warm glow in Carole's heart for some inexplicable reason—she braided Mitzi's fine hair into a long, silky flaxen plait. When Mitzi stood before the mirror admiring her new hair-do with wide, delighted blue eyes, Carole felt again that lump in her throat and the quickening of her heart. Oddly, she felt like hugging the little girl but was still shy in the presence of a child.

The day dragged on interminably. Late in the morning, Ferron came back and said the sheriff was there with a couple of deputies, and they were searching the house. Carole's heart began to pound.

"The girl's husband found a flashlight on the lawn last night that he swore belonged to his wife." He glared at

Carole. "Did you have a flashlight when you came here last night?"

"There was one in my jacket pocket. I must have lost it when I ran away and you tackled me."

"Her husband said the moonlight was shining on something on the lawn and when he went to see what it was, it was the flashlight," Ferron explained to Max. "The old man argued that it could be one his hired man had dropped, or he himself, but her husband declared it belonged to his wife and produced one like it that was his. He said he bought them both for this trip and they were shaped differently than the average flashlight. The sheriff seemed to believe him and got a search warrant since it was found so close to this house.

"But don't worry, little lady," he said, casting a baleful look Carole's way, "a hundred men couldn't find you here. It's the perfect hideout."

"Yeah," Max smirked at Carole, "and weren't that thoughtful of the old man's wife to fix it up, just for us—her beloved son-in-law and his dear friend, Max!" He guffawed long and loud, slapping his hands on his thighs.

Carole turned away in disgust, but a chill crept through her, causing her stomach to quiver and her skin to feel damp and clammy with fear. Ferron was right. There was no way the sheriff could find her. The cavern *was* a perfect hiding place. And as long as Ferron and Max kept the child in their clutches the old grandfather would never divulge the old mansion's secret. Gloom settled like a heavy fog upon her. There was no escape.

16

After Ferron went away to spy on the old man and the searchers, Max demanded more food. Carole sliced bread, made ham and cheese sandwiches, hot chocolate, and opened some jars of delectable looking golden peach halves she had found while prowling in the cupboard. Max fell upon the repast with gusto and put away an astonishingly large amount. Carole waited until he had finished and gone back to his couch and travel book before she and Mitzi had lunch. Again she felt a brief flash of pleasure in preparing the simple meal.

Ferron returned much later in the afternoon to report the searchers had left the house but the sheriff was putting pressure on the old artist. "He seems to think the old man is hiding the girl, or at least knows something he isn't telling. They questioned him about a child that Carole said she saw on the trail and later in a window of the castle. The old codger angrily denied any knowledge of a child. But the sheriff told him he may be taken into town for questioning. The sheriff is also curious about where the old man's hired couple has gone. He doesn't seem convinced that they are away on an extended trip. He's threatening to try to contact them."

Ferron was explaining this to Max but Carole heard it plainly from the little bedroom. She heard the concerned note in Ferron's voice and her heart leapt with hope.

"I'm gettin' a little anxious about that old geezer," Ferron lowered his voice but Carole had keen hearing and she was straining to hear every word through the thin bedroom wall. "He looks kinda sick. The strain may be gettin' to him. I sure don't want him to die on us. We need him to front for us right now. And if the sheriff finds that hired couple we could be in trouble. If it gets too hot around here we may have to split. But if we do, we can take the dame for a hostage." Ferron laughed his mirthless bark. "She's a cutie anyway, so her company won't be so bad." He laughed again. Max joined in with his own unpleasant cackle.

Carole felt her blood turn to ice. She shivered although the room was warm. Someway she had to escape! It was bad enough being the prisoner of these beasts here in the castle-dungeon where the old man was a buffer, but she shuddered to think what might happen if they took her away from here alone.

Suddenly they heard Mr. Prentice's voice, and both Carole and Mitzi went to the bedroom door. Mitzi rushed to her grandfather and he knelt stiffly on one knee to wrap his arms about his tiny granddaughter, his eyes warm with love and pleasure. Carole felt her eyes mist. The crochety old man surely can't hate his daughter and love her child as he obviously does, she thought.

"You brought my storybook!" cried Mitzi with delight.

Her grandfather rose rheumatically to his feet with his arm still about Mitzi's small shoulders. Placing a large Bible storybook, similar to the one in the tower, in Mitzi's arms, he glanced over at Carole. "Maybe the nice lady will read you your favorite story tonight, in case Grandpa can't get back in time." Leveling a steady look at Carole he asked, "Would you mind?"

"I'd be glad to," replied Carole.

"You're very good to Mitzi, and I appreciate it," the old artist said sincerely, still regarding her with a level, steady gaze.

"She's a darling little girl. It's my pleasure," Carole heard herself saying while part of her mind was thinking, "Is Mr. Prentice trying to relay a message of some sort to me?" He had turned away but in her mind's eye she could still see his intent, penetrating stare.

At that moment Mitzi gave a cry of happiness, "Ebenezer!" she exclaimed as she raced across the room to throw her arms about the gigantic black cat who had strolled in from the open tunnel door. The pair made an impressive picture. The supple feline rubbed his huge glossy black head against the diminutive child's fair cheek, emitting gutteral purrs that could be heard across the room. Mitzi giggled with pleasure when his whiskers tickled her cheek.

"Was that your cat I heard in the wee hours of the morning?" Carole asked the old man.

94

Laughter twinkled in Mr. Prentice's eyes, "Yes, I'm sure it was. I'm used to it by now so I don't notice. I think he hears or smells a big bobcat that hangs around our area and he goes kinda wild. He gets up on the highest place around and screams to the intruder that this is his territory."

Carole moved across the room and stooped to stroke the cat. She was so intent on the picturesque scene of Mitzi sitting on the floor with the huge cat curled up in her lap that she didn't hear the artist's warning shout. Just as her finger touched his sooty, glistening fur, he sprang from Mitzi's lap, with back bowed, hissing and spitting. He struck out savagely toward her hand with a claw-extended paw, barely missing. Carole jumped back in fright then backed away, throwing her hands up to protect her face from attack, as the huge feline seemed crouched to pounce upon her.

Mr. Prentice had hurried forward and now stood between her and the cat and was scolding him soundly. Ebenezer spit once more, then calmly turned and walked disdainfully away down the tunnel with the measured dignified, graceful tread of a monarch.

The old man turned to Carole with distress written plainly on his face. "I'm sorry. I hope he didn't scratch you." When Carole assured him shakily that she was all right, he continued. "I forgot to tell you that he doesn't like strangers. In fact, he doesn't really like people. He tolerates me and knows I'm boss, but the only one he really took to was my daughter, Joy—and now, Mitzi. It's strange but he almost seems to know she is Joy's daughter. He was only a year or so old when Joy moved away, but they were inseparable."

His dark eyes mirrored sadness as he looked away into space, seeming to have forgotten their presence. "I've been a fool," he mused. "I drove Joy away and broke her mother's heart by my stubborn selfishness—and my pride kept me from rectifying that past mistake. I could have been enjoying my granddaughter, as well as my daughter, for the past five years, but I have sat here and nursed my bitterness and self-pity. I deserve my misery!" he finished vehemently.

"Sure you do!" said Ferron contemptuously. "But let's cut the dramatics and get back to the house before you have visitors again and aren't available to answer questions."

The old man shook his shaggy gray head as if to clear his mind. Carole recalled Ferron's earlier concern that the old artist looked sick, and observed that he did, indeed, look drawn and gray. She wondered if, for just a moment, he had forgotten where he was, when he spoke of his daughter.

"Now," he turned back to Carole, "you will read Mitzi her favorite story before she goes to bed?" When Carole assured him she would, he kissed his granddaughter goodnight and walked with a weary, shuffling step out the door into the tunnel, followed by Ferron.

Max locked the door behind them before he went to rummage in the cabinets and refrigerator for a snack. Finding cookies and a glass of orange juice, he went back to his couch to play a game of solitaire and munch his snacks.

Carole did not want to appear eager, but she was almost sure the old artist had been trying to convey a message to her. She casually herded Mitzi back into the small bedroom and quietly slid the bar. Then nonchalantly she asked Mitzi which was her favorite story. If Mr. Prentice was trying to get a message to her, it must be in the storybook.

Mitzi excitedly turned the pages of her book to the favorite story and handed it to Carole, who studied the two pages and then turned to the ending on the next page. There was no message. Disappointment welled up inside Carole, black and despairing. She felt like crying again. This must all be getting to me, she thought. I was never such a cry baby before or plummeted so easily into bleak despondency. She had always been a cheerful optimist.

Mitzi was bouncing up and down in anticipation but settled herself cosily next to Carole as she began to read. The story was about Queen Esther—a story Carole had never read before, so in spite of her gloom the well written children's story penetrated her troubled mind and she read the remainder of the story with real interest.

When she finished, she was about to close the book but Mitzi spoke with a pleading voice, "Would you read it again—please?" Carole, unused to small children, didn't know they liked favorite stories read over and over. Carole complied—there was nothing else to do, anyway. But when she finished the second reading and the child begged to hear it again, she thought, "This is a little much."

"Okay," she told Mitzi, "I'll read it once more but that is enough." She was beginning to feel cross with the little girl and she knew it was mainly a reaction to disappointment at not finding any words written from the old man. As she began reading again, suddenly she saw something she had not noticed before. A word she had just read had a light pencil line under it. She had to look closely to see it. She stopped reading and glanced on down the page. On both pages and the ending of the story on the following page, she found several other words lightly underlined with pencil.

"Wait a minute," she answered Mitzi's puzzled expression. Shifting the book so she had more light, she read a few scattered words. There—is—an—outside—door—key—in—bottom—of—chest—Be—careful.

Excitement exploded inside her, and her heart began a rapid jig. But she knew she couldn't let on to Mitzi lest the little one inadvertently give away her secret. Willing herself to calmness, she finished the story—trying to appear unhurried. Handing the book back to Mitzi, she spoke in a natural voice—knowing every word she spoke carried clearly through the thin partition to their captor. "Pick out another story and I'll read it to you after supper. Okay?"

Mitzi agreed joyfully, and was quickly absorbed in scanning the pages of her book.

Carole unhurriedly went to the bathroom, ran a glass of water and drank it slowly. Then she strolled carelessly over to the chest-of-drawers—the only chest she saw in the room. She pulled out the first drawer and looked rapidly through the contents—clean, white undergarments, a trifle large for her but she catalogued them in her mind for use later when she showered again—if she didn't succeed in escaping quickly. "I've found some clothes I can wear," she said conversationally to Mitzi, knowing Max could hear her pulling out drawers.

The message had said the key was in the bottom of the chest so she pulled out the bottom drawer and tried to search calmly and methodically. It contained folded slacks, sweaters and socks. She carefully moved each piece, stacking them on the opposite side, one at a time, then ran her hand along the four sides and along the bottom. There was no key! Forgetting Max, she took the drawer completely out, dumped the contents on the floor, and looked under the drawer. There was no key taped under it. She peered inside at the bottom of the third drawer, feeling its sides and bottom. Nothing!

Turning over the bottom drawer she examined every inch of it inside and out. Then, feeling despair and gloom clutching at her again with icy fingers, she searched each piece of clothing, thoroughly shaking it out, then folding it again as she placed it back into the drawer she had returned to its place in the chest. When the last piece was back in the drawer, she sat back and let the tears slip down her cheeks. There was no key—no escape!

Suddenly she became aware that Max was up and walking across the other room. She must not let him see her tears! Nor Mitzi! Scrambling up, she went into the bathroom and ran the water with force so he could hear it and washed her face in cold water. Max had tried the door and was now knocking on it.

"Just a minute," called Carole. She turned off the water faucet and went to the door with a towel in her hand, still drying her face, partly hiding her eyes, and hoping he wouldn't notice that they were reddened.

"It's time for supper," announced Max in his unpleasant nasal voice. "And I'd like to have something besides a canned meal! There's some steak and potatoes, so fix baked potatoes and steak!"

Not accustomed to being ordered about, Carole felt her anger rise but she quickly squelched it. To anger Max was courting disaster. Besides, there was more than herself to think of—little Mitzi needed her. She remembered Max's desire to discipline the child and she meant to give him no excuse to use force on either of them.

So she tried to speak pleasantly. "I don't know how to cook steak and potatoes, but if you will tell me, I'll do my best."

Max's broad face grimaced as if in pain and he spoke sarcastically, "You are the dumbest broad I ever seen! They ain't anything to fixin' spuds but puttin' 'em in a hot oven! But come on, I'll tell you how, if that's what it takes to get a decent meal." He turned away and went to the refrigerator to take out the steak.

It was all Carole could do to hold her tongue but hold it she did!

With much instruction from a grumbling Max, Carole managed to cook a fairly good meal. Mitzi had remembered that her mother wrapped potatoes in foil, after scrubbing them, and the baked potatoes, with lots of fresh, sweet butter, were delicious . The steak—which Max had pounded for her after seeing her awkwardness—was passable; there seemed to be a knack about steak that she didn't get in one lesson. The salad and frozen peas—with directions on the box— needed no expert cook.

The kitchen was a mess after her lesson in the culinary arts, so she and Mitzi set to work washing dishes and straightening up the kitchen. The robber went back to his couch when his hunger was sated, with a terse, uncomplimentary, "I've eaten better steak but I guess it'll do till breakfast." But Carole didn't let his remark bother her. He had eaten quantities of food, so it couldn't have been that bad.

When the dishes were once more clean and in the cabinet, Carole was hanging up a dish towel when she spied a red box sitting on a shelf above the stove. "I wonder what's in that box," she remarked to Mitzi as she took it down from the shelf. Peeking inside, she saw that it contained recipe cards. When Mitzi saw what was in it, she lost interest and went to look at her storybook again. She was having difficulty deciding on which story Carole should read as a bedtime story.

If I have to cook perhaps I can learn something from the recipes, she mused. It would be a help if she didn't have to ask about every little thing she prepared, besides it was embarrassing. Seating herself at the table, she opened the box and thumbed through the category cards. Since it was all Greek to her, she might as well start at the first card, she decided.

Pushing back the cards, she heard a faint sound as if something had clicked against the side of the box. Pressing the set of cards away from the front of the box, she looked inside. Lying on the bottom of the box was a large key! Stunned, she sat and stared at it. Could this be the key the castle owner had said was in a chest? Probably not. Her cautious mind did not want to be disappointed again. Slowly she closed the lid and looked—really looked—at the recipe box. It was shaped like a little chest! This *was* the back door key!

Carole's heart was behaving like a jackhammer. Casting a glance at her captor, she saw he was engrossed in another game of solitaire. Picking up the recipe box, she went into the bedroom, then crossed to the bathroom and closed the door. Carefully, she extracted the key from the small chest. She looked about for a place to hide it and finally settled on putting it into the top of her sock and folding the sock down below the top of her left boot.

She had no idea when she would get a chance to try the key but as soon as opportunity presented itself, she meant to be ready!

Looking at her watch, Carole saw it was 7:00 p.m. Night again! Had she only been away from David a little more than twenty-four hours? It was unbelievable. It seemed eons ago when she had walked down that path to the river in such anger.

Loneliness and longing, so intense that it was almost more than she could bear, pulsed through her. To think that David was so close that, if she were free, she could probably walk to him—only she wouldn't walk, she would run—in a few minutes. So close and yet so far!

"David, please forgive me for all the pain I have caused you," she whispered in the solitude of the tiny bathroom. "I love you, love you, love you!" If only she were in the comfort of his arms! Joy of joys!

She came out of the bathroom and stretched herself on the double bed. Mitzi was sitting crosslegged on the other half of the bed, still perusing her storybook. Carole closed her eyes and tried to rest. She felt tense and restless, but if she had the chance to use that key later, she would need to be rested. The climb over the mountain, in the dark with Mitzi, could be a strenuous one. They would have to climb up and then to the right a ways, she figured, so they would come down in the stand of trees, instead of next to the house. When they got to the river, she thought, they would probably have to go down into the river bed and try to find a place to cross. She couldn't take the chance of being captured again.

Carole tried not to think about the possibility that she would have no opportunity to try the key. She had to find a way! Maybe Mr. Prentice could help get Max away long enough, but she knew he would have to be cautious. If he succeeded in helping them escape and were caught, he would probably seal his own doom.

Presently Carole heard Ferron return and ask if there was food cooked. She had put a large plate of food, covered with foil, in the heated oven and a salad in the refrigerator for him. She half expected to be ordered to come and serve him but she heard Max explain where she had put his meal, then the clink of silverware and the rattle of dishes as Ferron set out the food. Then there were only the faint sounds of eating. As soon as he finished, Ferron went away again saying, "There's something going on across the river but I don't know what, so I'm keeping close tabs on things."

What was going on across the river, Carole wondered. Here in this hole in the ground she could hear nothing and see nothing! It was frustrating and nerve jangling.

Mitzi's eyes were drooping so Carole took her into the little shower and showed her how to take a shower, turning on the water for her, as she had said she was accustomed to a tub bath. When Mitzi was back and dressed in the long white nightie that her grandfather had brought for her earlier, she climbed into bed and Carole read her the promised story—the baby Moses was her selection this time. After her little "Now I lay me" prayer had been said, Carole tucked her in and kissed her goodnight. Before Carole could have counted ten, Mitzi was sound asleep.

Carole tried to read a book but couldn't concentrate, so she laid down with her clothes on. She felt she was waiting for something—an opportunity to use that key, or to be rescued. But as time wore on she grew drowsy and finally drifted off to sleep.

17

Much later, Carole awoke to Ferron's voice, urgent and strident, in the next room. She was disoriented and couldn't think where she was. Then Ferron's words registered in her mind and instantly she was wide awake. "Get a move on, those dogs will be here any minute."

"What dogs?" came Max's nasal query. Ferron had, from all indications, awakened Max, too.

"I told you once," shouted Ferron, "the sheriff is using bloodhounds. You can hear them bawling across the river."

"What's that to us?"

"If they bring those hounds into the old man's house, they can trail that dame right to the closet that leads to the tunnel. And they'll take that closet apart till they find out how to get into the tunnel. We've got to use strong bleach water and mop every place that woman has been! The hounds can't scent through bleach, I'm sure. Let's go! Is that outside door locked good?" Max grunted an affirmative. "Okay. We'll lock the door to the tunnel and there's no danger of their getting away."

Carole had listened to the discourse with bated breath. When the sounds of their departure and the grating of the key in the lock died away, she sprang up. Her opportunity had arrived!

She shook Mitzi and instructed the sleepy child to quickly get into her play clothes again while she tried to get the door open. Mitzi could hardly keep her eyes open, and as soon as Carole turned away she fell back asleep. Carole shook her again, none too gently, and cried urgently, "Mitzi, get dressed! We're going to try to get away from these mean men and go find your mommy!"

"Mommy" was the magic word. Mitzi jumped out of bed and began to dress herself with feverish haste, her eyes bright stars of anticipation.

Carole raced to the heavy door, extracted the key from her sock and fitted it into the lock. It turned easily. Carole grabbed the large bar-like handle and pulled it with all her might. The door stayed stubbornly closed. Carole turned the key the other way in the lock and pulled at the door again. No movement! Frantically, she turned the key back the other way, confident she had been right the first time. Again she tugged at the huge door handle. And then again! And again! There was not the slightest movement! Almost in tears from frustration and fear that the robbers would return before they escaped, Carole felt like beating at the door with her fists and screaming at the top of her lungs.

"Easy, Carole," she said aloud, "this requires a clear

mind. Take it easy." She stood back and forced herself to breathe deeply and stop her frantic yanking. "I know the key is turned right," she reasoned aloud, "so that is not the problem. And it is the proper key, because I can hear and feel the click when I turn it. So what can it be? There is no other lock on the door. The door must just be very heavy." She pulled again on the door, putting all her strength into the tug. The door stayed stubbornly closed.

She felt a tug at her clothes and saw Mitzi standing at her side. Mitzi was usually very neat but now her shoes weren't tied or her shirt buttoned and her blond hair was tumbled about her flushed face—but she was poised for flight. It would have been laughable if the situation had not been so grave.

"I haven't got the door open yet, Mitzi. Run and get my jacket and a heavy sweater for yourself out of that bottom dresser drawer." Mitzi instantly sprang to obey. "And find some scarves for our heads," Carole called. "It will be cool outside."

She turned back to wrestle with the troublesome door. In a few minutes she was totally exhausted but the door had not budged a fraction of an inch. Sick at heart, her face hot and flushed, her legs and arms aching and trembling from her strenuous, frenetic efforts to open the door, she finally sat down upon the floor and buried her face in her hands. Despair washed over her in nauseous waves. They were buried here in this dismal dungeon and there was no escape!

She was vaguely aware that Mitzi was back. She had brushed past Carole and was standing at the door. "Come on, Aunt Carole," the child's anxious voice expostulated, "Let's go!"

Carole raised her head and looked at the child. The little thing's tiny arms were wrapped about Carole's jacket and a very large sweater. All ready to go and somehow she, Carole, had not been able to do her part. She stared at the child with dull eyes, speechless. The light will go out of those excited blue eyes when I tell her I have failed, she thought miserably.

"Come on, let's go," implored Mitzi as she dropped the jacket, sweater and scarves on the floor and reached for Carole's hand. Backing against the heavy door, she pulled back on Carole's hand. As she braced her back against the door—wonder of wonders—the huge door moved noiselessly outward! Carole realized her presumption that since the door sported a huge handle, it swung inward!

"How dumb can I get?" Carole declared.

But Carole wasted no valuable time in feeling foolish. She sprang to her feet, grabbed up the warm clothes, and followed Mitzi out into the night. They were free!

Leaving the key in the lock, Carole pushed the huge door back into place, and looked about her. The door on the outside looked like a boulder and fitted neatly into the mountain wall so that no one would dream there was a door here.

They were standing on a narrow, slightly sloping shelf with a cliff jutting out above them. The moon was riding high over the trees casting its dusky light over the side of the mountain.

Quickly Carole slipped into her jacket and put the adult-sized sweater on Mitzi, belted it tightly about her and folded up the sleeves. It reached nearly to Mitzi's feet. She hurriedly tied Mitzi's shoelaces.

"Come, we must hurry," she said urgently. Taking the tiny hand, she led the way off the narrow ledge and started the steep climb toward the top of the mountain. The slope was covered with rocks—from very small stones which rolled under foot and made climbing difficult to huge boulders which had to be skirted or climbed over. To further hamper their progress, dense brush grew in every open space where there was earth and their roots could take hold; their briery branches caught at them as they struggled upward.

Little Mitzi, after several moments of climbing, was winded and panting, and Carole was nearly as bad. They leaned against a large rock to rest and catch their breath for a minute, then pushed on, toiling up the steep hillside and threading their way through the brush. Their progress was snail-slow and Carole found herself looking back over her shoulder at nearly every labored step, expecting pursuit.

Suddenly the sky above them began to darken. Alarmed, Carole stopped and looked toward the moon. Clouds were stretching out tentacle-like arms to encircle and cover the moon, their only source of light! In a matter of just a few minutes, it was so dark that Carole could scarcely discern Mitzi's shape beside her. Mitzi whimpered in fright and clung more tightly to Carole's hand. Fear clutched its icy fingers about Carole's pounding heart. They had been moving at a snail's pace anyway, and now the whole hillside was blanketed in heavy darkness. It was foolhardy to move at all lest they fall into a hole or off the cliff. The only thing to do was sit down and hope the moon would move out from under the clouds. At the moment that possibility looked bleak.

"We'll have to sit down and wait for the moon to come out again," Carole told Mitzi, with much more cheerfulness than she felt. They sank down upon the ground and Carole pulled Mitzi close to her. Opening her own jacket, Carole enclosed Mitzi's small frame inside it and wrapped her arms about her.

"Are—are they going to catch us?" quavered Mitzi.

"Not if I can help it!" declared Carole vehemently.

The night was very still except for the sighing of the breeze in a small cluster of trees nearby and the soft nighttime mutterings of birds lodged there. Mitzi and Carole were nervously alert and, when an owl launched into the sky from the small grove of trees, both cried out in fear.

Carole had never been afraid of darkness but as time wore on, the blackness became oppressive and pressed in upon her. Every rustle in the brush or flutter in the trees rasped abrasively upon her taut nerves. If only that moon would come out!

Suddenly, out of the night faint sounds began to emerge, sounds that Carole at first was unable to identify. But as she strained to hear, and the volume increased and became more distinct, it dawned upon her what it was—the baying of bloodhounds! These were the dogs the sheriff had brought in to search for her! Hope surged in her breast. Those dogs—and searchers—were just over the ridge. Someway they must get to them!

She stood up quickly and at that moment a powerful searchlight swept across the mountainside, passed swiftly over her standing figure, and then returned to rest upon her in all its blinding glare. For a brief, elated second she thought the sheriff's search party had found them. Then she heard a hoarse shout and knew it was Max. In a blind panic she turned away from the brilliant light and tried to flee. But it was only seconds, it seemed, until Max's cruel hands were on her arms and she was being propelled back through the brush toward the cave. Ferron turned off the powerful searchlight and switched on a flashlight. In a few leaping steps he was up the incline. Picking Mitzi up, he flung her across his shoulder like a sack of feed and followed Max back toward the cavern prison.

A numb despair enveloped Carole. She scarcely felt the slap and the sting of the bushes or the pain of bumped knees and thighs as she was dragged and pushed around and over the rocks. The ground she and Mitzi had picked their way over so carefully awhile before was covered quickly. In a few minutes they were back in the dungeon. The heavy door swung shut and Carole heard the key lock them in once more.

18

Max shoved Carole into a chair, backed off and stood glaring maliciously at her, his hairy, ham-like hands on his hips. Ferron dumped Mitzi to the floor and she immediately ran to cower against Carole's side. Carole aroused from her stupor of hopelessness to wrap both arms about the trembling child and to draw her close. She had never been a violent person, but as she glimpsed the terror in Mitzi's eyes and held her trembling body, she thought savagely, "If I had a gun, I would kill both of these animals and feel no remorse!"

Max reached out a sinewy arm and gripped Carole's chin in a vice-like hold. "Where did you get that key, Queenie? Did the old man sneak it to you?"

"No, he didn't," snapped Carole. "I found it in that recipe box over there on the cabinet when I was looking at the recipes."

Max continued to glare at her suspiciously for another minute, then obviously accepting her answer, he released her chin. It felt bruised from the cruel grip. He continued to stare at her venomously.

"Ferron, you say the word and I'll work this chick over so good she'll be too sceered to even think of running away again!"

Carole braced for the worse. She was petrified with fear but felt instinctively that to plead or cry would be like waving a red flag before a bull's eyes. To hurt and maim was this man's pleasure—to hear her express distress or fear would only stimulate his bestial nature and goad him into more cruelty, she thought numbly.

She saw that Ferron was also watching her with his flat, expressionless, glacial eyes. She felt like a small rabbit mesmerized by the eyes of a coiled rattler. Ferron's good-looking face bore a half-smile as if he knew her terror and was savoring it to the hilt.

At last he spoke nonchalantly, as if it mattered little to him either way. "We may need her for a hostage, and a battered hostage isn't as good as one in good shape. Besides, Max, when you get started punishing someone, you don't know when to quit." He laughed as if it were a shared joke.

Max joined in the laughter with his own unpleasant guffaw. "Yeah, you're right, Ferron. I don't know when to quit!" He laughed harshly again, as if Ferron had complimented him highly. Carole cringed inwardly.

Abruptly Ferron changed the subject. "Max, why don't you go up and help the old man mop the tower room and the stairs? But keep a sharp lookout and don't let the sheriff or any of those searchers see you! I'll stay here and watch the girls for awhile. They won't escape again."

After Max left, Carole said she would put Mitzi to bed and escaped into the bedroom. Swiftly Carole changed Mitzi back into her nightwear—she was getting quite adept at this—and tucked her into bed.

When she touched her lips to the little one's forehead, Mitzi reached up and caught her around the neck and whispered tearfully, "I want my mommy! I want my mommy!" and suddenly the small body convulsed in sobs of anguish. The child was hysterical. Carole gathered her into her arms and rocked her gently back and forth.

"There, there, baby. Be a brave girl, now. Aunt Carole will take care of you. And you'll see your mommy soon. You'll see. There, there, baby, please don't cry. Ferron will hear you and be angry. There, there—" She continued to talk softly and held the child's shuddering body until she finally ceased sobbing and lay limp against Carole's shoulder.

Carole laid the still, exhausted child on the bed, thinking she was asleep. But the puffed eyelids came open and Mitzi's reddened eyes regarded her solemnly.

"Next to Mommy and Grandpa, I love you best of all," she whispered. She closed her eyes and was quickly sound asleep. Carole kissed the damp little cheek.

Tears pricked Carole's eyelids and a lump formed in her throat. How Ferron could not love a dear little daughter like this was more than she could fathom.

By her watch it was 11:30, and Carole was weary in body and spirit. She wasn't sure she could rest as her mind relived

109

her brief taste of freedom. Bitterly she wondered if she had someway failed Mitzi and herself. It seemed that everything was conspiring against them in their efforts to escape. Twice they had been so close to freedom. Despair and a feeling of utter desolation threatened to overwhelm her. Would she never see David again, or dear Gran, who must be worried sick? I must not continue in this vein of thought, she decided.

Leaving a small shaded lamp on for light, Carole stretched out upon her bed, too weary even to pull off her boots.

If David were here, she thought, he would plunk down on the other side of the bed and hold me. Longing for David welled up inside her until it was a physical pain. Tears, hot and stinging, blurred her eyesight. She rolled over and, with her head muffled in the pillow, wept heartbrokenly.

Her tears finally spent, she rubbed her eyes and rolled onto her back, staring at the ceiling. If only I could push time back forty-eight hours, I would change so much, she thought. But I can't. I can only hope to profit by experience and never make the same mistakes again. But will I have the opportunity? She shuddered as she recalled Max's cruel strength and Ferron's pitiless, cold eyes.

She sat up, removed her boots, and lay back down. There was a possibility—she had to face it squarely now—that she might never come out of this alive.

She had been thinking about that when the robbers had brought her to this cavern—could it have only been this morning? If she died, where would she go? It was a question Steve Morgan had asked. She didn't like to think about death, but now she must.

Mitzi's little prayer said, "And if I die before I wake, I pray Thee, Lord, my soul to take." That sounded like the Christian went to be with the Lord Jesus, and ministers spoke in glowing terms about heaven, so it must be a desirable place to go. If I *knew* I was going to be in heaven, then I would not have to worry about the alternative place, she contemplated.

Steve and Manuel seem to know they are right with God. Steve said I only need to believe that God's Son, Jesus, paid the price for my sins by dying on the cross, and that I simply invite Him into my heart and let Him rule in my life. Could it really be that living for God was not just obeying a set of almost impossible rules? No one had ever mentioned that there might be any immediate benefits. But Steve and Manuel spoke of a joyous, fulfilling, new way of life. It was almost too good to be true!

It seemed that all her preconceived ideas were being exploded. She had thought all children were repulsive, undisciplined, selfish brats because the two or three she had seen at close quarters were, but dear little Mitzi had proven that a false assumption. She had thought all Christians were unattractive, obnoxious, sanctimonious fanatics, but Steve and Manuel were none of those things—she would admit that now. She had thought David would desert her forever if he became involved in a profession because her parents had deserted her, and she had never given David a chance to prove otherwise. In the past, she had always let two or three bad examples brand all others. She squirmed under her self-applied searchlight.

When Gran had arrived and taken them away on this camping trip, she had been fed up with the life she and David were leading. She had seriously contemplated divorce as David spent more of his time inebriated. She was ashamed of him and his dependence upon alcohol. Carole had not wanted him to drink, but when he declared he had turned to Christ and planned never to drink again, she hadn't wanted that either.

I want my own way, she reflected. I always have. Well, this time I acted like a spoiled brat and had my own way, and it may cost me my life! She shivered at her own thoughts.

Manuel and Steve had told of their unsatisfying, selfish lives. Both had declared that when Christ came into their lives He had changed them. Could He do that for her? A great longing welled up inside her, like the yearning she felt when Manuel played his haunting music. She didn't really know how to pray but there was no one here to help her so she closed her eyes and whispered haltingly:

"God, I—I have always wanted my own way but it has only gotten me into terrible trouble. Would you forgive me for being so bad and come into my life? Take it over and make me what you would like me to be. I sincerely believe your Son Jesus died to pay for my sins and that He rose from the dead so that I could have new life through Him. Steve said this is all I have to do. Thank you, amen."

Carole opened her eyes and lay very still. She didn't feel any different. She was rather disappointed. Both Steve and Manuel had spoken as if a drastic change had come into their lives. What had she expected? A bolt of lightning to strike? Lights to flash? Come to think about it, neither man had intimated that they had any special feeling when they accepted Christ. They just said they were changed. And, after all, Steve had said this was all there was to it. "It is that simple" were his very words. I'll have to accept his word for it, Carole thought. A tiny thrill touched her.

"I'm a child of God," she whispered aloud, very softly. "A child of God." Every time she repeated the words, it seemed a bit of her anxiety slipped away, until she felt completely washed inside and out. Relaxing with the thought, she slipped almost instantly into a deep, restful sleep of real peace.

19

When Carole awoke the next morning, it was 9:07 by her watch. Mitzi was still sound asleep. Her long blond hair spread upon the pillow framed her small pointed face. Perfectly formed rosy lips were parted slightly, and curled flaxen lashes lay upon her gently rounded cheeks which had not quite lost their soft baby look. Carole's heart felt strangely warm as she studied the child. Suddenly she realized—to her amazement—that this child had become very dear to her and, when she had to relinquish her to her mother, it would be a real wrench to give her up.

Carole made another astounding discovery. During the night, hope had been reborn in her heart! Last night, before she had committed her life to God, she had felt that death was imminent—leering at her from every corner, ready to pounce and rend her apart. But this morning, although the same rocky prison walls surrounded her, she felt an inexplicable lightness, almost an expectancy.

Suddenly those momentous, wondrous words rose into her consciousness again, and she said them softly aloud, "I'm a child of God." A bubbly feeling of well-being and delight welled up inside.

She thought of David's declaration that he had accepted Christ into his life and found it no longer dismayed her. Indeed, she now felt a new kinship with him and with Steve Morgan and Manuel. What a joy it would be to share this newfound experience with them! To her utter amazement, she found herself relishing the thought of one of those formerly despicable camp worship services. She marveled.

She looked about the rocky, uneven walls shrouded in shadows cast by the dim night lamp. Strangely, the small room did not stifle or close in upon her now. She felt like running and leaping over the mountain slopes in exuberant joy. Her happiness was a thing of the spirit, unrelated to circumstances or setting. This must be what Manuel called salvation. And she had it, too!

No one else was astir so Carole tiptoed into the small bathroom, showered, shampooed her hair and slipped into the fresh garments she had found in the dresser drawer. Everything was a little large for her but they were clean. She braided her hair tightly again in a long thick plait down her back and donned a baggy pair of maroon slacks and a bulky sweatshirt. Instinctively she tried to tone down her natural beauty and to appear as young and tomboyish as possible. These unprincipled thugs were not to be trusted and she wanted to do all in her power to be unattractive to them. The viciousness she had sensed in these two men frightened her.

"But now I have God on my side," she whispered. "Dear God," she prayed fervently, "don't let these men harm Mitzi or me. And protect poor old Mr. Prentice from them, too. And please help us to escape or someone to find and rescue us. We'll have to leave it in your hands because somehow we have bungled every escape effort and exhausted every escape avenue. Thank you for giving me hope again. In Jesus' name, amen."

When Carole came out from the bathroom, she heard movement beyond the thin walls and soon Max's unpleasant nasal voice called to her, demanding breakfast. She wondered when her captors had changed places.

"As soon as I dress Mitzi," she answered. Quickly awakening the little girl, she urged her into her clothes. Being alone with the gorilla-like thief was not a pleasant thought.

Mitzi's delighted help with the cooking was invaluable to Carole. But Max still grumbled when Carole set a slightly scorched omelet—the only way she knew to cook eggs—before him.

Patiently Carole assured her ungrateful captor that she would serve them a different way next time, if he would tell her how he wanted them and explain how to get them that way.

"Queenie," his voice was laced with sarcasm, "I thought any broad knew how to crack open an egg and drop it in a skillet of grease. I like 'em over easy, which means you only cook 'em for a minute and then turn 'em over. You get 'em out before they're hard and you don't cook eggs over such a hot burner. That's what burned these," he finished uncharitably.

He wolfed down the three-egg omelet, however, with

four pieces of toast and two cups of coffee, so Carole didn't allow his derogatory words to intimidate her. But she carefully followed his cryptic directions and cooked two quite passable over easy eggs for herself and Mitzi. When she slipped them on their plates, added slices of buttery toast and home canned, wild strawberry jam and steaming mugs of hot chocolate, she was vastly pleased with her culinary achievement. Max would complain of something if she cooked another meal for him, she was sure, but her cooking skills were improving.

Presently, just as she and Mitzi were finishing their breakfast, Ferron came in to be fed. She carefully cooked two eggs over easy and was delighted at the near perfect plate she set before him. Ferron took one look at the eggs, and handed the plate back, instructing her to cook them hard. Somewhat chagrined, she choked back a bitter retort, fried them again, and returned them to the plate. Abstractedly, Ferron accepted the plate—with no thought of thanks, apparently—bolted down the food and disappeared into the tunnel again.

After Carole cleaned up the small kitchen with Mitzi's help, she stood at the sink and wondered what to do with the day. She surveyed the room: Max was napping on one bunk, Mitzi could be seen through the bedroom door sitting on a throw rug perusing her beloved Bible storybook. Carole's eyes swept the irregular walls of the cave. Several paintings were hung about the room. She had paid little attention to her surroundings before. Her only thought had been to escape them.

Carole stepped over to the nearest picture—a diminutive, dainty, spotted fawn pressed close to the side of his graceful, gentle-eyed mother. In the lower right-hand corner was the name "Esther Prentice." Realization suddenly struck Carole. The picture must have been painted by Mitzi's grandmother. The painting was quite good. The artist had made the two deer so lifelike, she almost expected them to go bounding away into the forest. The mother appeared to be listening intently and seemed poised for flight.

Carole, who loved paintings, forgot her aversion to being in the proximity of her captor and moved to another picture. This one had captured Thunder Mountain Manor in the afternoon. The glow of the afternoon sun was partially obscured by towering, rolling thunderclouds, silver and charcoal gray, rolling over Thunder Mountain at the rear of the mansion. Trees were bent before the fury of the oncoming storm. One could almost hear the crash of thunder, see the jagged streaks of lightning, and feel the lash of rain driven before the gale. The name in the corner was again, "Esther Prentice."

Hung next to the storm picture was an autumn scene— also of the castle. Bright rays of golden sunlight streamed into the panorama from the right-hand corner of the picture. The mountainside was ablaze with color—vivid varied shades of orange, red and rust, interspersed with multi-hued greens, grays and browns. To the right and left of the house the bright emerald of the evergreens contrasted sharply with the quaking, golden leaves of the aspen. Showers of waxy, yellow leaves, set free by a sudden gust of wind, frolicked in the bright sunlight and upon the green lawn. This picture, too, had been painted by Esther Prentice.

Entranced with the paintings, Carole had completely forgotten her jailer. Out of the corner of her eye, she suddenly became aware that Max was watching her. Trying not to show the panic that rose into her throat, she moved toward the door of the bedroom where Mitzi was still looking at her book. Just as she reached the doorway, another painting caught her eye. It was a much smaller picture, no more than twelve by fourteen inches, she judged. A large, majestic preening peacock dominated the picture. His gorgeous, iridescent tail feathers, with their brilliantly colored spots, were in full fan as he promenaded before a pair of peahens displaying what an elegant fellow he was.

A little bell began ringing in Carole's mind. A peacock! Where had she read or heard something in the last two or three days about a peacock? She had it! In Joy's strange diary in the books on the top shelf of the tower bookcase, Joy had stated, "I found mother's secret today—behind the peacock."

Was that secret still hidden behind the peacock? This cave hideaway seemed to have been Esther Prentice's special cloister, even as the tower had been Joy's.

Carole reached out and raised the picture. Her heart missed a beat. Behind the painting was a small door. A secret compartment was hidden behind the picture of the peacock!

20

Carole suddenly heard heavy breathing and turned around with a start. Max stood at her right shoulder, a smirk on his face. In her excitement she had forgotten him!

"Lemme see what's hid there." He shouldered his way in, took down the painting and threw it carelessly on the floor. Shocked at his rough treatment of the lovely painting, Carole quickly retrieved it and noticed with distress that the frame was broken. However, the picture did not seem to be harmed, she noted with relief.

The little hinged door had no lock on it so by this time Max had it open and brought out its contents: two small, very worn, matching leather-bound books. Holding the volumes in one hand, he reached in once more and explored the small space thoroughly with the other. Convinced there was nothing else hidden there, he carried the books to the small table where the lighting was better. Curiosity overcame Carole's fear of the hulking robber and she followed.

Throwing the small volumes upon the table, he drew up a chair and sat down to examine them. Carole hovered as unobtrusively as possible in the background. At a glance, she saw that one was a Bible and the other was labeled simply: *Diary*.

Max laboriously read the title—sounding out the letters—B-i-b-l-e on the small worn book. A frown of disgust settled on his florid face. Tossing it aside as if it burned his fingers, he picked up the other leather bound volume. Carole realized he could barely read as he painstakingly attempted to sound out the word on the cover.

"It's a diary," Carole supplied.

Annoyed, Max quickly opened the book with a, "Don'cha think I know that!"

The pages inside were covered with neat, easily read, flowing script. Carole caught only a word now and then as Max flipped carelessly through the book. "I don't like to read," Max declared as he handed the book to Carole. "What does it say?"

Carole felt a feeling akin to pity. Her burly captor was curious but didn't want to reveal the very obvious fact that he was functionally illiterate.

Accepting the old, smooth, well-used diary, Carole quickly read the first page—which announced that the diary was the property of Esther Prentice. The next page was dated thirty years before. Carole read a couple of lines aloud. Hoping to bore him, she read in a disinterested monotone. She couldn't wait to fly into the diary and find out the secret which had given Joy the courage to leave home, but she didn't want to share it with this insensitive thug.

"I am about to be married! Charles is so handsome and a perfect gentleman, and very wealthy as well. He is an artist—already successful and acclaimed as a gifted painter. What he can see in mousy, little old me, I will never know, but I'm not asking questions. I'm just reveling in the wonder and joy of being chosen and loved by such a brilliant and talented artist! I can paint, too, but mine will never—I am certain—compare with his superb talent.

"He has bought me the most gorgeous wedding dr—"

Max cut in, "Is the whole thing about some silly dame?"

Leafing through several pages, Carole assured him this seemed to be the case.

"Then count me out," Max said brusquely. He rose from the table to begin another game of solitaire in his accustomed place.

Silently jubilant, Carole gathered up the two leather volumes and retired to her bedroom where Mitzi had been absorbed in a coloring book. As Carole entered the bedroom, Mitzi ran to proudly show her handiwork, which Carole dutifully praised. Satisfied, the little girl returned to her crayons and color book and Carole was free to explore the mysterious diary.

Sitting crosslegged in the middle of the bed, she began flipping through the pages. She quickly saw that the diary covered a twenty-five year period, with long lapses of time between entries. Only about half the pages were filled and most of the comments were brief. Esther had apparently written in the diary only when some momentous happening had occurred or when she needed to voice her emotions.

Carole settled down to earnest reading, beginning at the first page. Her heartbeat quickened with anticipation—the diary was about to reveal its secret to her!

There was a rather lengthy, glowing account of the wedding and a blissful honeymoon. For months there were brief, written glimpses of the happy couple settling into a lavish apartment, Esther's adjustment to servants and household management—all a great adventure to the shy, newlywed wife.

In the second year, plans were drawn for a permanent home—a manor-house—back in the wilderness area near the river. Esther was somewhat alarmed to find they would be so far from people. She had always lived in the city. But handsome Charles had swept away all her doubts in his usual forceful way. He wanted seclusion so he could paint without interruption. However, he let her plan anything her heart desired to go in the new home. Rapturously, she planned it as an English tudor castle complete with two tower rooms, one above the other with battlements.

The cave was discovered on a hike over Charles' vast wilderness estate and at Esther's insistence was incorporated into the plans as a place to escape to in case of intruders. Much later in the diary, Carole discovered that the cave became Esther's special retreat—to paint, to dream or to write in her diary. She often came through the tunnel into the cave and out onto the hillside to paint. There was a little stream in the valley below, she wrote, where she painted wildlife as they came to drink and browse.

In their early married life there were many excursions out for shopping, showings of Charles's paintings, a few parties. But these became farther and farther apart—to Esther's growing dismay. One entry was a bitter cry of anguish. "How can I bear this isolation! Charles has become a recluse and I have become his prisoner. He does not actually forbid me to go into town or to the city, but if I do go, he punishes me for weeks with martyred, offended silence. If I did not love him so much, I would leave this castle of despair forever! But where could I go? I have no one. And I could not support myself. And dear Charles, how could I live without you? I love you so much!"

But joy rang on the next page. Esther was to bear a child! Loneliness was forgotten in the adventure into motherhood. Charles was ecstatic and lavished every care and comfort upon her that money or love could obtain or bestow. He even came out of his self-appointed exile and took her visiting to share their good fortune with their few close friends, and to consult the very best doctors.

He insisted upon an extended stay in the hospital when little Joy was born, while he hovered in the background, solicitous and loving. Life was good again!

Then they were home at the castle with a nurse in attendance for the baby, plus the strong young couple, Stella and Jasper Parsons, who lived-in and cared for the house and their needs. At first all was well and Esther's life revolved about her new infant. After that, there was no entry in the diary for a long while. Joy was two when the account was resumed.

It was spread over most of a year. Carole noted she was nearing the end of the written pages, and almost half of the diary pages were blank.

The nurse had gone away, and only the young couple with Joy and her parents remained in residence at Thunder Mountain Manor. Stella, the housekeeper, was kind and a good worker but a woman of few words. The lonely mistress of the luxurious castle mourned that her husband had again shut himself away in his second floor studio, absorbed in his painting. The terse, few lines in her diary reeked with loneliness and despair. She painted and cared lovingly for her child, but nothing could take away her desire to be with other people.

Charles was once more a total recluse and could not—or would not—understand why Esther was not content. If she timidly tried to explain her feelings or asked to be allowed to leave Thunder Mountain Manor—even to grocery shop with Jasper Parsons, who alone left the castle to obtain supplies for the manor house—Charles would fly into a towering rage, accusing her of being a gadabout and of not loving him and their lovely child. Then he would stalk off to his second floor studio and she might see nothing of him for days, unless she went to him, meekly asking forgiveness and listening to his scathing chastisement. She finally ceased trying to communicate her feelings to him and tried to be content with the crumbs of kindness and love he chose to occasionally cast her way.

In one thing she unselfishly rejoiced. Charles always took a little time each day for his small, adorable daughter. If he was angry with Esther for some small infraction of the personal rigid rules he had laid down for his wife, he would summon Stella Parsons to bring Joy to him in his studio. And Joy loved her father with all her little being.

121

There was a time lapse of ten years before Esther again wrote in her diary. Joy was twelve. The first entry expressed extreme sadness. Although Esther and her daughter were very close and Joy still loved her father passionately, Joy was now beginning to yearn for the companionship of other children. Esther taught her school lessons and she never saw anyone except an occasional hunter or fisherman—from afar because she was not allowed to talk to strangers.

There was no open rebellion but Joy began to confide her loneliness to her mother. She was as much intimidated by her father's fierce rages, even though they weren't directed toward her, as Esther was. Esther encouraged her child to read, played games with her, and tried to make up for the friends she missed. She was careful never to divulge her own loneliness or discontent as she felt that would be disloyal to Charles.

Two years passed without an entry and then on Joy's fourteenth birthday Esther wrote in large, red letters, "I am so happy! I was reborn today! Great-Aunt Lacy sent me a small booklet explaining the way to God. I have always read—and taught Joy—from the Bible Mother gave me when I was sixteen (a companion to this diary) and I taught Joy to pray little prayers, but I never knew one could know Jesus in a personal, real way. Now he is my Saviour and friend! I must introduce Joy to Him! And I must tell Charles. Surely he will want to know Him, too."

Carole's heart leaped in pleasure. She had met Jesus as her Saviour only hours before, and Esther had very likely accepted Christ right in this room, too! She felt a new kinship with this woman whose diary she was reading.

The account was resumed several days later. "Joy has invited Jesus to be her Saviour! My heart could burst with happiness! But Charles was very angry when I tried to tell him of our new friend and would not let me finish. I fear he thought it might change our feelings for him. He shouted at me never to mention God to him again.

"Even Joy attempted to explain to Charles what God

meant to her and the simplicity of having God's Son in one's heart by just inviting Him in. Her father had never before raised his voice to her (only at me in her presence), but he yelled at her and caused her to cry heartbrokenly. Then he turned on me and said I was turning his daughter against him. I have never seen him so furious. I suppose I will be made to pay with another of those awful, condemning silences, but some way, with Jesus in my life, I do not fear. 'Dear God, if only I had known you sooner, how much easier my life would have been. I love you!' "

Carole laid aside the book. She was dimly aware that little Mitzi had fallen asleep on a large pillow on the floor, a fat crayon still clutched in her hand. There were a few more pages but something was gnawing at her, an inexplicable something. She even forgot that she had not, as yet, found the secret Joy had spoken of as being in Esther's diary. What was bothering her?

Thoughts and lines from the diary were whirling about in her brain. A horrifying thought was gradually taking shape in her mind. Charles Prentice was a selfish, domineering tyrant. His will was law and he imposed his will on his loved ones. Esther and Joy had submitted to his will because they loved him. Wasn't she, Carole Loring, a selfish, domineering tyrant also, though? And hadn't David submitted to her will because he loved her? Her face grew hot with shame as she faced herself. She had known this before but had never had the courage or the desire to accept it.

She had a fear, it was true, that David would allow his profession to rule him to the extent that he would forsake her. But she had never given him a chance to prove himself.

Painfully she faced the facts. She had demanded things to conform to her wishes regardless of David's desires. Her determination to have her own way at any cost had almost wrecked her marriage and nearly destroyed the man she loved. David could not adjust to her mode of living and, giving up his beloved teaching rather than lose her, he had resorted to alcohol to dull the shame of being dependent on his wife for his and her living as well as the frustration and hurt of having no fulfilling work.

"God, please forgive me for my selfishness. Help me to yield myself to your will," she prayed, humbly. "Teach me, Lord, to be what you would have me to be. And please give me another chance to undo the wrongs I have done to David and Gran."

Suddenly she heard Ferron's voice. He sounded agitated. Marking her place in the diary, she laid it aside and crept softly to the closed bedroom door to listen.

"I don't like it! The sheriff is trying to contact the old man's hired couple. He keeps asking questions about where to find them. Prentice is stalling but they'll find 'em, if they keep digging. If they are brought here, they'll know about our hiding place. We had better pack some chow, a couple of blankets and our clothes and get ready to move out at a minute's notice. We'd have to take the dame and the kid so the old man won't talk. We could dump 'em when we don't need 'em anymore."

Carole felt her flesh creep. She didn't like the sound of that word "dump." And to leave the questionable safety of the cave with these two unscrupulous hoodlums was a terrifying thought.

"You mean we would just leave the old man here to spill his guts to the sheriff?" questioned Max.

"He won't talk as long as we have the kid! We would take the old geezer's Land Rover. When we get to Granite, we'll take the back roads till we get a couple of hundred miles away. Then we'll dump the Land Rover in a canyon where it won't be found for a while, and head for Canada. Al owes me a favor. We'll call him and see if he can get us across the border safely. He has connections."

"I never did trust that smart-mouthed Al," growled Max. "You sure he won't squeal on us to the cops?"

"He wouldn't dare! He knows I'd never rest till I carved him up in little pieces." Carole shuddered at Ferron's boast and the sadistic chuckle that accompanied it.

Max was apparently pacified. "You dig up some grub and I'll get our duds together," he said. "Then we'll be ready to take the girls and get out of here."

"Okay," Ferron agreed, and Carole heard his steps retreating. A door opened and closed and she knew Ferron had returned to the castle to gather supplies. She heard Max moving about in the other room and half expected him to call and demand her help in packing the men's clothing. Then she remembered they had few clothes that she had noticed and what they had were kept in a couple of small duffel bags.

Carole retreated to the bed, fear pulsing with every heartbeat. What would the robbers do to her and Mitzi? Blind panic threatened to engulf her. She wanted to run and run and run, but the rocky prison walls enclosed her. Her breath came in short, labored pants as she collapsed upon the bed, pressing her face into the pillow.

"Dear God, please help us. I'm scared to death. Please don't let them hurt or kill Mitzi and me. You took care of Esther and all those people in the Bible, so I know you can take care of us."

As she continued to talk to God her fears slowly subsided and in their place came a peace that flowed through her like warm oil, soothing and healing. It was almost unbelievable and Carole sat up crosslegged in the middle of the bed to ponder this strange happening. She was no longer afraid! God had answered her prayer! Joy surged through her until it seemed her very toes and fingertips tingled with exultation. She was God's child! He loved her and was watching over her!

21

After a while she picked up the small diary and decided to finish the few remaining pages.

"I've decided to practice Romans 10:9 and 10," Esther had written. "I shall begin today." Those were the only words on the page. Mystified, Carole picked up the small, well-worn Bible and tried to locate the book of Romans. Although she owned a beautiful, expensive leather bound volume at home, she had never opened it. After resorting to the contents page, she found the book, chapter and verse, and read:

"That if thou shalt confess with thy mouth the Lord Jesus, and shalt believe in thine heart that God hath raised him from the dead, thou shalt be saved.

"For with the heart man believeth unto righteousness; and with the mouth confession is made unto salvation."

Carole had to read it over a couple of times carefully because of the strange, old English words, but rather quickly she grasped the gist of their meaning. To be saved one had only to believe sincerely that Jesus died for your sins and rose again, speak out your belief, and you are saved.

I have done that, thought Carole. And so had Esther. Then what did she mean when she said she was going to put it into practice?

Opening the diary, she studied the two sentences, "I've decided to practice Romans 10:9 and 10. I shall begin today." Still mystified, Carole turned to the next page. "I practiced Romans 10:9 and 10 today. I told both Stella and Jasper about what God had done for Joy and me, and they both wanted to become children of God, too. I am bursting with happiness. Now I shall write everyone I know—that is another way of speaking out my faith. 'Dear God, bless these words that I will write to exalt your name!'"

Several weeks later, Esther wrote, "Most of the persons I wrote have answered. I fear that many of them felt the castle solitude has made me a little odd, but three—Leona, Rufus and Joanna—thanked me for my concern. Rufus said he is already a Christian. Leona and Joanna both said they'd think about what I said. I'm glad I wrote."

Carole felt somewhat sad. There was no one she could talk to like that. She almost laughed out loud when she pictured herself walking up to cold-eyed Ferron or herculean Max, who took pleasure in inflicting pain, and declaring that God loved them.

Then a strange thought surfaced in her mind. I wonder if anyone has ever told either of them that God loves them. Maybe—just maybe—if someone had done so years ago, they would not be the heartless brutes they are today. But it's too late now, she concluded sadly and regretfully.

Turning back to the diary, she suddenly remembered, I haven't found the secret that gave Joy the courage to defy her father and flee the loneliness of Thunder Mountain Manor. Was there no secret after all? she wondered. There were only two more pages. She read eagerly.

The next to the last page had been written on Joy's seventeenth birthday. "Joy, how my heart cries out to give you the birthday gift you most desire—your freedom. My heart is torn apart as I try to decide if I dare encourage you to flee from this castle of despair. Your father is a selfish tyrant, but he loves you, and it would break his heart if you left him. Would I be disloyal to my husband, and your father, if I bid you to steal away before this place warps you forever? My heart says 'Fly away, dear child! Run away quickly while you still have your youth—and become whatever your heart dictates. The money hidden here I have squirreled away for many years to help you live should you ever decide to go away. It is yours. Take it and go, with my blessing and with God's blessing also, I am sure.' Dear child, if only I had the courage to really speak these words to you. What a coward I am! Am I more afraid of Charles's fierce wrath than a frightful future for my lovely daughter? God, give me the courage to set Joy free!"

Carole's heart pounded with excitement. So that was

Esther's secret that had set Joy free! What had happened then? She quickly turned to the final entry which was dated a week later.

"Charles is almost beside himself with rage. Joy somehow found my diary, read it, took the money, and fled Thunder Mountain Manor. Charles accused me of talking Joy into leaving. I could truthfully say I had not spoken a word to her. And after he settled down he seemed to believe me. Did I lie, dear God? I think not. But I did tell Charles quite truthfully that I had considered encouraging her to go because she needs to live her own life.

"When he cruelly abused me verbally, I did something I have never done before. I turned away and left him ranting. I went to my cave retreat and when he tried to follow me so he could continue his vociferous castigation, I locked him out of my refuge and did not return to the castle the rest of the week although he returned repeatedly and ordered me out. I just refused to take any more. He finally sent Stella to tell me he was sorry and would I please forgive him. I had about determined to follow Joy, and I think he knew I had.

"Perhaps I should have stood up to him long ago, because now he treats me with respect and our fellowship has been much improved. I am glad because I sense that I will not be long in this world. My old condition has returned and the doctor is not very hopeful.

"I miss Joy so much but Charles does permit us to correspond as long as I never mention her name. She is training to program computers so should be able to make her own way in the world. Dear Jesus, perhaps I shall see you soon. I am very tired. Goodnight."

That was all.

Carole sat for some time thinking of the poignant drama she had witnessed through the vivid word pictures painted by the old artist's wife. Mr. Prentice, through his tyrannical actions, had caused his family much grief, but as she pictured his lined, melancholic face, she realized he was reaping a bitter harvest. No doubt he deserved even the anguish he was going through at the present, but still she felt very sorry for him. That he loved little Mitzi, he showed plainly.

Max interrupted her meditations with a loud knocking on the door. He informed her that they would probably be moving on that night and ordered her to get lunch quickly, and then pack some clothes for herself and Mitzi as they were coming along.

Fear leaped in Carole's heart again but she quickly subdued it. God was with her and she must let Him be responsible for their safety.

Ferron came for lunch carrying a large duffel bag, obviously food packed for travel. She set out ham and cheese sandwiches, hot asparagus soup from a can, hot chocolate and instant coffee. The men didn't object when she carried a tray for herself and Mitzi into the bedroom. She set it on a scatter rug on the floor and, sitting crosslegged on the rug, they ate their lunch like a picnic. Mitzi was delighted and kept up a steady chatter. Carole noticed the men in the other room had almost nothing to say but bolted their food and left the table. She wondered if the robbers were worried about being captured.

When Carole returned to the kitchen area with the tray and began to clear the table, Max demanded that she get their clothes packed first. Not too many, he warned. She obediently packed a few things in a canvas bag she found in a closet. Setting it in the corner of the bedroom, she added her coat and the heavy, adult-sized sweater for Mitzi.

An odd thing occurred as Carole was clearing away the remains of lunch. As Mitzi was bustling about helping, she began to sing a little Sunday School song softly.

"Jesus loves me this I know, for the Bible tells me so."

She sang it several times and Carole noticed Max watching the little girl intently with a strange, brooding expression on his homely face. It made Carole uneasy so she sent Mitzi to the bedroom on some pretense and tried to finish cleaning up the kitchen as quickly as possible so she could follow her. She breathed easier when Max started another game of solitaire.

He was absorbed in his game when suddenly he began to hum a little tune absentmindedly. It was the little "Jesus Loves Me" song that Mitzi had been singing! Carole was shocked. It seemed so incongruous coming from the lips of the sadistic, burly robber, so inconsistent with what she had observed about him.

Could this criminal have attended church somewhere in his distant childhood or had he just picked it up from Mitzi? Then she remembered his intent interest in Mitzi when she began to sing the little song. Had it opened a door in Max's mind, firmly closed for many years?

As she mused, Max continued to hum. It was definitely "Jesus Loves Me"! He even mouthed a few of the words as he continued his game. Carole decided suddenly that she must get to the bottom of this strange phenomenon. She put the bowl she had just wiped into the cupboard and turned from the small sink.

"Max," she queried, "is your mother living?"

Max raised his bulldog head and stared at her in astonishment. "What'cha wanna know for?"

"The song you were humming. It's about Jesus. I thought perhaps your mother took you to church when you were a child."

Max glared at her as if she had taken leave of her senses. "My mother take me to church?" He threw back his shaggy head and howled with laughter. Carole wished she had minded her own business and let well enough alone. She turned back to her dishes.

But Max wasn't through. Abruptly he stopped laughing. He sprang from his chair, strode across the room and stopped about two feet from Carole. She saw him coming and backed away, fear beating in her throat. Max's face was twisted with hate.

Skewering her with his strange, muddy-yellow eyes, he

130

leaned toward her and snarled, "You wanted to hear about my mother? Okay! I'll tell you about my mamma. She was a snivelin', whinin' junkie and a hooker to boot." He paused for the news to properly shock Carole. It did! "She had the dirtiest mouth on the block and could outswear the best. She kept Tina, my little baby sister, quiet by dipping her pacifier in beer and by the time she could walk she was cryin' for the stuff. Tina's a hooker on the streets of Seattle today so's she can satisfy her cravin' for booze.

"I wouldn't pull my 'mother' "—he spat it out like a dirty word—"out of a burning building, if she was still alive, which she ain't. She died of an overdose of horse when I was fourteen and I was glad! Glad! I celebrated the happy occasion by stealin' some wine and gettin' drunk! She made Tina and me steal and beg and do other things I don't wanna talk about, to keep her in dope."

Carole was horrified and pity formed a lump in her throat. But she knew this tough victim of terrible abuse would not welcome an open display of sympathy or pity. She wondered if the victims of Max's cruelty were being made to pay vicariously for his mother's abuse of himself and his sister.

"Is Tina pretty?" inquired Carole, wondering why she was keeping this strange conversation going.

"She used to be, but she ain't no more. She's twenty-four and she looks like forty. Wine's got her like dope had my mother. The sooner she dies the sooner she gets out of her misery." Suddenly his shoulders sagged and he turned away as if the weight of the world rested there and it was an intolerable load.

Max loved his baby sister, Tina! The impact of the realization hit Carole like a clout over the head. Big, tough, merciless Max could love! It was astounding.

"There is hope for Tina," Carole said softly to Max's departing back. Max stopped abruptly and stood for a second before he turned slowly to face Carole.

"What did you say?"

"I said there is still hope for Tina." She had his rapt attention. She waited a moment for it to sink in. "God could help Tina, you know."

Hope flared briefly in Max's yellow eyes and then faded as fury began to glow there. His face slowly suffused with a purple-red color, the scar glowed lividly and his hands tightened into fists. Carole's stomach bunched into knots. She wished fervently she had never started this conversation. Was he going to hit her? "God help me," she prayed silently. His voice, when it came, was an ugly shout.

"God? Where was God when He gave us a mother like we got! That let us go hungry! I had to *steal* to keep me and Tina from starving when 'dear' mother was spaced out for days at a time. And the pious talks I got from the police captain and the station chaplain when I got caught!" His speech was punctuated with vile words.

"Where was God when they threw me in jail and I almost went crazy with worry about what would happen to Tina?" He paused, remembering. "I guess I did go a little crazy, 'cause I ripped the washbasin off the wall and tore the mattress to little pieces. That got me three months in the detention home."

Max had relaxed his hands now and his voice had calmed. He seemed to have almost forgotten Carole. "They finally told me they had put Tina in a foster home. They put me in the same home when I got out. If we'd stayed there things mighta been different. The lady there took us to church and she had a little girl who went around singin' all the time. That little song the kid's been singin' was her special song. She liked me and—and—"

Max's voice changed to a savage growl, "Then the stupid welfare people let us go back to Mamma! Where was your God then, Queenie?" His belligerent voice and amber eyes burning into hers demanded an answer.

Carole swallowed hard. How could she answer this hard, bitter man that the world had treated so unjustly? She breathed a fervent, silent prayer and suddenly a stillness stole over her spirit.

"Max," she reasoned gently, feeling her way along, for such thoughts were new to her. "I believe God cannot do things for us unless we invite Him to do so. If we give our lives to Him, then He can direct us and make things work for us.

"And if we don't give our lives to God, then the devil must be our master and is responsible for the terrible things that happen—such as your mother being a drug addict. If a drug addict has a child, God has nothing to do with its suffering. The parent is responsible and the devil is behind it all."

Carole was amazed at the words coming from her own mouth. And more amazing yet was that Max was listening. She continued, "Because I felt my parents dumped me and let others raise me, I tried to tie my husband to me so tightly that I drove him to drink. I almost made an alcoholic out of him. But on this fishing trip I came to God and realized what I have been doing.

"If David had become an alcoholic, God would not have been to blame. But perhaps God did let us come on this fishing trip so we would have a chance to hear about Him. At first I didn't want to listen, but now I'm glad I did."

"You ain't facin' prison for a long time like me if I tried to straighten up my act," growled Max. His eyes began to take on an ugly belligerence again. "It's easy for you to talk of livin' for God. Soft-livin' and plenty of ever' thin's, all you ever knew." His eyes began to glitter with malice, and his hands bunched and unbunched.

Prickles of fear went down Carole's spine. She should back off before he decided to start punching her. But it seemed she could not resist one last shot.

"You live dangerously, Max. What if you take a bullet in the heart from a policeman's gun and die? Where would you go?"

She spoke softly and kindly, but Max's yellow eyes seemed to burst into flames, and his face went livid. In two strides Max reached Carole, and he grabbed both her shoulders in his big vise-like hands and shook her. "Shut up!" he shouted. "I oughta break every bone in your body."

Carole felt his hot breath on her face and the deadly power in his hands. "God, help me," she gasped under her breath.

Max released her so abruptly that she nearly fell. "Go back to them dishes," he ordered, and turning his back on her, he retreated to his game of cards.

It seems I lack something when it comes to explaining God's love, she thought ruefully. Finishing the dishes quickly, she retired to the bedroom out of Max's sight. He was ignoring her completely, but she felt the room was charged with tension.

Carole played a game with Mitzi. Then she went back to the two small volumes that were Esther's while Mitzi took up her coloring book again. Carole read little bits here and there in the Bible. She had never thought she would enjoy the Bible but now, strangely, she felt a great desire to read it even though she hardly knew where to begin.

Suddenly she heard the tunnel door open and Mitzi went flying. She knew her grandfather's step. Mitzi, after receiving her grandfather's hug, took his hand and tugged him into the bedroom to see what she had been coloring and drawing. Max followed them as far as the bedroom door and stood lounging against the doorjamb. He apparently doesn't trust the old man when he's with us, thought Carole. Afraid we'll hatch up another escape, I suppose.

Carole was sitting in the middle of the bed with her feet tucked under her, Esther's Bible in her hand. The diary lay on the bed near her. Max spied the diary, walked over to the bed and picked it up. A sly look came into his eyes as he turned toward Mr. Prentice.

"Say, old man, Queenie here has been readin' us your old woman's diary. It's too mushy for me but I'll bet she," indicating Carole with a nod of his head, "read ever' page.

Women go for that mushy stuff."

The old artist raised stiffly from his stooped position where he was examining Mitzi's coloring book. He looked first at Max and then at Carole. Carole felt her face go red. She had never considered until this moment that Mr. Prentice might object to her reading his wife's diary.

"What diary?" he asked.

"The one hid behind the peacock picture," the brawny robber volunteered. "I don't know how Queenie knew it was there, but she did." Max looked as smug as the cat that ate the canary. You old tattletale! Carole thought resentfully. He was deliberately trying to put her in a bad light with the old man.

Mr. Prentice moved forward and took the diary from Max's hands, and slowly turned pages for a moment or so. "This is my wife's writing. I didn't know she had written a diary. How did you know where it was?" he demanded of Carole.

"Joy's diary said she had read a secret in her mother's diary, and that it was hidden behind the peacock."

Mr. Prentice's eyes grew cold beneath his shaggy gray brows. "For someone who has been in my home only four days, you have certainly gotten around. And where was Joy's diary hidden?"

Carole felt like a schoolgirl called before the principal. "She—she didn't exactly have a diary, but it's like one. Th—the books in the top shelf of her bookcase in the tower room all have a little message in them—like a—a diary."

The old man's voice, frosty and accusing, matched his fierce dark eyes. "So you took the liberty to read all my family's secrets?"

Carole glanced up to see that Max was hugely enjoying her discomfiture. Her face hot with shame, she replied miserably, "I am truly very sorry, Mr. Prentice. I just never thought!" The thought flashed into her mind that poor Esther Prentice had borne this tyrant's reproofs for most of her married life.

Without another word to Carole, the aristocratic, old artist turned on his heel and left, carrying the little diary with him, his back stiff and disapproving. Max, with a satisfied smirk on his face, returned to the other room.

"Mr. Prentice," Carole muttered to herself, "if you didn't know how your wife felt about you, you are in for a rude awakening." But in spite of the fact that he probably deserved whatever he got, she felt pity for him. This was a trying time for him and he looked ill. If he did not know of his wife's feelings for him, this was a bad time for him to be enlightened.

After the men left, Carole felt depressed. Mr. Prentice was very angry with her. She had tried to witness to Max and had failed miserably. And she was still shut away in this horrible cave prison and might never see David and Gran again. How she longed to feel David's strong, comforting arms about her. Tears filled her eyes. She lay down with her head in the pillow and let the tears flow. But she had forgotten Mitzi. Almost at once a small hand was stroking her head and, startled, Carole looked up into Mitzi's distressed little face.

Tears of sympathy hovered perilously near to spilling over in Mitzi's eyes. "Are you okay, Aunt Carole?"

Carole dashed the tears from her eyes with the back of her hand. "Of course I'm all right, Mitzi. I was just being a crybaby." Mitzi still looked troubled and unconvinced so Carole suggested they play a game. Quickly forgetting everything else, Mitzi ran eagerly to get the Chinese checkers.

22

David was at the point of despair and total exhaustion. He had scarcely slept or eaten for four days—though he had tried to at Steve Morgan's insistence. Every time he lay down, his imagination took over. In vivid detail he could picture Carole mauled by grizzly bears, swept away in the swift waters below the swinging bridge, or abducted by vicious men. Terrifying nightmares filled his troubled mind.

Late this afternoon he was making his slow, searching way back toward camp. All day he had followed the deep, swift, winding river for miles but had turned back toward camp an hour ago. The river had been searched before but every place was being searched and re-searched. He had hunted carefully, going up the river, and was doing the same returning. He probed the depths of the clear river, the banks, and under the banks where there were recessed spaces, until his eyes were sore and red from strain. He plodded along almost in a daze, his eyes darting here and there; searching, always searching.

Where was God? He seemed to have deserted David. After the first shock of knowing that Carole was truly missing, David had turned quickly to God for encouragement, and God had seemed to wrap him in a cocoon of love and warmth. But as the hours became days, David was fast losing contact with the reality of God. In fact, nothing of this whole nightmare seemed real. His wife, whom he loved better than life itself, could not have vanished as if she had never been! It was unreal! It was almost eerie.

David sank down upon the ground, too weary in body and spirit to go further. He stared into the water swirling about a submerged boulder. Carole could be lying submerged like that somewhere in this rushing, tumbling river. He shuddered. Carole, so beautiful, so vibrantly full of life, could not be dead! But if she was alive, where was she?

When he was around Gran, he tried to be encouraging and optimistic for her sake. He thought of her now. The past four days had been almost unbearable for Carole's little grandmother. She blamed herself for bringing Carole here.

"Carole didn't want to come, but I swept aside her

objections and all but forced her to come," she told David and Steve.

When they tried to tell her that she must not blame herself, she would just shake her head and say that facts were facts.

This morning, as usual, when David left for the search as soon as it was light, she was waiting and had accompanied him for an hour or so. It was about all she could manage. Indelibly stamped on his memory was her haggard face, as she moved slowly back toward camp, her eyes red-rimmed with dark smudges beneath. She had lost her bounce. Indeed, she seemed to have aged before his eyes. The only slightly worthwhile thing that had come from this was that he and Gran had been drawn together, trying to give comfort to each other. David was surprised to find she was a person he could love and greatly respect.

David refused to let Gran harbor any thought except that Carole was alive. Carole was her life and if she were dead, he was not certain Gran could rise from the ashes of despair, or even wish to. She was a tough little lady, but he could see this ordeal had almost devastated her.

He knew the pangs of guilt that were plaguing Gran because they were also needling him constantly. Gran had brought Carole here, but he was the one who had upset her and then had not tried to coax her out of her anger as he usually did. He was convinced he had come on too strong with the news that he had given his life to God, and that he planned to go back to school to prepare to teach. He had thrown the whole ball of wax in her lap and said, "Play ball with me or lump it!"

Also, he had seen her leave camp. He should have realized the danger and not allowed her to go alone—especially when he heard Steve's warning to her. He had been tempted to follow her, but knowing she was angry with him, he had drawn back from incurring her wrath.

"I'm too sensitive for my own good," he scornfully told himself, now. Always, when Carole spoke harshly to him, each word was like a knife stab in his heart. "If I had the gumption of a real man, Carole would not be out there alone somewhere! A husband's duty is to protect his wife and I'm the poorest excuse for a husband there ever was!" Groaning, he dropped his face in his hands.

"It isn't enough that I made her life miserable with my alcoholic binges, but now I fail to protect her, too," he castigated himself. But word-flogging didn't help—it just made him more miserable.

He felt a hand on his shoulder and jerked his head up in alarm. He hadn't known anyone was around. Steve was bending over him, solicitude mirrored in his hazel-green eyes. The face David lifted to Steve was covered with a four-day, reddish-gold stubble, and his usually electric blue eyes were glazed with fatigue and worry.

"Any news?" asked David eagerly.

"None," replied Steve as he lowered himelf wearily to the sand and rested his back against a boulder. "The sheriff's department is still trying to locate the Parsons—Mr. Prentice's hired couple. The sheriff is still convinced something strange is going on in that old mansion. He has repeatedly questioned the old man, but doesn't get anything out of him except that he let his hired people go on an extended trip and that he is completely alone."

David nodded.

"Mr. Prentice is an irascible old guy and quite wealthy. The sheriff could come up with charges of harrassment brought against him if he keeps badgering him. The old artist has threatened as much. Actually, the sheriff really doesn't have any reason to question the man's words. The only thing that seems to connect your wife's disappearance to the old castle is the flashlight found on his front lawn."

"Would it be possible that a wild animal, like a mountain lion, could have chased her across the lawn and she lost the flashlight in fleeing?" asked David fearfully.

Steve regarded David thoughtfully for a moment. "Anything is possible, David, but it is very unlikely she was harmed by a wild animal. For one thing, we have found no blood, bits of clothing or any evidence that she was attacked by an animal. Though I can't account for the flashlight on the lawn, I still feel that she must have walked back into the woods, became lost and will yet be found. There are edible berries and plants in the forest and abundant water, so a person could survive a long time. Don't give up hope, my friend. Keep your faith and trust in God."

"I'm not sure I have any faith left," answered David honestly. "I keep wondering why God did this to me when I was trying to serve Him."

"Why do you think God did this to you?" countered Steve.

"Doesn't God direct everything?"

"God intervenes in man's affairs when prayer is offered up to Him, but He would be interfering with man's free will if He jumped in and restrained man every time he was about to make a move that was unwise or not His will."

David lowered his eyes, thinking through this new thought.

"David," Steve spoke kindly but frankly, "God did not send Carole for a walk in the woods that night. She went of her own free will. You must not fall into the trap that so many fall into of blaming God for what He had nothing to do with."

David's eyes sparkled fire. "You mean God is punishing Carole for—"

"Whoa—I didn't say that!" said the older man. "I'm saying God had nothing to do with it, either way. I personally don't believe God causes bad things to happen to people but lets people go their own way. But when these persons take God in as a partner, He will help them pick up the pieces and something good will come out of it for His children. The Bible says that all things work for good to those who are His people. David, can you just trust Carole into God's hands?"

"But if Carole is dead, she wasn't a Christian and—

and—"

"How do you know she isn't a Christian? The day she disappeared, I told her the simple plan of salvation. It takes only a moment to talk to God and accept Christ as Saviour. I'm still convinced she has very good chances to be alive, but even is she is not alive she very easily could have found God in her last moments of life."

David spoke thoughtfully, "Steve, one thing still bothers me, though. I seemed to have such an awareness of God when Carole first disappeared, but now He seems to have withdrawn from me."

"God is still with us whether we feel His presence or not," Steve declared emphatically. "You're worn out and worried, and have been wondering if God was behind all this trouble. We can't walk by feelings, David, because too many things affect our feelings. God stated in the Bible that He would be with you always, and I'm confident He is even now."

David seemed to shake himself, his shoulders lifted and he took a deep, relieved breath. "I'm okay now. But would you mind praying with me before we go back to camp? God must think I'm a pretty poor example of a Christian, the way I've been doubting."

Steve laughed, "We all have our doubts at times, but the Scriptures and prayer are good tools to use against them." He bowed his head, "Heavenly Father, we thank you for sustaining us in this search. Help David to cope with this trial that has come his way. And, Father, be with Carole wherever she is. Protect her from harm and bring her to understand your love. Help us to find her or guide her back to us. We thank you. Amen."

Steve drew a small Bible from his pocket. "There is a verse in Isaiah 41:13 that has pulled me through many a rough time. When I'm in real trouble I quote this verse over and over until it pushes out any doubt that God is taking care of me and is on top of my problem." He flipped some pages and read a verse bordered in red.

"For I the Lord thy God will hold thy right hand, saying unto thee, Fear not; I will help thee."

David silently repeated, "Fear not; I will help thee," as he followed Steve to camp. When he arrived, he found his spirit buoyed up and his faith again high. "We'll find Carole," he assured Gran, who had come out to meet him. Seeing David encouraged, and even sitting down to eat a meal, Gran was able to eat, also, and hope sprang up again in her despairing heart.

23

Carole played Chinese checkers with Mitzi for a couple of hours. Mitzi loved the game. But she didn't want Carole to let her win. The next two or three games Carole won, and she could see that Mitzi was crestfallen over every defeat, although she tried to be brave about it. So Carole played to win only part of the time. The rest of the time, when she would see a good move for Mitzi, she would point it out exclaiming, "Oh, no, you are about to jump five of my men." or, "Don't you dare move that marble, you'll mess up my move!" With a triumphant giggle Mitzi would jump Carole's marbles or move a marble. Carole was certain the sharp little girl saw through the subterfuge but pretended not to catch on because it was so much fun to win.

At last Mitzi began to yawn and Carole felt tired, too, so she suggested a nap—to which Mitzi reluctantly agreed. Carole knew there was a good possibility they would have to flee with the robbers later, so she felt a good rest might help greatly should they have to go. She lay down beside Mitzi, not expecting to sleep, but the next thing she knew, Max was hammering on the flimsy door.

Groggy from sleep, she rose from bed. "Just a moment," she called as she went to splash cold water on her face.

Max seemed perturbed. "We may have to split anytime so you better get some supper on. Might not have a chance for a hot meal in a long time."

"Has something happened?" Carole asked.

Max ignored her question. "Since you can't cook meat worth eatin', I'll cook us some pork chops. You peel some spuds."

Carole had never peeled potatoes before but she supposed anyone should be able to get the peeling off. However, as always seemed to be the case, it proved more difficult than she had imagined. Noticing her awkward use of the knife, Max disgustedly produced a potato peeler from a drawer and showed her how to use it. Then, scowling, he went back to his pork chops. I will forever appreciate the people who prepare my food, Carole thought, if I ever get out of this mess alive.

Max was an excellent cook, and under his direction and expert handling of the pork chops, the meal looked very good—mashed potatoes, gravy made by Max with the pork chops, green beans, pickled beets, and even a coconut pudding from a package mix.

The meal was nearing completion when Max turned from the stove where he was stirring the gravy. "You make me think of her," he said suddenly.

Carole looked up in surprise from beating the potatoes with a small mixer. "Of who? Your mother?"

Max scowled. Any mention of his mother had an adverse effect on him. "Not her! Like Mrs. Lawson—the woman me and Tina stayed with for awhile."

"Oh—" Carole hardly knew what response to make. "I look like her, do I?"

"Not look like her," explained Max patiently, as if Carole were a simpleton. "She had short straw-colored hair and freckles and weren't pretty a bit, but—" He was obviously struggling to express in words what he meant—an unusual task for the surly criminal. "She—she was real people, if you know what I mean." His face reddened and Carole realized she was being paid a compliment.

"Thank you, Max, I feel honored to remind you of your Mrs. Lawson." And strangely, she did. The foster mother had obviously been the only element for good in all of Max's sordid past.

Max turned back to the stove, ending the conversation.

Ferron came in as the food was being placed on the table so he must have told Max to have the meal ready at a set time. Carole again took her own and Mitzi's plates into the bedroom. The men talked in low tones as they wolfed down their meal. Ferron had completely ignored Carole and Mitzi and seemed vastly troubled, even angry.

"That old coot would have to do this to us!" was all she could make out of their conversation. She wondered what Mr. Prentice had done.

Ferron went away as soon as the meal was over and Carole and Mitzi cleaned up the kitchen. Max commanded them to get it finished quickly.

But they had not quite finished when the tunnel door opened and Ferron came through, half supporting and half dragging Mr. Prentice. Mitzi went running to her grandfather but Ferron curtly ordered her out of their way. With Max's help, he carried the old man into the bedroom and placed him on the bed.

Carole and Mitzi followed them into the bedroom. Mr. Prentice seemed barely conscious. His breathing was deep and labored; his skin looked flushed. Mitzi, ignoring Ferron's frown, rushed around the bed and climbed up on it to take her grandfather's hand and press it to her small chest. Carole noticed how dry and parched his skin looked.

Mr. Prentice's eyes fluttered, then slowly opened. Mitzi's face was ashy as if she realized the old man was very ill. The artist's long, slender, sensitive fingers closed on Mitzi's small hand. "I—love—you—kitten," he whispered weakly.

"I love you, too, Grandpa!" Mitzi replied with childish sincerity.

Smiling weakly, Mr. Prentice slowly turned his head

toward Carole who had gone to stand beside the bed. "Please—take—care—of—Mitzi," he whispered, as with great effort.

Carole leaned over so she could catch his words. "Yes, of course I will!"

"Could—you—get—me—some—water?" he implored. "I—am—so—thirsty."

Carole quickly complied, lifting his shaggy head to drink. His breath had an odd fruity odor, she observed. Suddenly it hit her! The old artist must be a diabetic and he was slipping into a diabetic coma! The same thing had happened to a close friend in college. The two robbers had left the room and were talking in low tones. Carole went swiftly into the other room. "We must find Mr. Prentice's insulin! He's going into a diabetic coma!"

Ferron shot her a withering look. "Don't you think I know that! And there isn't any insulin. He's used it all."

"But he'll die unless he gets it."

"What's it to you if he does?" Ferron retorted.

Carole was shocked. "He's a human being!" she declared. "We must get him some insulin or get him to a doctor."

Sarcastically and mockingly, Ferron answered, "Should I take him into town and say 'Here is my father-in-law. I've been keeping him prisoner for almost two weeks. Now he's sick and I give up my chances at staying free to get help for him?' No way! He stays and *we* go—before that nosey sheriff comes around again, can't rouse anyone, and gets an order to break in. Get your duds, you're going with us."

"But we can't just leave him here alone to die!" Carole remonstrated.

"Says who? And besides, he won't be alone. We're leaving the kid here, too."

The horror of what Ferron proposed to do struck Carole in the pit of the stomach with the force of a sledgehammer. "Leave that tiny little girl alone with an unconscious, dying man? You—you can't—"

145

"Who are you to tell me what I can or cannot do?" Ferron's voice had taken on a dangerous edge.

But Carole was too horror-stricken and appalled to notice. "Dear God, help!" She prayed silently as she strove to make Ferron conscious of the horror of what he was about to do. She tried to speak calmly.

"Ferron, Mitzi is one of the dearest children I have ever known. She is your daughter—your own flesh and blood. She is a very sensitive child and if she is shut up alone in this cave with her unconscious grandfather she may never recover from the terror of it. Please let me stay with her. Please! I'm begging you!"

Ferron's obsidian eyes had gone as cold as death. "I don't want to hear another peep out of you! Get your bag. You're going with us!"

Carole felt her heart turn to ice. The numbness of bitter defeat and devastating despair engulfed her as she turned to follow Ferron's orders.

"Queenie ain't goin' with us." It was Max's voice. Carole stared at Max in astonishment.

Ferron's head jerked around and he, too, stared at Max. "What did you say?" he demanded.

Max's voice was calm but emphatic, "I said Queenie ain't goin' with us," he repeated.

Ferron laughed, a bark that was light but not mirthful, and said smoothly, "Of course she's going, Max. We need her for a hostage in case the cops get after us. The kid's no good to us now that the old man is out of it, but the dame will be a perfect hostage."

The air was charged with tension. Carole hardly dared breathe.

"Queenie ain't goin'," Max's voice had softened into almost a whisper.

Carole saw a muscle twitch in Ferron's jaw, and his voice changed to a hearty, "Aw, come on, Max! What has that dame done to you? Are you going soft?"

Max's hands curled into fists. Carole felt cold fear lance

through her body as she saw his eyes darken and narrow into muddy-yellow slits. Max's voice was a menacing snarl, "She ain't comin'!"

For a long suspenseful moment Ferron locked eyes with the burly thief. Carole could see the pulse pounding in a vein in his neck. Then abruptly, Ferron dropped his eyes and turned away.

"Sure, Max, if that's what you want, that's what you get." His manner and tone of voice were indifferent, as if it didn't matter to him if Carole went or stayed, but when his eyes flicked to Carole's, they were dark orbs full of black hatred!

Ferron's eyes—so cold and snake-like—had always filled Carole with terror, but now she sensed that God had intervened in her behalf. Wonder and awe welled up in her. Although she didn't gloat, neither did she drop her eyes as she looked at Ferron with a steady, calm gaze until, with an ugly oath, he turned from her, grabbed the large canvas bag of food and left by the tunnel door.

Carole didn't know whether to thank Max or not. But he never looked her way, just took up the two duffel bags and quickly followed Ferron. The door swung shut and she heard it being locked.

24

As she heard the last click of the door and stillness seemed to echo in the empty cave, Carole let out a relieved breath, closed her eyes and thanked the Lord audibly. She and the other two were still prisoners in the cave, but she was certain Ferron had planned to kill her as soon as she was no longer of use to them. The danger was still grave—they might never be found here in the cavern—but she would take first things first. Besides, God had just intervened for them and He could do so again.

She hurried back into the bedroom. Mr. Prentice lay very still except for his labored breathing. Calling and gently shaking him brought no response. He was already in a coma! How long could he live without insulin?

Mitzi was still holding his hand in her small hands but now it lay limp and still. Tears brimmed in her eyes as she looked up at Carole fearfully. "Aunt Carole," she quavered, "I can't wake Grandpa at all! Is Grandpa going to d-die?"

Carole looked at the distraught child and for a moment she, too, wondered if he was going to die. Then she had a sudden thought. She hadn't known God very long, but He'd already answered some big prayers for her, so this seemed to be the time to pray.

"Mitzi," she said, "you know Jesus. Let's pray, shall we?"

Mitzi looked up at her with troubled eyes and studied Carole's face for just a moment. Then she silently nodded, and bowed her head.

Carole took Mitzi's small, cold hands in a warm clasp and bowed her head. Since this was all new to her she didn't pray a very fancy prayer, but it was a prayer that came from her heart.

"Dear God, you see this poor old man here. He doesn't even know you. Please don't let him die in this condition. God, someway, help Mitzi and me to get out of this cave and bring help, or bring help to us. Please! Amen."

Mitzi opened her eyes and stood looking anxiously down at her grandfather. And Carole, observing the old man, realized that he was very, very sick. She reached down and touched his hand. It was frighteningly cold. A horrifying thought came to her mind. Is he dying now? Is he dead already? She leaned down and put her ear to his chest and was relieved to hear a faint thump-thumping sound.

Panic traced its way into her heart again. What would they do if old Mr. Prentice died? How horrifying it would be to be shut up in this dungeon with a dead man. But wait! She and Mitzi had prayed. God had heard her before. He'd heard her last night. He'd answered her request to stay here with Mitzi and the old man instead of going with the robbers as a hostage. Now she and Mitzi had prayed for help, so they'd just have to trust it in God's hands.

She slipped off the old artist's shoes and covered him with a blanket. Mitzi hovered around the edge of her grandfather's bed, her sensitive little face troubled and distraught. Carole decided she must get her away from him. After all, there was nothing they could do now except keep him as comfortable as possible.

"Mitzi, let's finish cleaning up the kitchen."

The child did not want to leave her grandfather, but with a little urging, she reluctantly followed Carole from the room.

Just as they entered the larger room, Carole heard an odd scrabbling noise. It seemed to come from the rocky ceiling, directly above the kitchen table. Glancing up, she saw that fine gravel was sifting out of the ceiling. Stepping farther into the room, Carole peered up into the shadowy ceiling, straining to find out why gravelly dirt was falling.

At that moment, a dark figure appeared—right in the middle of the ceiling! A pair of eyes, glowing green and evil, riveted her to the spot. She stood petrified with terror.

Suddenly the dark figure launched itself into the room and Carole broke out of her stupefied state. With a shriek of terror she backed away toward the bedroom door, colliding with Mitzi behind her. Both went down in a tangle of legs and arms.

Swiftly righting herself and Mitzi, Carole cast a fearful glance toward the intruder, half expecting to see a wild animal crouched to spring upon them. But before she could get a good look at the animal, Mitzi let out a rapturous squeal and ran toward it calling, "Ebenezer! Ebenezer!"

It *was* Ebenezer! The artist's huge black cat was standing right in the middle of the kitchen table, his wide green eyes all but shooting sparks, his black glossy fur standing out until he looked almost twice his usual huge size.

As Mitzi reached out eager arms for him, he subsided somewhat and allowed Mitzi to stroke his glistening fur while keeping vigilant, baleful, distrustful emerald eyes upon Carole.

"Don't think I want to touch you," muttered Carole. "That's the farthest thing from my mind!" Her stomach felt like a freight train had crashed through it and her body still tingled and twitched in reaction to her fright.

But a sudden realization shot through her numbed brain. Ebenezer had come into the cave through the ceiling! He was quite large. If Ebenezer could get in, perhaps the opening he had entered was big enough for them to get out!

But first she had to get him off the table and away from the opening so she could investigate. "Mitzi, could you coax Ebenezer off the table and into the bedroom or over next to the tunnel door?" She took one step toward Mitzi and the cat arched his back and spat at her, his green eyes glowing with malice.

Carole inched her way around the room to the bunks and sat down slowly, the huge feline's malevolent eyes following her every move.

It took some persuasion on Mitzi's part to coax Ebenezer down off the table and into the bedroom but she finally managed it. Carole waited a moment before she crossed the room to the table. But when Ebenezer did not return and she could hear Mitzi's voice speaking endearments to her pet, Carole finally felt it safe to advance.

Climbing onto the sturdy wooden table, Carole peered up at the dim, rocky ceiling. She could see what looked like a break in the stone but was still unable to touch the ceiling. She got down and set the kitchen stepstool on the table. Once more she climbed up on the table and then up the steps of the stool. When her head reached the level of the opening, cool, damp air brushed her cheeks. Her breath quickened and she climbed another step. She could see into the opening!

The irregular cave ceiling dipped and slanted downward here, and in the side of the sloping section was a fissure three or four feet wide. The crevice was not deep. Indeed, to Carole's probing eyes it looked quite narrow. Were her hopes of an avenue of escape doomed to disappointment?

Cautiously, Carole descended the steps of the kitchen stool. "Mitzi," she called, "could you bring the flashlight that is in your grandfather's coat pocket?"

The child answered in the affirmative and after a moment or so she ran into the room with the small light in her hand, trailed by Ebenezer. He stopped in the doorway, however, to Carole's immense relief. She thanked Mitzi and urged her to return to the other room with Ebenezer. Curiosity shone in Mitzi's bright eyes but she complied with Carole's wishes. In her heart Carole blessed Joy for training her child in simple obedience.

Back at the top of the stepstool, Carole shone the light into the cleft in the rock. It sloped slightly upward. The narrow break in the rock extended outward perhaps six feet and then the flashlight's spear of light picked up what appeared to be the branch of a bush or small tree. The crack in the rock extended to the outside!

Now the big question was, could she and Mitzi get through such a small hole? It looked wide enough but very narrow in depth. Flashing the light along the fissure, Carole saw that it was much deeper at some places than at others. She would have to wriggle her way through it like a snake.

And what if it were not deep enough and she became wedged in the narrow opening? The thought of that possibility caused a claustrophobic panic to close in upon Carole. She detested close, cramped spaces. Her skin crawled at the very thought. It was bad enough to be imprisoned in this forsaken cave-dungeon, but to be stuck in a narrow crack in the rock such as this would be maddening. I just might go berserk, she thought.

She studied the inside of the crevice as thoroughly as

she could with the small beam of the flashlight. The large cat had been able to come through so she was quite confident Mitzi would have no difficulty. She looked down at her own trim figure. It would be a tight fit but the possibility was very good that she could squirm through.

"Dear God," she whispered fervently, "please help me to know if I should try this. Don't let me pull a stupid stunt." She scanned the length of the crack again. "I believe I can do it," she decided. But her heart quivered in dread. Was she doing the right thing? She stood very still and began to talk to God again. Her heart slowly calmed and she was at peace.

"It is the only path of escape I can find," she declared to herself as much as to God, "and we might not be found for a long while. Mr. Prentice needs help now, if it is to do him any good." She determined to try to escape through the fissure. Having made up her mind, she felt better.

Climbing down from her perch on the stepstool, Carole called to Mitzi. Mitzi came running immediately with Ebenezer right behind her. This time he chose to ignore Carole who was standing on the kitchen table.

"Mitzi, the hole that Ebenezer came through is not very large but I want to try to get out of the cave through it. Are you brave enough to crawl through a hole to the outside? It is right up there." She motioned above her head. "You would climb up the stepstool and I would lift you into the opening. Do you think you can do that?"

Mitzi looked from Carole, to the hole, and back again. "Is it a dark, scary hole?" she asked fearfully.

"It is dark," Carole admitted, "but you can carry the flashlight and then shine it back down the little shaft when you get out, so I can see to crawl out."

"We need to get out and get a doctor for Grandpa, don't we?" Mitzi questioned logically.

"Yes, we do, and the quicker the better."

"Okay, I'll go."

"First we must get your sweater and my jacket. That air through the crack in the rock feels very cool and damp. Also

I want to find a piece of rope, if I can, I'll tie it to your feet and if for any reason at all we need to get you back in the cave, I can pull you back in."

The jacket and sweater were quickly retrieved from the bedroom. When she couldn't locate any rope, she tore a sheet in strips and knotted them firmly together to form a rope.

Now all was in readiness. Taking a deep breath she called Mitzi and helped her onto the kitchen table. "Mitzi, see if you can get Ebenezer to go out with you." She would just as soon not be left alone with the cantankerous creature who seemed to have taken such a dislike to her.

But although Mitzi coaxed and even got down and tried to propel him toward the table, he was uncooperative and refused to be coerced or persuaded. When Mitzi tried to shove him toward the table, he went limp and lay down. He was too big for her to carry, so Mitzi left him and climbed up on the table. He took no interest in her actions at all but sat there, calmly washing his giant paws. They gave up trying to persuade him and Carole prepared to hoist Mitzi into the cleft in the ceiling.

As an afterthought Carole put one sweater on the child and laid an extra in the mouth of the opening, instructing Mitzi to pull it along with her. The small flashlight she put in the mouth of the crevice also and urged Mitzi to be very careful that she didn't drop it since it was their only light.

"Take your time and go slowly," she advised, "and don't climb out the other side until you are certain everything is okay."

They were standing together on the stool and Carole was about to boost Mitzi up when Carole saw a brilliant flash at the other end of the fissure. Mitzi was standing on the top of the stool with Carole below her. Both could see into the crack in the rock. She gripped Mitzi's arm and cautioned her to wait.

Fear constricted her throat. Were the robbers back? Or could it be searchers? There! The flash came again and a dull rumble came to them down the shaft. Carole let out a deep sigh of relief. It was lightning and thunder. A storm must be brewing. She was glad they had warm clothing. They would, in all likelihood, need it.

Carole lifted Mitzi into the fissure. She noticed the child's face was pale but there was a determined set to her chin. She was obviously very frightened, but not a complaint passed her lips.

"Easy does it," she cautioned as Mitzi crawled slowly into the hole, dragging the sweater with one hand and holding the flashlight in the other.

Thankfully, Carole saw that Mitzi could crawl quite freely—of course, she was very small. Carole knew she would not fare so well. She continued to speak encouragingly as Mitzi crept slowly along the shaft. Carole let out, bit by bit, the sheet-rope she had tied to Mitzi's feet.

In a very short time Mitzi called back, "I'm outside. What do I do now?"

"Tell me what you see."

"There's a big bush and rocks and there is a little roof over me, kinda like a baby-cave 'cept there's not any sides. And the lightning is real bad," she ended fearfully.

"I'm going to tie my jacket to this end of the sheet-rope. I want you to pull it through. Okay?"

"Okay," agreed the little girl, "but first I wanna put on the other sweater. It's cold out here."

Soon Carole's jacket was lying beside Mitzi on the outside of the cave and Mitzi was directing the beam of the flashlight back into the fissure. Carole's heart constricted once again with fear as she surveyed the narrow crack she proposed to wriggle through. "Dear God, help me to be as brave as Mitzi," she petitioned. Her heart was pounding. Taking several deep breaths, she finally calmed down somewhat and boosted herself into the upward slant of the cleft in the rock.

The top seemed to press down upon her as she began her slow, torturous way toward the other end—and freedom.

She tried to think of freedom instead of the hard rock which seemed to be conspiring to trap her. There was plenty of room on either side but she had to continually shift her body to find the deepest spots in order to push through. Inch by inch, she dragged herself along, twisting and creeping, using her hands—which were quickly stinging from contact with the rough stone—to propel herself.

It was such grueling exertion that she had to stop and rest often. But she was making progress. She had maneuvered herself about halfway through when she heard a scrabbling, scrambling sound behind her and felt something brush against her leg.

Shocked and alarmed, Carole lay perfectly still for a moment. Then it hit her—Ebenezer was crawling through the crack in the rock beside her! Horrified, she realized that she was in the center of the crevice and that he would have to crowd close to her.

Barely breathing, she lay very still. Her throat felt dry and parched. Ebenezer seemed to despise her. What would he do if he were crowded? Would he attack her?

She willed herself, with a great deal of effort, to lie perfectly immobile. Slowly turning her head away from the animal that was advancing on her right side, she prayed faintly, "Please help me." She wanted to scream and run, but there was no place to run. She didn't even dare move over lest he feel he was being threatened. One of the underlined verses from Esther's Bible flashed into her mind: "I will fear no evil for thou art with me."

Through the material of her jeans, Carole could feel the form of the large cat as he edged his way up the length of her, touching her body as he moved. She was glad she was wearing long sleeves, hoping that when he came to her arms, Ebenezer wouldn't be tempted to take a bite or scratch her. The thought was terrifying. Carole tried not to think, just to shift her mind into neutral and wait. Her heart seemed to have stopped beating.

Now the cat was moving against her elbow. He was

155

more crowded here. Then she felt the feline's furry body as he moved inch by inch from her elbow to her hands. Carole felt his warm breath on her hand, and she was terror stricken. Any moment she expected to feel his sharp, fierce teeth plunge into her hand. But he moved on. Not daring to move a muscle, Carole felt a feathery something touch her hand, and realized it was the cat's tail. Carole softly exhaled as she heard Ebenezer continue on down the narrow passageway.

She still didn't move until she heard Mitzi, on the other end, give a glad shout of welcome to her pet. Then she collapsed—as well as she could. Her body was drenched in perspiration, and it was damp under her head. She realized that tears had been running down her cheeks. She had never been more terrified in her life.

A great relief swept through her. I have survived this, she thought. God *is* with me. I can make it the rest of the way. She began to inch her way forward again with tortoise slow movement. Finally her reaching fingers were able to curl around the edge of the hole. She was almost out! Just beyond the pale light that Mitzi was shining into the crevice, she could see the child's anxious face.

Carole started to ease forward again, but to her horror she suddenly realized she couldn't move. Twisting her body over a little, she called to Mitzi to shine the light over to her right, and tried again to move. But the crevice had narrowed considerably. She couldn't advance. Fighting the panic that threatened to overwhelm her, she told herself sternly, "Carole, be calm, be calm, be calm." She shifted her body as far over as she could to the right, but that didn't help. Slowly, inch by inch, she wriggled her body back to the left. Each time trying to squirm forward, but the rock seemed to have her body in an awful vise from which she could not break free. Terror tore at her brain.

She willed herself to lie very still, closed her eyes and prayed. "Dear God, Father, don't let me be this near to coming out and not be able to make it. Please help me. Help me now." The panic passed. She opened her eyes.

"Are you okay?" Mitzi's little face was peering into the opening.

"I'm okay. I'm just bigger than you and it's harder for me. But give me time. I'll make it." Her voice sounded confident.

Lying motionless, Carole surveyed the opening as well as she could by the dim light that was shining to her right. It seemed that just about the middle was the deepest part. She shifted her body to the place that she felt was the best and began to wriggle forward. Briefly she could move just a little. Then, again, she was caught. Perspiration ran down into her eyes. Panic began to rise again. She could not be this near to freedom and fail! She just couldn't! A sob broke from her trembling lips. "Father, help me!"

Carole's reaching fingers had curled around the lip of the hole. Praying for strength, she gave herself a mighty boost—and moved a fraction of an inch. She felt that the skin was literally being scraped from her body, but ignoring the pain, she clenched her teeth, took a firmer grip, and dug her toes in again. She gave a mighty boost once, twice, three times. Suddenly she was free!

Perhaps the greatest relief of her whole life poured over her. She felt tears running down her cheeks as she whispered, "Thank you, Father, thank you!" The way was easy now as she slipped effortlessly out into the small space under the stone overhang. She grabbed startled little Mitzi with both arms and hugged her, laughing and crying. "We did it, Mitzi! We did it! We're free! We're free!"

25

Carole quickly turned off the dim flashlight, realizing the batteries were about exhausted, and looked about. They were on a small shelf with an outcropping of rock over their heads. It was not high enough for Carole to stand under although Mitzi could stand up easily. There was one large bush directly in front of the opening of the crevice. Apparently that was what Carole had seen when she'd looked through the opening the first time.

It was very dark except when lightning zigzagged across the sky, which was frequent. Thunder continued to roll. Carole stepped out onto the hillside and felt the keen cut of the wind.

Looking up she saw the clouds, black, roiling and tumbling, surging across the sky. A storm was certainly brewing. Even as she stood there with little Mitzi clutching her hand, she realized it would be unwise to move on until the storm passed.

Suddenly an extremely hard gust of wind struck the two exposed on the hillside, and it seemed like a bucket of water was thrown on them as rain began to descend in torrents. They both quickly ducked back under the overhang and crouched as far back against the wall as they could. Carole pressed Mitzi behind her and sat down, wrapping her own jacket partly around the shivering child. The rain didn't hit them with force here, but they did get well splattered, and the wind was very cold.

The rain poured in sheets for what seemed a long, long time. Peals of thunder continued to roll, growing louder and louder, cracking over their heads like cannon fire. Jagged lightning zigzagged across the sky, brilliant and blinding. Mitzi was terrified and began to whimper.

"Put your hands over your ears and close your eyes," Carole shouted above the roar of the storm. Mitzi promptly clapped her small hands over her ears, closed her eyes tightly, and snuggled deeper into Carole's jacket.

I know now why they call this Thunder Mountain, Carole thought, as the clamorous, fiery exhibition continued in its awesome fury.

After what seemed an eternity, the rain began to slacken, the lightning came less frequently and the thunder seemed farther and farther away. Shortly the storm was over.

Carole could hear water running and knew that little rivulets of water were coursing down the hillside. She waited a few more moments before she ventured forth.

In her mind she tried to visualize where they were. If her calculations were correct, they were directly over the hill from Thunder Mountain Manor, so if they climbed straight up to the crest and then to the right just a little, they would come down about where the woodhouse was. She didn't want to go directly to the castle in case Ferron and Max had, for some unknown reason, returned. She certainly did not want to risk being captured again!

She and Mitzi came out of their shelter and stood on the hillside once more. They were wet but not as drenched as they would have been if there had been no shelter. The wind cut through them but it was good to be alive, even if they were wet and cold.

Suddenly Carole realized that the huge cat was not with them. "Where's Ebenezer?" she asked.

"He didn't like the storm and ran away as soon as he got out," Mitzi answered.

Carole was relieved that he was gone. He had no doubt returned to the castle.

"Mitzi," Carole said, "we're going to climb over the mountain. We'll have to climb as quickly as we can because our flashlight is going out, and also we want to get into shelter as soon as possible."

They turned the flashlight back on and began to scramble upward as fast as they could over the wet, rocky hillside. But boulders, loose stones, and dripping branches of low shrubs growing thickly here and there, blocked their progress and tore at their clothing. They could see only a few feet ahead of them, but as long as they were climbing Carole felt they were making progress. It wasn't long before they came out on a level space and she presumed they were at the top of Thunder Mountain directly behind the manor. She turned to her right and they traveled quickly along the ridge of the mountain.

The wind caught them fully here and the force of it was difficult to struggle against. After they had walked for a few minutes, Carole felt it was safe to begin the descent. The flashlight was very dim now, and they had to move cautiously. Carole didn't relish the thought of dropping into a hole or tumbling over a cliff. Slipping and sliding over the wet, irregular terrain, Carole heard a sound and turned the dim light on Mitzi's face. Her lips were blue from cold and her teeth were chatterng. We must get down quickly, she thought. If only we could see better!

Suddenly, far below them Carole observed the light of a flashlight beam. Her heart quickened. Then she saw another light and then another. Three small pinpoints of light were bobbing along together. She strained to see through the darkness. Then she spotted another faint light that she supposed was above the side door of the castle. The lights were visible briefly, and then they disappeared as if they had gone behind a building, perhaps the woodshed. Carole wasn't sure.

Did she dare call out? Could they hear her from this far, anyway? She flashed her dim light again on Mitzi's little face and realized she must get this child to a place where it was warm, as rapidly as possible. Surely, she thought, there isn't a possibility that the thieves are still hanging around? She just had to take the chance.

"Dear God," she prayed, "please, don't let those robbers catch us again."

Cupping her hands around her mouth, Carole called as loudly as she could, "Hello, down there! Hello, down there!" Her voice echoed. Did anyone hear her? She called again, "Hello, down there. Hello, down there."

Then she saw one bobbing light and then another and then another spring out from behind the building—or whatever they had been hidden behind—and a strange man's voice drifted up to her.

"Hello, up there. Who is there?"

"It's Carole Loring," she called. "It's Carole and Mitzi,

please come and help us."

And then, joy of joys, she heard David's voice. "Carole, is that you? Where are you? Do you have a light?"

"Our light's really weak," she called back. "Please come up and help us."

"Stay right where you are." David's voice rang with excitement. "We'll be right there. Keep calling so we'll know which direction to go."

Then she saw the lights flit swiftly across the ground and soon they were rushing toward her up the steep slope. She called out periodically, then one of the lights began to pull away from the others. It seemed to be bounding over the rocks. Her joyful heart told her, "That's David."

She sat down upon the rock and pulled Mitzi into her lap, wrapping her coat around the shivering child. Then she turned on their faint light.

She was so excited it didn't seem her pounding heart could stay inside her body. David! How she had longed to feel his arms about her and now soon she would! Moments later the beam of a powerful flashlight flashed up past them and then came back to rest upon them.

"Are you all right?" David called.

"We're fine, just cold. Please hurry."

In another moment David was there kneeling beside her. With a glad cry she threw both arms about his neck and he drew her tenderly into his arms. She could feel the roughness of his coat and his strong arms about her, and suddenly the terror of the past few days, the strain, and the uncertainty seemed to crash down upon Carole. Burying her head in his shoulder, she wept uncontrollably.

David tightened his arms about her, murmuring endearments and stroking her hair.

Mitzi, who had drifted off into exhausted sleep while lying in Carole's lap, was completely unnoticed by David. She suddenly raised up and struggled to disentangle herself from Carole's jacket. "Aunt Carole," she said, her voice quivering, "are you okay, Aunt Carole?"

161

Carole had forgotten Mitzi! She raised her head and dabbed at the tears with her sleeve. "Of course, I'm okay, Mitzi. Aunt Carole is just being a crybaby again."

David had laid the flashlight upon the ground and now Carole saw the shock and bewilderment in his eyes as he stared at Mitzi.

"Who's this?" he inquired.

"This is the artist's granddaughter, Mitzi." Her face quickly clouded. "David, we must get help for Mr. Prentice. He's in the cave and is very ill. He's in a coma."

"In the cave?" David queried.

"Yes, the robbers locked us in the cave—"

"What robbers?" a strange voice asked. Carole looked up, startled, and realized that two other men had arrived. One was Steve Morgan, the camp boss, and the other was a stranger.

"Sheriff, this is my wife Carole," said David. "Carole, this is Sheriff Murphy."

Concern written on his face, Steve knelt down in front of Carole and Mitzi. "Are you okay, Mrs. Loring? You've given us quite a scare."

"Yes, I'm fine, but Mr. Prentice is in a diabetic coma in the cave."

"You spoke of robbers and a cave?" Sheriff Murphy broke in.

Carole struggled to explain. "There's a cave on the other side of the mountain from Thunder Mountain Manor, and there's a tunnel that goes through from the castle into the cave. The robbers have been keeping Mitzi and me captive there for the past four days. Mr. Prentice ran out of insulin and now he's in a diabetic coma. The robbers locked the three of us in the cavern and went away in his Land Rover. Mitzi and I escaped through a crack in the ceiling of the cave. Please, we must hurry or Mr. Prentice will die if he doesn't get some insulin quickly."

"First, we'd better get you and the little girl into some warm clothing and out of the cold," David spoke up.

162

Steve said, "I'll carry the little one." He reached to take Mitzi but she had seen enough of strange men for the past two weeks, so with a shriek she threw her arms around Carole's neck and clung there tearfully.

Carole, with a catch in her throat, wrapped her arms about the shaking child. "Mitzi, Mitzi, it's okay. Mitzi, will you let my husband carry you?"

Finally, after much coaxing, she allowed David to take her from Carole's arms. David drew her inside his warm coat and wrapped it around her until only the top of her head was showing. Swiftly they began the descent. Steve and Sheriff Murphy, with Carole between them, followed. Soon they were crossing the lawn of the old castle.

Suddenly the sound of a motor vehicle was heard and lights swept around the mansion from the direction of the road that wound toward Granite. A jeep ground to a stop, spewing gravel in the driveway. Both doors burst open and two rather stout persons, a man and a woman, descended from the jeep and hastened up the flagstone walk toward the front door of the castle.

When the sheriff called, they turned in his direction and the older man broke into a run. "Sheriff," he called, "Sheriff! They told me in town you would be here."

"Jasper," the Sheriff exclaimed. "I've been trying to contact you."

Carole realized suddenly that this must be Stella and Jasper Parsons, the caretakers of the artist's manor home.

"We've been worried about Mr. Prentice," Jasper said. "When he didn't contact us to come back to work, we began to feel like something was wrong. So Mother and I came back to Granite. We heard there was a lady lost near the castle and some strange things seemed to be going on, so we came out as quick as we could."

The Sheriff said, "It's a good thing you're here. Do you have a key to the tunnel that goes into the cave?"

Stella Parsons had been standing quietly. "Yes," she

answered, "there's an extra key. I know right where it is."

"Can you let us in the castle door?" the Sheriff questioned.

"Of course," Mr. Parsons said, "we're the caretakers, ain't we?" And without another word he turned and strode quickly toward the castle.

Stella said, "Sheriff, something has happened to Mr. Prentice, hasn't it? We've both been so worried."

"Yes, he's in a diabetic coma. He's locked in the cave and that's what we need the keys for."

"Good heavens!" the woman exclaimed. "We knew something was wrong!" She turned and scurried toward the castle door as fast as her plump legs could carry her. Carole and the three men followed close behind her. Jasper quickly extracted a ring of keys from his pocket, selected one and opened the heavy front door.

Stella was back in a moment with the tunnel key. It didn't take long for them to go through the house into the tunnel, and soon Jasper was opening the cave door. What would they find? Carole's heart began to pound as they approached the door at the other end of the dank, darkened tunnel. Would poor old Mr. Prentice have died there alone?

Thrusting open the heavy door, they burst into the room. The sheriff strode to the bedroom, the others right behind. Quickly lifting the old man's arm Sheriff Murphy felt for his pulse.

Before Carole reached the bedside, she could hear the old man's labored breathing. He was alive! He was alive! Perhaps they were in time.

"His pulse is pretty weak," the sheriff declared. "Jasper, would you bring a kitchen chair?" As he was instructing the handyman, he was wrapping a blanket around the unconscious old man.

Placing him in the chair, Steve and the sheriff each took an end and, with Jasper steadying him on one side and Stella hovering solicitously on the other, began to transport him from the room. Carole followed with David still carrying Mitzi, who, exhausted from their ordeal, and finally warm and comforted, had gone to sleep in David's arms.

The ground to the campground was hurriedly covered. As they neared the camp, Carole glimpsed several figures sitting around the campfire. As the crunch of their steps was heard, everyone jumped up and several figures advanced to meet the sheriff's group.

Carole saw her grandmother coming and ran to meet her. When Gran saw it was really Carole, she too began to run, crying and laughing as she came. Carole threw her arms about her tiny grandmother, her heart bursting with happiness.

"Carole, Carole," her grandmother choked. "You'll never know how worried we have been. Are you all right, child?" Carole assured her she was fine. Gran drew herself out of Carole's strong embrace and looked her over from head to toe. "You look all right," she said. "Where have you been, young lady?"

Carole laughed shakily, "I've been in a castle tower and in a castle dungeon. It's a long story, Gran, but as soon as I get into some dry clothes and we get Mr. Prentice on the way to the hospital, I'll tell you every detail."

The sheriff quickly called his deputy on the radio in his jeep. The deputy promised to send a helicopter out with a doctor immediately.

The sheriff explained to Carole and David that a helicopter was kept at a small field in the vicinity of Granite for emergencies. He looked keenly at Carole. "I would like to hear your story as soon as you get into dry clothes. We'll need everything you can remember about the robbers. Do you know if the jewels are hidden in the castle?"

"The jewels were never mentioned in my presence," said Carole. "I'll put Mitzi to bed, change my clothes and be right back."

David carried Mitzi to the tent for Carole, dropped a warm kiss on her chilled lips and hurried out to see what he could do to help the sheriff.

Carole dressed Mitzi in her own long warm flannel gown and tucked her in her own cot. Mitzi only half awakened, reassured herself that Aunt Carole was still present, and promptly closed her eyes again in deep sleep.

Carole kissed the sleeping little girl on the top of her flaxen head. "Dear Jesus," she whispered, "thank you for bringing us safely here. It still seems like a dream that we are safe. And please help poor Mr. Prentice to live. Thank you again—"

26

Carole shed her damp clothing. Her body hurt in several different places from the scraping it had endured during the escape through the ceiling crevice. But thankfully, she wasn't really injured. Donning warm, fresh clothes from the skin out, Carole felt almost her old self again. She found a dry sweater and cap, and taking one last look at the sleeping child, she went out the tent door, leaving a lighted battery lantern in case Mitzi should waken and be frightened.

Mr. Prentice had been placed on a cot in the warm dining room tent to await the arrival of the doctor and helicopter. Stella was hovering about his unconscious form, massaging his hands and feet.

Manuel came to Carole and placed a steaming cup of hot chocolate in her hands which she accepted gratefully. Manuel, with warm dark eyes glowing, said simply, "Senora, it is a verra good to have you back."

As she came out of the dining room tent, David came to meet her. "The sheriff wants to hear as much of your story as possible before the helicopter arrives." Steve drew a chair up to the fire for her in the circle of campers waiting with her grandmother and Sheriff Murphy. David took a seat to her left.

Unashamedly, Carole reached for David's hand as she began her narrative. She told her story as simply and quickly as possible, sticking strictly to the facts. As she finished, and before the sheriff had opportunity to question her, the helicopter was there. Within minutes Dr. Morton, who apparently was Mr. Prentice's regular physician, had examined the old man, administered a shot, and both doctor and patient were airlifted out of the camp.

After the departure of the helicopter, Sheriff Murphy questioned Carole thoroughly, taking notes as he did so. When she was finished he, Steve, and the Parsons went away to the castle. The sheriff planned to search the tower, the cave and the bedrooms the robbers had used. Steve and Jasper were needed to help. David and the other men offered their assistance but the sheriff said two were enough.

When the sheriff had gone, the campers, Gran and David were full of questions and Carole had some questions of her own about the search for her. David and Gran told the story about the search, interspersed with comments from the others. As they talked together, Carole noticed the dark circles under Gran's eyes and the tiredness in her face. David's deep blue eyes were red-rimmed and he appeared to have lost weight.

"Dear God," she prayed silently, "help me never to put my family through anything this terrible again."

Suddenly Carole realized Mitzi had been alone for a long time. She jumped up. "I must check on Mitzi. Gran, I think you had better get to bed. You look so tired."

Her grandmother rose and said she believed she would go to bed. "And my rest will be sweet tonight because you are safe." Carole and David walked with her to her tent, one on either side. She kissed each goodnight. "I can hardly express how much help David has been to me during this ordeal," she told Carole. "I gave you up for dead a dozen times but David would not allow me to believe that. He was a tower of strength. You have a husband in a million. Latch on to him and hold him fast."

"Believe me, I plan to," Carole said softly. They bid Gran goodnight and, hand in hand, strolled to their own tent.

Inside the tent, Carole bent over Mitzi. The child was sleeping deeply and peacefully.

David entered the tent behind her, took her into his arms and kissed her, then held her away from him and hungrily searched her face. "You know," he whispered huskily, "I wasn't sure I'd ever see your beautiful face again, alive. Carole, can you ever forgive me for upsetting you the way I did?"

"Forgive you?" Carole spoke in a shocked voice. "I'm the one who should beg your forgiveness. Can you ever forgive me, David, for the atrocious, stupid way I behaved?"

"It was my fault," David objected. "I should have taken better care of you."

"It was never your fault," Carole declared. "It's all mine. I wanted my way and I got my way. I'm so sorry, David, for the anxiety I put you and Gran through."

He folded her in his arms again and she felt as if she never wanted him to let her go. Presently, though, they drew apart and sat down in a couple of chairs inside the tent.

"Carole," David began. "About my teaching. . ." Carole was watching him very intently. "Do you want to talk about this?" he asked.

"Yes," she said.

"Carole, you don't think that I would ever let teaching or anything else come between us, do you? I do want to teach, but you're the dearest thing, outside of God, in my life, and nothing, *nothing* will ever come between us. Do you understand that, Carole?"

Carole's dark eyes were serious. "It's okay, David," she said. "I do understand."

"You do?" David's face showed his incredulity.

"Yes, I do," Carole said. "Because you see, I'm not the same person who went away. I've found God, too."

David's eyes shone but he seemed to be struck absolutely speechless!

"Perhaps I should say that God found me and finally knocked some sense into my hard head. Things will be different now. I want you to teach."

Her eyes began to twinkle. "Besides, I'll be very busy myself when we get back home."

At last, David found his voice. "What do you mean?"

"I'll be reading books on infant care and collecting the necessary paraphernalia," she said. "I've decided to ask my husband if we can have a baby."

With a whoop, David caught Carole around the waist and whirled her around and around, until they were both laughing and dizzy.

Carole and David were so absorbed in their own private world they didn't see Mitzi sit bolt upright in shocked horror. With a resounding shriek, she leaped from the bed and tore into David with both fists flailing and small feet kicking—an enraged little tigress.

"Hey—hey! What—what—" Completely baffled, David backed away from the irate little girl. She charged in again crying wrathfully, "You let Aunt Carole alone!"

"Mitzi! What are you doing? Stop that!" Carole's shocked words halted the child in her steps.

Tears brimmed over and rolled down Mitzi's cheeks. "He was hurtin' you!"

A lump as big as a pumpkin seemed to fill Carole's throat. She knelt down and put her hands on the weeping child's small, shaking shoulders. "No, Mitzi, David wasn't hurting me. We were only playing."

The small shoulders sagged and the tears continued to pour down her pale cheeks. "I—I'm s—sorry, Aunt Carole, I woke up and thought Max was hurtin' you. I—I musta been dreamin'."

David knelt down beside Mitzi and spoke earnestly, "Honey, no one is going to hurt you or Carole again. You are among friends now. Okay?"

Drying her eyes on the long sleeve of the flannel gown, Mitzi seemed to be thinking. Suddenly she looked up at David and gave him a dazzling smile. "Okay," she said.

David gathered her tiny figure, swathed in the adult-sized gown, into his arms and tucked her back into bed. Carole kissed her goodnight again. "I wish my storybook was here," she told Carole wistfully, "so you could read me a story."

"I'll *tell* you one," promptly volunteered David, to Carole's utter amazement. "Will that make up for scaring you?"

Mitzi eagerly agreed that it would and lay back in delighted anticipation.

For the next ten minutes David spun a tale that had Mitzi laughing and clapping her hands in pleasure. Then he skillfully swung the story into a quieter vein until when he had finished Mitzi was relaxed and almost immediately fell asleep.

Astounded, Carole said, "I didn't know you could tell stories!"

"I used to babysit my little brother and sister," David replied, grinning. And with a special caress in his voice, he added, "And I can't wait to tell some to our own."

Carole's eyes shone as she tucked her hand into David's.

27

The next morning David, Carole, Gran and Mitzi accompanied Jasper Parsons into Granite to visit the old artist. Stella remained behind to put the mansion in order. She had volunteered to keep little Mitzi, but seeing the look of distress in Mitzi's sensitive little face and feeling a wrench in her own heart, Carole quickly assured Mrs. Parsons that Mr. Prentice had placed Mitzi in her care.

As they traveled over the rough back road into the little town of Granite, Carole wondered if the robbers had gotten completely away. Probably, she thought. They had heard no news and if the sheriff had any, he hadn't relayed it to them this morning before they left camp.

They drove directly to Granite's small hospital. When they entered the old artist's room, Carole realized that he was still a very sick man. His eyes were closed and his breathing was still labored. The nurse in attendance whispered that he was conscious but very weak, and they wouldn't be allowed to visit long.

In whispered tones Carole explained that Mitzi was the old man's granddaughter, and the private nurse assured them that it would be okay for her to go in because he had been asking for her. "He has also been asking for Joy, whom I presume is his daughter? If she can be located, it would be very wise to bring her here. I believe it would speed his recovery immeasurably."

Carole explained to the nurse that she had acquired Joy's address and they would be contacting her in the very near future.

When they entered the room, Mitzi ran quickly to her grandfather's bedside and took his hand. The old man's eyes slowly opened. At first he seemed to have difficulty focusing his eyes. But when he turned his head and saw Mitzi, a gentle smile came to his lips and he pressed the little hand that was holding his. Carole moved into his line of vision and his smile broadened to include her. He whispered something and she leaned forward so she could hear him.

"Carole," he whispered, "thank you, for taking care of Mitzi."

Jasper moved forward and spoke to the old man— David and Gran stayed in the background. Mr. Parsons assured his employer that he needn't worry about anything at the castle, that he was taking care of everything, and the old gentleman uttered a whispered, "Thank you."

Mr. Prentice moved his eyes from face to face and then

lifted a hand and motioned Carole closer. "I read the diary," he whispered, slowly. "I'm sorry I was angry with you. You've been so kind to my granddaughter and me. You seem to care." He hesitated, "Could you find Joy for me? I'm sorry for the grief I have caused her—and her mother." His eyes closed and two tears ran down the side of his face. He seemed oblivious to them.

When he opened his eyes again, with great effort it seemed, Carole urged him to be quiet, telling him that he could talk later when he was stronger.

He raised a frail hand in protest. "No, I must talk now. I have been a fool. I can't undo what I have done, but I will spend the remainder of my life trying to make amends to Joy and Mitzi. It's too late for Esther. I'm so sorry, so sorry," his voice trailed off weakly.

Carole took his trembling, frail hand and pressed it. "Mr. Prentice, we'll do everything in our power to find Joy quickly and bring her to you. Now, we must go as we don't want to tire you." Her eyes were misty. "But remember, it's never too late with God. You can have what Esther and Joy found."

"Yes, I know, and thank you," murmured the old man, as he closed his eyes. His hand relaxed and Carole realized he was asleep, sleeping the sleep of the exhausted.

When they left the hospital, Jasper drove them directly to the airport. Mrs. Parsons had found the address of the place Joy had been living when her mother had died several years before. That was the last time they had heard from her. So they had come prepared to search for Mitzi's mother. They had brought along clothes for a stay of several days in Spokane, if necessary.

They chartered a small plane, and the office girl told them the pilot should be back in about thirty minutes. Carole decided to call the sheriff's office to see if there had been any word of the two thieves. The sheriff had just returned from the castle area and was in the office when she called. He had news.

The robbers had been apprehended coming into a nearby town at a road block on a back road. It seemed that Ferron had fired on the deputies and had been shot and killed. Max had surrendered and was in jail. He had been kept overnight at the small town of Rocky and was being transported this morning to Spokane where he and Ferron had committed the robbery a couple of weeks before.

Carole returned to David, her grandmother and Jasper to report what the sheriff had told her.

"You know," she said thoughtfully, "I have a strange feeling that Max, underneath his tough outward appearance, has a longing to know God. David, would you go with me to visit Max after we locate Joy?"

A frown crossed David's face. "Carole, I would prefer that you have no more dealings with that man. I shudder to think what he could have done to you. From what you have told us, he's an animal."

"Yes," Carole agreed, "he is. But buried beneath that savagery there is a soft spot. He loves his sister. He stood up for me against Ferron, his fellow conspirator, so that I could remain with the old man and Mitzi. I still feel he can be salvaged if he will allow God to work in his life."

"Perhaps you're right," David conceded, grudgingly. "I'll go with you. I certainly don't want you going alone."

Gran seconded this heartily. Gran had been quiet on the trip and Carole noticed that she looked very tired.

"Gran, you look so tired. Why don't you stay here and rest while we go to Spokane?"

"That is what I've decided," Gran conceded. "I had planned to go with you, but suddenly I realize I am exhausted. I'll take a room here in Granite and just rest for awhile." She laughed, "I suppose that I'm getting too old for such adventures as we've been through the last several days."

Carole reached over and hugged her. "I'm sorry, Gran," she said.

"Don't be!" Mrs. Drake answered. "I'm just thankful that you and Mitzi and the old gentleman are alive."

173

"If you feel like it, and if Mr. Prentice is feeling like having visitors, perhaps it would be good if you could drop in on him while we're gone," Carole said. "I understand he has no friends to speak of."

"I think perhaps I shall," Gran agreed. "After a good night's rest I'll be fine. And a good comfortable bed will be better than a camp cot."

At this point a young man walked briskly toward them and inquired if they were ready to leave. Carole hugged her grandmother good-bye and David shook hands with Mr. Parsons, thanking him for bringing them out. Then she, David and Mitzi boarded the small four-passenger plane.

The trip to Spokane was uneventful. Renting a car at the airport, they proceeded to the address Stella had written out for them. A middle-aged lady came to the door. When she saw Mitzi, she let out an exclamation of joy and gathered the little child into her arms. Then she invited them in, preceding them down a small hallway, asking a dozen questions at one time. Where was Ferron? How did they get Mitzi?

Carole explained that they were friends of Mitzi's grandfather and introduced herself and David. Mrs. Carroll, Joy's landlady, waved them to chairs and insisted on bringing tea, all the time talking a mile a minute and telling them what a terrible mistake she had made in letting Mitzi go with Ferron.

"He seemed like such a nice, handsome young man," she said, "and even brought me a note in Joy's handwriting. But I guess he'd forged it, " Mrs. Carroll said ruefully. "Joy has lived with me for several years and I should have known her handwriting anywhere.

"I didn't know until yesterday that Mitzi was in the wrong hands." Mrs. Carroll had finally stopped flitting about the room, and was seated. "I haven't been able to talk with Joy herself, even though I called every day. Her condition was very serious for awhile as she had complications—infection set in. She had eye surgery, you know, serious eye surgery. They have had her lying very still so she wasn't even able to

174

talk on the phone until yesterday.

"Finally she called me. She asked how Mitzi was and I was horrified to realize I had let Mitzi into the wrong hands. Joy just about went to pieces when I told her where Mitzi was. Joy seemed very afraid of her husband. They wouldn't let Joy leave the hospital, but they sent a policeman down and I went to the police station to explain the situation."

"And what was the reaction of the police?" David asked.

"At first the policeman didn't seem greatly perturbed. He seemed to think if Mitzi was with her father, it was okay. But when Joy told him who Ferron was, and that she was fearful of what he would do to Mitzi, the policeman said they would try to find Mitzi."

The woman drew a long breath after telling her story. "Poor Joy has been so distraught," she continued, shaking her head. "We must call and tell her we have Mitzi because that poor child has been beside herself with fear and grief."

Mrs. Carroll went dashing into the next room to call, but was back within a minute. "Joy isn't answering her phone," she exclaimed. "So why don't we go to the hospital? It isn't far. Could we go now?"

"Sure," David said.

They all hustled into the car and in just a few minutes entered Memorial Hospital. As they were walking down the hospital corridor, Carole's heart began to surge with anticipation. They were about to meet Mitzi's mother—the old artist's daughter. Carole felt she almost knew Joy from the diary she had written in the books in the castle tower.

Joy's room was on the first floor of the south wing, and it took only a few brief moments for them to reach the doorway. The desk nurse had informed them they couldn't stay long because Joy's eye surgery had left her very weak. But when Carole explained they were bringing Joy's little girl to her, the nurse's stern face broke into a wide smile and she said, "That makes a difference. This is the best medicine we can give that poor woman!" And she led the way to Joy's room.

There were three other beds in the room, but immediately they knew which one was Joy's. The girl had short, very blond hair, perhaps a shade darker than Mitzi's, but she had the same pixy face, and a look of frailty about her.

Joy appeared to be sleeping as the nurse walked to the bedside and laid a hand on her arm. "Joy, you have visitors," she said.

The uncovered eye snapped open quickly and her face went radiant with joy as she saw her daughter. "Mitzi! Darling!" she called excitedly.

But Mitzi hung back, apparently afraid of this strange person with a huge gauze bandage over one eye and the left side of her face still quite swollen. She didn't look much like the mother that Mitzi knew.

Carole nudged Mitzi toward her mother and leaned over and whispered, "It's your mother, honey. She's had her eye operated on but she's the same mommy."

Mitzi went forward timidly and as soon as her mother spoke her name again she raced the remainder of the way and jumped upon the bed to be smothered in her mother's arms.

The nurse, standing by, looked somewhat disturbed, fearful the little girl would accidentally bump her mother's eye. But though she hovered in the foreground, she said nothing.

"Mommy, you're squeezing me too hard," Mitzi finally said breathlessly, and everyone laughed. When Joy released her small daughter, tears were running unashamedly down her face.

Mrs. Carroll stepped to the side of the bed and kissed Joy lightly on the cheek. "These folks are friends of your father, Joy," she explained.

"Of my father?" Joy looked puzzled.

Carole crossed the few steps to the bedside and

presented her hand. "I'm Carole Loring," she said, "and this is my husband David. Mitzi has been with your father."

"Mitzi has been with my father? How did he get her? I thought she was with Ferron." Joy took Carole's hand and acknowledged the introduction to David with a nod as she asked the questions.

"Please be seated," the nurse said, pushing a seat forward for Carole. "I'll bring two more chairs."

Mitzi had forgotten her fear now that she realized this was really her mother. She was fascinated with the bandage and what had happened to her mother's eye. Joy had to explain to little Mitzi why her eye was covered and her face swollen. By this time the nurse had brought in two more chairs.

Joy had calmed down somewhat by now. As she looked from one to the other of her visitors, her face mirrored the bewilderment she was feeling. "I still don't understand. Ferron had Mitzi. What has Ferron to do with my father?"

Carole said, "Would you like us to begin at the beginning? I think that is the only way we can fully explain the situation."

"Please do."

So, Carole, with David dropping in a comment now and then, proceeded to tell Joy in as few words as possible how she had become involved. She told how Ferron had taken Mitzi to Mr. Prentice's home to use as a hostage against her father so he would provide a secure place for himself and Max to stay.

She finished with, "Max has been captured, but Ferron was killed."

Joy's face registered shock. "Ferron is dead?" she said. "I can hardly believe it! And yet," her face was thoughtful, "I feel no sorrow. He was such a brutal man. I've always been afraid he would kill somebody. And Max was also a very terrifying person. I lived in fear the short time my husband and I lived together. I was thankful when he no longer had a need for me and moved out."

"Were you married to Ferron very long?" Carole said gently.

"I'm still married to him," Joy said. "I just couldn't seem to bear the thought of going through a divorce. But Ferron has been gone for several years. As soon as he found out we were going to have a child, he knocked me around. Then, declaring he didn't want to be tied down to a brat, he left. I haven't seen him since. At first I was fearful he would return, but as the months and then years went by, I scarcely thought of him at all."

Carole nodded sympathetically.

"I believe he married me just to have a place to hide after one of his burglaries," Joy continued. "I was a convenience as long as there were no strings attached to his freedom. I had lived so long in seclusion I'm afraid I was a very poor judge of character. And Ferron could be very charming—and he was so handsome. He swept me off my feet."

A fleeting thought of snake-like eyes crossed Carole's mind, but she just smiled her encouragement as the young woman paused.

"A close friend at work was apprehensive about him, but, of course, a person in love cannot be told anything," Joy continued. "But that," she said, "is enough about me. My father? How is he?"

"Your father is still very weak, but he is conscious and he gave us a message for you," Carole said.

"A message for me?" Joy's one good eye revealed both bewilderment and hope.

"Yes. Your father said to tell you he loves you very much, and he wants you to forgive him for hurting you and your mother. He wants to see you as soon as possible."

Joy's face paled. Her lips began to tremble. Tears trickled down her cheeks. It was a moment before she could say anything. "He—he wants to see me? He is sorry? I can hardly believe it—and yet I have prayed so long," she whispered.

178

Joy turned to the nurse who had come back into the room. "How soon can I go?" she inquired. "I want to see my father."

"We'll have to talk to the doctor about that," the nurse said, shaking her head. "I'm sure that it won't be immediately. Your condition has been very precarious, you know."

Carole and David stood. "We must go," Carole said. "I'm afraid we have overtired you. But we will take a hotel room and return tomorrow."

"No, no," Joy interrupted. "You must stay in my apartment! Mrs. Carroll, I want them to stay in my apartment. That will be fine with you, won't it?"

Mrs. Carroll quickly agreed. Although Carole and David protested, Joy and Mrs. Carroll were adamant. So it was decided that Carole and David would stay with Mrs. Carroll as long as they were in Spokane.

Mitzi had been taking all of this in and suddenly she let out a delighted squeal, as if it had finally registered. "Aunt Carole, you'll be staying with me!"

Joy gave Mitzi another squeeze. "Yes, dear, and we'll be eternally grateful to your Aunt Carole for taking such good care of you. Thank you, so very much," she told Carole earnestly.

As they were walking out the door, Joy called Carole back. "What does my father think of Mitzi?" she asked.

Carole smiled. "He adores her," she assured Joy. "Calls her 'kitten' and tells her he loves her."

Joy's eyes were misty. "That's what he called me when I was a little girl."

Later, at the apartment, Mrs. Carroll would not allow them to leave until she had prepared lunch. Then Mitzi insisted on giving them a grand tour of her small, attractive room and proudly showed off her books and toys. Promising Mitzi they would return soon, after awhile they left to visit Max at the jail.

28

It took some convincing for the sergeant at the desk to allow them in to see Max. He told them Max was very much a problem prisoner and was being kept in a cell by himself. Regarding Carole with a doubtful look, he said, "You'll have to go down the corridor past the other prisoners and sometimes they can be pretty obnoxious. A lady like you doesn't know what she's letting herself in for."

"Please," Carole pleaded, "we need to see Max. He did a favor for me recently and we want to do what we can for him."

Finally, reluctantly, the sergeant called a deputy to escort them to Max. "You can't stay long," he cautioned.

Walking behind the deputy, they soon arrived at a large door which the deputy unlocked. After they entered, he relocked it behind them. Carole had never been locked in prison before and it was a very eerie feeling. They passed through a small room, then through another locked door. Stretched before them was a long hall with barred walls along either side. As they walked down the corridor, prisoners crowded to the bars and Carole quickly saw what the sergeant had meant. Shrill whistles rent the air and crude remarks were directed at Carole. But she held her head high and tried not to look either way as she followed the deputy down the full length of the prison corridor. They finally reached the next to last cell where they could see Max lying on a bunk.

"Max, you've got visitors," the guard said, as they stopped before the cell with only one occupant.

Max raised himself to a sitting position on the narrow bunk. "Who is it?" he inquired indifferently.

"See for yourself," the guard said insolently. "I'm not your butler."

Max stood up and lumbered over to the bars. When he saw Carole and David standing there, a frown creased his homely features. "What cha' want?"

"Hello, Max," Carole said. "This is my husband, David."

Max favored David with only a cursory glance, then glared at Carole with his muddy-yellow eyes. His thick lips drew back into a sneer. "And I guess I'm s'pposed to be delighted to see you! What do you want?"

Carole hesitated, uncertain how to answer. It did seem foolish to visit the person who had held her captive for several days and had threatened her life. But it seemed she had to try to help him somehow.

"Max, we want to be your friends if—"

Max grabbed the bars with both hands, as if he were trying to rip them apart. His face twisted with venom and malice, and his voice was so filled with loathing that Carole recoiled as if she had been struck. "Yeah! *You* are the friend that soft-soaped me into leavin' you behind when we needed you for a hostage. You're the reason my only friend is dead! That sweet talk of yours about a God who can help people and who cares for 'em is why I'm shut up in jail!" His face was purple with rage.

Out of the corner of her eyes, Carole saw the guard take a step forward, alert and poised for trouble. What she said must be said quickly because she knew the visit was about to be terminated. David, at her shoulder, pressed her arm and whispered tersely, "Let's get out of here." But she couldn't go yet!

"Max," she spoke gently, "God does care for you and for your sister, Tina. If you'll give me Tina's address, I'll visit your sister and see if there is a way we can help her!"

Max threw back his head and laughed harshly. The guffaw seemed to fill the passageway.

Carole felt her face flush with embarrassment but she stood her ground. "Would you like us to visit Tina?"

"She'd laugh in your face!"

"Perhaps. But she should have a chance, if she wants it."

"Why do you care what happens to her—or me either?" Max queried suspiciously.

"Because God cared for me and came to help me when I was at the end of my rope. I would like to repay Him a little by helping someone else. David and I want to be your friends—and also Tina's."

Max stood for a second with distrust written plainly upon his rough features before he rudely turned his back on them. "Me and Tina don't need your help!"

"I'll not bother you again, Max, but if you change your mind and want us to visit Tina, I'll leave our address at the desk. Good-bye," she said softly. Max did not acknowledge her offer or farewell.

David took Carole's arm, and they followed the guard back down the corridor lined with barred cells on each side, their steps echoing on the bare concrete. Once more Carole had to face the gauntlet of ogling, bold eyes, whistles, and shouts of "Hello there, Cutie," "What's your name, doll?" and even a couple of obscene remarks. They were almost to the heavy steel door when a voice rang down the corridor, "Wait, Queenie. Come back!"

Startled, Carole stopped. The guard was placing the large key in the door. "Sorry, lady, he's had his chance," he stated as he swung the door open and stood back for them to exit.

The shout came again, "Bring her back, guard! Queenie, come back!"

The guard shook his head obstinately.

"Please—just for a minute!" Carole turned her midnight blue eyes, velvety and pleading, upon the man.

The guard blustered, still shaking his head.

Her delicately formed lips curved into a coaxing smile and a dimple appeared in one cheek. "I promise to be only a minute or two."

Grudgingly, the guard gave in. David chuckled silently as he followed Carole and the guard back to Max's cell. How often he, David, had succumbed to those melting eyes and dimpled charm!

Looking somewhat sheepish, Max stood waiting at the bars. "It won't do no good, Queenie, but if you're bound and determined to waste your time, I'll give ya Tina's address. I ain't seen her in a couple of years but I allus try to know where she is."

Carole was deeply touched. It had taken a deep love for Max to swallow his pride and grab at what he apparently felt was a very frail straw to obtain help for his sister. Intuitively, she hid her feelings. Businesslike, she whipped out a pad and pen and took down the address. "We'll let you know how she is," she promised. Max only grunted ungraciously, turned his back on them, and went back to his narrow cell bunk without a word of thanks.

David followed Carole from the jail in amazed silence. He could hardly believe the change in Carole even yet. He had loved her—almost worshiped her—but he knew her faults well. He had often been the victim of them. She had a violent temper and was always the self-centered little princess who must be pampered and indulged. Now she had let Max treat her abominably, and had not only kept her cool but had looked beyond his crude demeanor to see something that was apparently worth taking ridicule and rebuff to salvage. This was not the Carole he knew! David was awed and humbled. What a miracle God had wrought!

They went back to the hospital to inform Joy of their plans. Carole also told Joy she planned to call and leave a message for Mr. Prentice. "Do you wish to tell your father anything?"

"Yes," Joy exclaimed. "Tell him I love him, forgive him and want to see him as soon as I am able to travel." She paused, a glow came to her tired face, and she spoke softly, "Maybe now we can talk about all that's in mother's diary."

"Will do!" declared Carole. "After we call Granite, David and I plan to fly to Seattle to see if we can locate Max's sister.

We expect to be back in a couple of days or less but we'll keep in touch."

"Can I go, too?" asked Mitzi eagerly.

"No, Mitzi," Joy said, "You must stay and keep Mrs. Carroll company."

Seeing her woebegone expression, Carole hugged her and assured Mitzi they would return soon.

29

Several hours later they were cruising slowly down Lemon Avenue in Seattle in a rented car. At the address of the cheap apartment house Max had supplied, the stringy-haired, slovenly apartment manager eyed them curiously before assuring them that Tina would be on Santiago Street, probably near the fortieth block.

Carole had told David that Tina was—according to Max—an alcoholic and a prostitute. Carole had not let her mind dwell on the girl's unsavory occupation or what she would be like, but now her imagination took flight.

She was well acquainted with the horrors and repugnance of alcoholism. In their wide circle of friends, where social drinking was the norm, there were a number who, though usually disclaiming it, were confirmed alcoholics. Several were blubbering, whining women who were forever telling all who would listen of their woes. Would this woman be like them and a "woman-of-the-night," as well? Carole felt revulsion rise in her. She felt queasy and panic threatened to overwhelm her. What had she let herself in for? This Tina was probably like her brother—foul-mouthed, loud and crude—and a drunk as well.

Could God really do anything for someone like that? She had blithely assured Max that God could. Now, she felt her faith weakening. She glanced at David and saw the strained, tense look on his face and wondered if he were fighting the same battle as she.

"Honey," David said, casting an uneasy look her way, "do you think it is necessary for you to have personal contact with this Tina? Couldn't you just contact a minister or mission in this area and put it in their hands? After all, they know how to deal with this sort of person and you don't."

His argument sounded logical and for a moment Carole almost embraced the idea. She wanted to, indeed, she longed to push this distasteful task onto anyone else's shoulders. Then she thought of Max, whom life had seemed to treat so unfairly. For some strange reason—unknown even to herself—she had to do this personally, for Max.

They were nearing the corner where the landlady had said Tina would be loitering. Carole's stomach still had butterflies; her palms felt damp and clammy.

David pulled over and parked. His face looked so grave and distressed that Carole giggled nervously. David looked reproachfully at her. "I just don't like to see my wife associating with riffraff like this girl!"

"Now who's a snob?" she bantered—much more lightly than she felt.

David colored slightly. "Perhaps I am. I guess I would think it very commendable for any person, other than my wife, to have a try at helping a down-and-outer."

"Just stick close to me," Carole said, squeezing his hand.

"Like a leech!" David vowed fervently.

They sat in the car and watched the passers-by—persons of all ages, mostly poorly-dressed or in dirty work clothes. Carole spotted a young girl who stood out. She looked no more than sixteen, was dressed in a short, tight skirt, and was eyeing the men who passed with boldly mascaraed eyes. Revulsion, mingled with pity, surged through Carole. How could a pretty girl—like this one could be, if properly and attractively dressed—sell herself to any man she could entice? She shuddered.

David had seen the girl, too, and saw Carole's reaction.

"You can still back out!"

Carole shook her head stubbornly. "Don't tempt me. "I've *got* to do this!"

Sighing, David started the car again and moved slowly back into the line of traffic. They cruised slowly up the street for several blocks and saw no redheads, although they saw three other women who were obviously plying the same profession.

David said suddenly, "There!"

Standing on the corner, talking to two very rough-looking young men, was a petite redhead. She was dressed in faded blue jeans, a bright yellow blouse, and wore sandals. Her hair was a glistening auburn, feathered back on each side. Her fair skin was pleasantly sprinkled with freckles.

As they drove past, Carole studied the face of the young woman who was talking animatedly. She looked about twenty-five—the age Max had declared Tina to be. The face was not pretty but had a drawing quality about it. Carole felt her hopes plummet. She prayed fervently in her heart that this girl would not be a prostitute—and then realized how foolish such a prayer was. Either she was or she wasn't. But she hoped passionately that she wasn't, because there was something compelling about this woman that Carole reached out to—though she only saw her face briefly as they slid by.

David parked halfway down the block and locked the car. Neither said a word. David took her cold hand as they walked slowly back up the street toward the corner. The two men were continuing on down the street, but the girl had stopped another man. The woman was talking persuasively and the man seemed to be protesting, though they could not hear the conversation because of the street noises. The man—a mechanic from the looks of his clothes—was still shaking his head "no" as they approached Then he turned abruptly from the auburn haired woman and strode quickly away—almost like he couldn't get away fast enough.

The woman seemed completely unperturbed but

turned her gaze in the direction of Carole and David, passed over them indifferently and seemed to be searching the faces of the pedestrians scattered along the sidewalk.

Carole was a few steps from the woman now. She was Max's sister! The eyes clinched the identification. They were the same strange yellow color, though hers were brighter and were highlighted with reddish-brown flecks.

"Tina Parrish?" asked Carole.

"Yes, I am." The amber eyes fixed on Carole were quizzical.

"Your brother Max gave us your address. We—" Carole was unprepared for the girl's reaction.

She grabbed Carole's arm with strong freckled fingers. "Max! You have seen Max? Where is he?" Her voice sparkled with excitement.

"He's in Spokane. He expressed concern for you and we told him we would look you up. Is there a quiet place we could talk?"

"Sure! Over on the next street there is a little cafe. I work there."

"We have a car. Should we drive over?"

"Your car would be safer where you can see it. Wait a minute and I'll ask Chet if he wants to drive over with us." She ran lightly down the sidewalk to talk briefly with a thin, dark young man lounging against a building a few doorways down. After an exchange of a few words, Tina came hurrying back with the young man in tow.

"This is my friend Chet." She hesitated, "I don't know your names."

"I'm sorry," Carole apologized. "This is my husband, David Loring, and I'm Carole." Both acknowledged the introduction to Chet. He grinned, said a shy "Hi," and nothing more. All four climbed into the rented car and David drove to the little cafe.

Inside, Tina waved and called a greeting to a waitress and the cashier, then led them to a back booth. David urged their guests to order whatever they wanted but they took only coffee as did Carole and David. They would eat when they had completed this mission.

"Now tell me about Max," Tina said as soon as they had ordered. "Where did you meet him?"

Carole glanced at David questioningly. "You go ahead," David said. "You know him better than I do."

Carole took a deep breath. "It's a long story and I hardly know where to begin."

"Just tell me everything. I have plenty of time." Tina clasped her thin, freckled hands together and pressed them to her lips thoughtfully, then laid them, still clasped, upon the table. "I suppose Max is in trouble. He always is. How I have worried about that boy! For a long time I have been trying to find him but he's as elusive as a flea."

"You two must be very close," Carole said gently. "Max said he worries about you, too."

"Well—we only have each other." Tina leaned toward Carole. "Is Max in jail?"

"Yes, he and another man robbed a jewelry store."

"He and Ferron?"

When Carole nodded yes, Tina said heatedly, "I don't like that man! He's so hard and cold. His eyes give me the 'heebie-jeebies'!"

Carole spoke emphatically, "We are in complete agreement there!" before continuing with her story. "Max and Ferron were surrounded by police. Ferron opened fire and was killed. Max wasn't harmed," she hastened to add when she saw Tina's face pale.

"Thank the Lord!" exclaimed Tina to Carole's astonishment. "Where did you meet Max—in jail?"

"No, he and Ferron captured me and held me captive for several days, along with Ferron's small daughter and father-in-law."

Mingled incredulity, astonishment and inquiry showed in Tina's expressive face. "I think you had better start at the very beginning," she suggested.

So Carole told the story, briefly, of her capture and

188

imprisonment in the tower and then the cave, of Max siding with her before he and Ferron left, and then the escape, with an occasional comment from David. She told also of their visit to Max in jail. Tina listened raptly, asking a question now and then to clarify something. Chet said nothing but his complete attention was on the narrative.

When she had finished, Carole looked squarely at Tina and spoke softly. "Max said you are an alcoholic. He is terribly worried about you."

Tina's lips trembled and tears filled her eyes. "Dear Max. I have caused him so much grief. I suppose I am actually to blame for his life of crime. He used to be always bailing me out of something, and it always cost money. Money he didn't have. So he got it! Usually through robbing a store or something. Finally it became a way of life, I'm afraid."

She took a tissue from her pocket and dabbed at her eyes. "But he won't have to worry about me anymore! I have been trying to locate him for better than a year but have been unable to find him. I—"

"Wait," Carole interrupted, "you said Max would not have to worry about you any more. What do you mean?"

"I'm a Christian."

Carole and David both exclaimed at the same time, "You're what?"

"A Christian. I found Christ through a young couple who opened The Home, a place for people like me, over on Walnut Street. They have a one-year program that a person who's on drugs or alcohol can enroll in. You have to promise to stay in the program for a year and follow the strict rules. A friend sobered me up enough to get me down there. I didn't think I could ever quit drinking, but those dear people loved me into a personal relationship with the Saviour. Jesus did what I couldn't do. He set me free from alcohol!"

Tina's voice quivered and her eyes filled with tears.

Carole felt tears springing up in her own eyes, and she laid a gentle hand on Tina's as she said reverently, "Beautiful! Beautiful! I—I'm utterly astounded. I came here to tell you that God could help you—and God has already been here." Her voice broke with emotion.

Tina's head jerked up. "You mean that you are Christians, too?" At Carole's affirmative nod, she spoke wonderingly. "I think I instinctively knew that! That is why you cared enough to try to help Max—and me! How long have you two known the Lord?"

"Less than a week," David interposed.

"I've passed the six-month milestone," Chet suddenly declared proudly.

Tina reached over and laid a slender hand over Chet's. "Chet came to The Home six months after I did. He's making great strides forward in his Christian walk. He helps me pass out tracts when he isn't working." She grinned suddenly. "He is still too shy to witness to people on the street, like I do, but he comes along and stays nearby to see that no harm comes to me."

"That's what you were doing when we came up—talking to those men about God?" Carole inquired.

"It's the least I can do after Jesus has done so much for me," Tina spoke with deep sincerity and humility.

Chet turned warm eager eyes upon Tina. "Tina and I are getting married when I graduate from The Home."

Tina's amber eyes glowed with love as they rested upon Chet. "Outside of God, Chet is the best thing that ever happened to me. He knows all about me and still loves me. He says I'm to be married in white." Her hand snuggled into Chet's lean brown hand which tightened upon it.

"I'm the fortunate one," Chet said emphatically. "We both had much to be forgiven for but now, in God's sight, we are as sinless as newborn babies. I like the feeling of being clean. I can look in the mirror now and not be ashamed to look myself in the face. It's great!" He suddenly seemed to come to the realization that he was talking and looked away embarrassed.

Carole felt David's hand cover hers on the table and glanced at his face. She saw by the moisture in his blue eyes that he, too, was much touched by the simple joy and love shared by these two who had been salvaged from the world's garbage pit.

"What about Max?" asked Tina eagerly. "Was he interested in God at all?"

"I don't know," Carole answered honestly. "He is careful to maintain his Mr. Tough Guy image, but I feel there is still something in his heart that cries out for something better."

"I must go to him!" Tina said.

"We will be flying back to Spokane tomorrow. Would you like to go with us?" invited Carole. David quickly voiced his approval.

Tina looked thoughtful. "I can get Babs to fill in for me while I'm gone, and I think I can swing it money-wise. I've been saving money for my wedding, but this is more important. Don't you think so, Chet?"

Chet looked somewhat downcast but agreed readily enough. Tina noticed his dejected face and spoke brightly. "I won't be gone any longer than necessary, and I'll call. And, remember, the others at The Home are there if you need help."

Chet brightened. "Don't worry about me. I'm just missing you already."

Back in Spokane the next day, Mrs. Carroll was pleased to have Tina as a temporary boarder, and after a quick lunch, David and Carole drove Tina to the jail, waiting outside in a small park across the street for her return.

After about twenty minutes, Tina came from the jail and walked dejectedly across the street to join them. In answer to their eager questions of how it went, Tina shook her head.

"Not too good. Max was very happy to see me but as soon as he realized I was alive and seemed to be doing okay, he went back into the old tough guy shell that you mentioned. He tried to act as if he knew *I* could kick that dirty habit if I wanted to. But he didn't want to believe that God had

191

anything to do with it!"

Tina was definitely deflated. "I guess I expected Max to be overjoyed at what God has done in my life and go running to God on the spot. But he won't even accept that Jesus had a part in it."

David spoke gravely, "Don't be discouraged. Things don't always go as we think they will or should. After all, God has our stubborn wills to contend with and I don't think He will ever force His will on us."

"You're right! Those poor, precious people at The Home had some trying times with me and my will. I almost gave up two or three times, but they wouldn't give up on me. And I'm not giving up on Max! I'm sure God isn't either! That old deputy told me I could only come once a day for a short time, but I'm going to talk to my Father about that." At their quizzical looks, she added, pointing upward, "The one up there," and laughed.

Later, Carole called her grandmother in Granite and was told that she was much more rested and that Mr. Prentice was gaining strength steadily but was anxious to see his daughter and Mitzi. Gran felt the sooner Joy could be transported to her father's bedside the better it would be for the old gentleman. Carole promised to see if it would be possible for Joy to travel soon.

When Carole, David and Mitzi visited Joy later in the day, they were delighted to find her sitting up in a chair. Joy said the doctor was very pleased with her progress and felt the infection was under control. Even the swelling had gone down noticeably.

"Your father is extremely anxious to see you," Carole told Joy. "He sent you a message. Would it be possible for you to fly to Granite in a chartered plane if a nurse could be found to attend you? He said he would pay all expenses, of course."

Joy's pale face suddenly seemed to shine. "This is almost more than I can believe! I have waited so long for a reunion with my father that I had almost given up hope. Now it is Father who is hastening our meeting! If Ferron had not kidnapped Mitzi and taken refuge in the castle, things would no doubt still be as they were. God uses the strangest things to bring about His desired result," she finished in an awed voice.

"Some pretty impossible things have come out of this situation to change our lives, too," Carole stated. "Until God allowed Mitzi to be dumped in my lap, I always thought I detested children. She changed my feelings completely about having a child. And I was terribly upset with David for becoming a Christian and hated the camp service. It took utter despair in the dungeon of the castle to make me know I needed God. I came out a different person."

David interspersed, "And I discovered that God can be just as real when terrible things that we don't understand come our way. He gives us strength and helps us bear what we think is unbearable."

Nodding gently, Joy said softly, "I can't wait to go home."

30

Two days later a plane glided to a stop on the small airstrip near the hospital in Granite. Joy was carefully lifted from the plane onto a rolling stretcher and whisked into the waiting ambulance.

Gran was in the small waiting room at the emergency entrance of the hospital when Carole, David and Mitzi followed Joy, on the rolling stretcher, through the doors.

Dr. Morton came striding briskly down the hall and followed the stretcher into a private room. "We'll make Joy comfortable and see that she has suffered no ill effects from the trip before we bring her father down," he explained, before he went in and closed the door.

"Charles is on pins and needles about his daughter and

Mitzi," Gran said. "Let's go tell him they have arrived."

Mr. Prentice was sitting up in a wheelchair when they reached his room. He still looked ill but much improved. Gran spoke from the doorway, "They're here, Charles. Here's little Mitzi. And as soon as Dr. Morton examines Joy, you can see her."

With a glad cry, Mitzi flew to her grandfather, who leaned over in the chair to wrap his thin, pajama-clad arms about her. He stilled the nurse's protestations with a curt, gruff, "I can hold my granddaughter, if I want," and proceeded to help her climb up on his lap.

"Mommy's here, Grandpa. Are you glad?" Mitzi asked anxiously.

"Yes, indeed, I'm glad!" Mr. Prentice declared forcefully. His voice was strong now. "Margaret," he addressed Gran, "would you please go tell Dr. Morton I had Joy brought here so I could see her, not so he could see her!"

Carole's eyes widened with amazement when Gran trotted right off to do his bidding. But she had no time to ponder this strange phenomenon. As she stood barely inside the room, the old artist beckoned to her.

"I'm sorry. I'm forgetting my manners," he apologized. "You and that fine young man of yours come on over here so I can properly thank you for everything you have been doing for me, my daughter and Mitzi."

Both Carole and David assured him it was their pleasure and they wanted no thanks, but he waved away their words. "Margaret—bless her heart, she has been so gracious and good to me—told me how you crawled through that hole in the rock and escaped so you could bring help for me. I wish there was a way I could repay you."

Carole protested, but he continued.

"And you cared for Mitzi as though she were your own. The sheriff told me how you talked those thugs into leaving you with Mitzi and me. You are a very brave, kind young woman—and after I treated you so badly." His keen old eyes swung to David, "And I'm sorry, young man, that we put you and Margaret through so much. You understand now why I didn't dare tell you your wife was a prisoner in my house? Those men would stop at nothing to insure their own safety."

David reassured the old artist. "It's okay, Mr. Prentice. We understand the terrible pressure you were under."

Carole's grandmother was back and said the doctor had given his permission for Mr. Prentice to see Joy. David pushed the wheelchair along the hall, Mitzi riding on her grandfather's lap. Carole and Gran walked quietly behind.

Joy was propped up on pillows. When she saw her father being wheeled in, she lay very still and pale, obviously waiting for him to make the first move. David wheeled him in next to the bed, and he sat gazing at Joy for a few seconds before he reached out his hand.

"Hello, kitten," he said softly. "I never realized how much I missed you until our little Mitzi came to me."

Joy reached out her hand and placed it in her father's. Her eyes filled with tears and her lips trembled. With a voice choked with emotion, she whispered, "I've missed you, too, Daddy."

Ignoring the gasp and protests from everyone in the room, the old gentleman raised slowly to his feet and took a faltering step. David sprang to assist him as he lowered himself to the edge of the bed. Like a small child, Joy flung herself into her father's outstretched arms.

Gran, Carole and David, eased out the door, taking Mitzi with them. "Is my mommy okay?" quavered Mitzi, tears gathering in her anxious blue eyes.

Smoothing back the fine fair hair from the troubled little face, Carole smiled. "Yes, honey, your mommy and grandpa are fine, just fine!"

A nurse came hurrying down the hall toward the small group standing together. "Is one of you Carole Loring?"

"I am," said Carole.

"There's a call for you. Come with me."

Carole followed her down the hospital corridor,

195

wondering who it could be.

As soon as she spoke into the telephone, she heard Tina's excited, bubbly voice. "Carole! Guess what! I've just come from the jail, and I had to tell you what a changed person Max is! Max has been thinking real deep about the things you said while they held you prisoner and how you still could forgive him and even offered to help him and me. He thought about me and the hold alcohol has had on my life. He finally admitted that I had to have had help from someone to get free from booze. He finally came to the conclusion that maybe it was God."

"Oh, I'm so glad!" Carole felt tears on her cheeks but ignored them.

"Carole, you would not believe the change in his attitude! He is no longer angry at the world. And he said to tell you that you probably saved his life."

"Saved his life?"

"Yes, saved his life. When the police surrounded their car, Ferron said, 'Let's shoot our way out of this!' Max grabbed a gun but suddenly your words rang loud and clear in his ears. 'You live dangerously, Max. What if you take a bullet in the heart from a policeman's gun and die? Where would you go?' He droped his gun like it was hot and jumped out of the car with his hands up, yelling, 'Don't shoot! I'm surrendering!' That wasn't like Max—he wasn't afraid of anything."

No, Carole agreed silently, that would not be like Max.

"He said the words you spoke to him in the cave room have been going over and over in his mind like a broken record. He tried to put them out of his mind but couldn't. You reminded him of the foster mother who took care of us for awhile when we were children. She was the only one who ever loved us."

"Max told me about her," said Carole. "I continue to be amazed at the things God uses to work out His purposes and plans. I felt I was such an utter failure in witnessing to Max.

Once he became so angry he grabbed me and shook me."

"Oh!" Tina paused at the thought. "I'm sorry Max gave you such a bad time, but I'm thankful he didn't seriously hurt you. God must have had His hand upon you. Others have not come out as well when Max was angry with them! It's a wonder he never killed anyone."

"We will continue to pray for Max," Carole said. "It is such a shame that Ferron died without making peace with God."

"Yes, but Carole, Ferron was different from Max. Max was cruel and did many wicked things, but he always had a tender spot deep inside. Ferron did not seem to have that. I feel that long ago Ferron hardened himself against any gentling influence. I never saw that man exhibit one kindness. He seemed totally hard, motivated by complete selfishness."

"What are your plans, now, Tina?" Carole asked.

"I plan to stay a week or so longer and talk to Max about God," Tina replied. "The sergeant is letting me spend more time with Max, now." She chuckled. "My Father had a little talk with him."

For a second Carole was puzzled, and then realized that Tina was again referring to her heavenly Father. "I imagine the sergeant is puzzling over the change in Max."

"He said I have had a good influence on him," Tina laughed. "He doesn't know the half of it!" Then she sobered, "I'm glad Max was charged with the jewelry store robbery only. The store owner is recovering, and he testified that Ferron was the only one armed, and that it was Ferron who shot him."

"That is fortunate for Max." Carole agreed. "Have they recovered the stolen merchandise?"

"Yes. Max is being very cooperative. He told the police where the jewels were cached. Everything was accounted for."

"Will Max be allowed to post bail?"

"He could, but he doesn't have any money, and so far I haven't come up with a plan to raise it, either. When I get back to Seattle I'll talk to my boss and see if he will help. I've worked there for a year and he's a very decent, nice guy."

"Do you think it would be good for Max to be out of jail at this time?" questioned Carole.

"I believe the directors at The Home would allow Max to live there while he is awaiting trial, and there is no better environment for someone with problems. Believe me, I know!"

"Would you allow David and me to stand good for Max's bail?"

There was utter silence for a minute. Tina was completely overwhelmed. Then she stammered, "But—but why would you be willing to do that? You hardly know either one of us. A—and you don't really *know* that Max won't skip and leave you holding the empty bag!"

"Do you think he would?"

"No, I don't!" she said emphatically.

"Then I don't either."

"But why are you doing this for a man who deeply wronged you and mistreated you and—"

"I wouldn't have two weeks ago, but now I don't look at things the way I did," Carole said earnestly. "If David and I can do some small thing to help establish Max, we would feel it a privilege. Will you accept our offer?"

"How can I refuse, when you express it that way?" Tina said. "And I do sincerely thank you."

"We'll fly up today and take care of it," Carole said.

Within hours, Max was out on bail and David and Carole were standing in the Spokane airport lobby, waiting for the plane which would take Max and Tina to Seattle. Tina had made the arrangements for Max to reside at The Home until his trial and Max had agreed to the arrangement.

Over soft drinks, the four discussed Max's plans. "I never tried to learn anything when I was in prison before," Max stated, "but when I'm sent back, I want to learn a trade. I've dabbled in welding a little bit, and I like the feeling I got when I saw that hot metal flowing on a pipe in a smooth, even bead. I think I'll see if I can become a good welder."

When Tina had said Max had changed, she hadn't exaggerated. He was as ugly as ever but now carried himself with a certain dignity, mixed with humility, that demanded respect. He thanked Carole and David sincerely for their help and sealed it with a huge, firm handshake. "I'll do my best to make Tina and you folks proud of me," he said, and they knew he meant it.

"But, Max," Carole protested, "you can't do it without God's help. David and I found that out. I want you to remember that we will be praying that you will make that important decision to receive Christ as your Saviour and live to please God."

"I'm thinking about it," Max assured them, "real hard." Then, as they began to leave, he said in a bantering tone, "And, Queenie, by the time I get out of prison, I hope you've learned to cook and can cook me a steak to celebrate."

"You're forgetting the fantastic omelets I can make," Carole shot back. Tina and David joined them in their shared laughter.

After seeing Tina and Max off on the plane, Carole and David did a little shopping, spent the night in Spokane, and flew back to Granite the next morning.

Gran was not at the boarding house when they arrived, but had left word she was at the hospital. When they entered Mr. Prentice's room, he was on his feet and dressed for travel, looking unusually fit for one who had been in such serious condition a week ago. But it was when Carole saw her grandmother looking radiantly lovely and ten years younger, that she knew something momentous was afoot.

After greetings were exchanged, Mr. Prentice informed David and Carole that they and Margaret were going home with him and Joy to be their guests at Thunder Mountain Manor. When Carole protested he and Joy weren't well

199

enough for visitors yet, he waved aside all objections, saying the Parsons were expecting them and all was in readiness. "In fact," he declared, "I hired another couple earlier in the week to assist the Parsons."

At that moment, a nurse brought Joy, also dressed for travel, into the room in a wheelchair. With her was Mitzi and the nurse Mr. Prentice had secured to care for Joy. "Anne is coming home with us," Mitzi exclaimed, running to Carole and grabbing her hand in delighted welcome.

Carole patted the small hand in hers by way of acknowledgment, but her mind was preoccupied. Gran and Mr. Prentice? Could this be why Gran had been content to stay in Granite and rest, visiting poor Mr. Prentice in the hospital while Carole and David journeyed to and fro.

They would make a handsome couple Carole had to admit. Gran was petite, trim, every inch a lady, and Charles Prentice looked like the distinguished, gray-bearded, successful artist that he was. The light that seemed to glow in their eyes every time they looked at each other reminded her of her first date with David.

But it must not be, thought Carole. She must protect her grandmother from her own foolhardiness!

31

Carole had no chance to speak privately with her grandmother until they were at Thunder Mountain Manor. Mr. Parsons had come for them in the Land Rover, which the police had returned after the robbers were apprehended. Gran was given a large, lavishly furnished room on the third floor. Carole and David were in the lower tower room to Carole's delight. But as soon as lunch was over, Carole went to her grandmother's room.

Gran was lying down. Carole offered apologetically to come back later but Gran assured her she was much too excited to sleep anyway. "Sit here in this chair by the bed, and I'll just rest while we chat."

Seating herself, Carole began uncertainly, "Gran, I hardly know how to say this. I can see that you are very fond of Mr. Prentice, but before this goes further, I feel there are some things you should know about him."

"Yes?" Gran raised her eyebrows quizzically.

"I read Mr. Prentice's wife's diary. Esther was a very lonely woman, almost a prisoner in this isolated mansion. Mr. Prentice became a complete recluse and expected his wife to share his self-imposed exile or suffer his anger. Joy could not bear the loneliness and finally ran away with her mother's approval."

Carole leaned forward, talking rapidly in her concern. "Gran, I know he is an extremely talented, acclaimed artist. He can be kind, gentle and sweet, but he can also be an irascible, egotistical ogre. His wife suffered much from his selfishness and his violent, unreasonable temper. Gran, could you accept a life like that?"

Gran laid a gentle hand on Carole's arm. "I appreciate your concern for my welfare, dear, but Charles has told me everything. He spared himself not at all but painted a black picture of what he put his wife—and Joy—through. But you see, Carole, that was before."

"Before?"

"Before he realized the kind of man he was. He told me about your finding Esther's diary—and even about his anger because you read it. Taking it back to his room, he read it through. Charles said that as he read it, he saw himself for the first time as he really was—a dictatorial, selfish tyrant. He didn't sleep at all that night, he was in such an agony of remorse for the grief he had caused Esther and Joy. In his torment and anguish, words from the diary have begun to sink into his heart. Words about the peace and happiness Esther and Joy had found. He's open, Carole, really open to the idea of knowing that source of peace and joy."

Carole was still troubled. "That's marvelous, Gran, but

what if you marry him and he resorts back to the same old pattern."

"Do you expect David to go back to his drinking?"

"No, but Mr. Prentice is older and more set in his ways."

"The God I serve is worthy of more trust than that," Gran chided gently.

"You are a Christian, aren't you?" Carole said.

"Yes," acknowledged her grandmother. "I accepted Christ last year and when I heard about Steve Morgan's Christ centered wilderness camping trips, I thought it might be the only way I could share that message with you and David. I'm older and set in my ways, too—like Charles. But when I told God what a failure I had been as a parent to you and what a waste my whole life had been, He just lovingly forgave me all, and told me to get up and get busy for Him. And I plan to spend the rest of my life doing just that."

"You were never a failure as a parent," protested Carole. "I am so sorry for the terrible things I said to you that day. They were cruel and untrue!"

"They were terrible, I'll agree, but the truth, nevertheless. But God has forgiven me. Will you?"

Carole stood up and threw her arms about her tiny grandmother. "I'm the one who needs to ask forgiveness. God has forgiven me for my willfulness and selfishness. Will you forgive me, Gran?"

Gran kissed her granddaughter tenderly, then lay back on the pillows. "I won't marry Charles until I know he's accepted Christ, but I honestly don't think it will be long before he asks God to forgive him, too. Oh, Carole, there's so much good we can do together. We've already talked about contributing a substantial amount of money to that place in Seattle where Tina found help."

"You mean The Home?"

"Yes. That's it. Charles and I have wasted a lot of our lives but we are anxious to get to work and also to put our money to work for good instead of ourselves. We aren't rushing into things, but we aren't young and we don't have a lot of time."

Carole sat back and gazed at her grandmother in amazement, a fond smile on her face. At last she stood up to leave. "David and I will pray that Mr. Prentice accepts Christ soon, too." Carole opened the door, then turned back to her grandmother. "I know you'll both be very happy, Gran. And, I think I might enjoy having a grandfather!"

32

The next morning when Carole awakened in the faint light of early dawn, she could not recall at first where she was. The ceiling rose high above the huge bed on which she lay. Her eyes roved about the enormous room. Velvet drapes of soft rose framed the gigantic windows of the octagonal shaped room, and the morning light filtered in through gossamer thin lace panels. Carole's gaze lingered appreciatively on the beautiful antique rosewood furniture and the sofa upholstered in the same soft rose as the drapes, all against a background of paneled oak walls.

Carole's aesthetic soul swelled with joy and pleasure. She remembered where she was—the magnificently beautiful home of Charles Prentice. Thunder Mountain Manor!

Gently pushing aside the cool sheet and eiderdown comforter, Carole crept softly from bed so as not to awaken David. A chill had invaded the room during the night, and Carole slipped into a warm, quilted robe before crossing the carpeted floor to the eastern window. The first blush of sunrise was spreading upward above the dense forest. Slightly to the right a clearing marked the camp where this adventure had begun.

Gran tricked us into coming to that camp, she thought, and none of us will ever be the same again!

She turned to look at David, still asleep in the rapidly

brightening room. Dear, kind, lovable David! He looked like a tousled little boy! Through her own willfulness she had almost lost him to alcohol, which almost certainly would have led to their eventual divorce. Her heart swelled with thankfulness to God for restoring their relationship to what it was when they were first married. Only now she knew that it was even better.

They had agreed that David should enter college in the fall, and she no longer doubted his declaration that teaching would never separate them.

Carole turned back to the glory of the huge red ball sliding up over the tree tops.

Suddenly Carole felt strong arms reach about her, breaking into her reverie. "Isn't the sun glorious out there?" she murmured to David, as she leaned back into his arms.

"Almost as glorious as my wife," David said, nuzzling her neck. At that moment there was a soft knock at the door and Mitzi's voice called, "Aunt Carole, come see what Ebenezer brought me."

"She's an early riser," commented David ruefully.

Grinning wickedly, Carole called back over her shoulder as she went to answer the door, "This is the way it will be when we have a child. Do you still want one?"

Mitzi stood on the threshold in a little pink nightgown, a shoe box in her arms. When Carole invited her in, she marched to the bed and placed the box upon it. Carole came over to see what the box contained.

"Ebenezer woke me up this morning scratching on my door," she said, eyes shining with pride and excitement. "When I opened it, this was lying by the door." Taking the lid off the shoe box she lifted a large pack rat out by the tail and held him up for Carole's inspection.

Carole screamed and backed away. "Mitzi, put it down!"

David broke into peals of laughter. "It's dead, Carole."

Carole could see nothing funny about it, "I know it's

dead but it's a dirty, repulsive creature! Please, put it down, Mitzi."

Mitzi looked from the large dead rat, dangling from her fingers by its tail, to Carole's distraught face. "It really isn't dirty," she declared solemnly. "Ebenezer is a very clean cat and he carried it in his mouth."

Carole shuddered again, but David chuckled at Mitzi's logic. "A pack rat isn't really a dirty animal," David said. "He is a curious, interesting creature."

Mitzi deposited the rat back in the box, "Ebenezer wanted to give me a present and it was the best he had," she told Carole.

David's lips twitched with the effort to restrain his merriment. "Mitzi," he explained, "Aunt Carole isn't saying Ebenezer's gift isn't a wonderful gift. It's just that grown ladies are afraid of rats and that sort of thing. Do you understand?"

"I—think so," Mitzi said. "But he really won't hurt you, Aunt Carole, see?" She was starting to lift out her present again.

Suddenly it burst into Carole's understanding what David was seeing. The dainty little girl, long silvery hair cascading about diminutive shoulders, small feet peeking from under a soft pink nightgown, expressive blue eyes glowing—holding that ridiculous dead rat by its long furry tail in her delicate white fingers.

Carole began to smile, then to chuckle and then to laugh uproariously. Mothering would never be dull. She could foresee that!

When she could talk again, Carole said, "It is a wonderful present, Mitzi. Ebenezer must love you lots to bring you his prize catch. Now, would you like to go up to the top of the tower with Uncle David and me to see the beautiful morning we are blessed with?"

"Okay." Mitzi hastily clapped the lid on the box. "Can I leave him here?" she asked.

"Why not?" Carole responded. The twinkle and approval in David's eyes warmed her heart.

David swung a delighted Mitzi to his shoulder and together they went up the winding stairway.